MR. AND MRS. GUNPLAY

By

Khalil Murray

The Equal Team Publications
P.O. Box 37232
Philadelphia, PA 19148

Mr. and Mrs. Gunplay

This book is a work of fiction. All persons, places, and situations in this novel are imaginary. Any resemblance to real persons, actual events, and situations is merely coincidental.

Library of Congress Control Number: 2011911140

ISBN-978-0-692-62226-1

First Edition: August 2012

10 9 8 7 6 5 4 3 2 1

Dedication

Myani, Khadafi, and Saeedah . . .

I'm dedicating this first book to my three
children, because when I thought of them in this
jail cell, my mind was granted freedom each and
every time. These momentary escapes were like
putting new batteries in my back. So, it's fair to
say that my children assisted me in preparing
this first book out of my ten-book series, and I
unshamefully admit that I sometimes miss them
more than I miss my freedom.

(City of Secrets)
10-book Series

MR. AND MRS. GUNPLAY

Chapter One

July 14th, 2010-7:03 p.m.

"Camay, this not how you supposed to be feelin' on ya fuckin' birthday," Tia advised her best friend, as she handed her a handful of napkins to wipe away her falling tears. Moments like this always made her wish that her best friend wasn't such a kind-hearted person. "This is exactly what ya mom was talkin' about yesterday. Robbie ain't no fuckin' body, and he only do you like this, 'cause he know he can get away with this type of corny ass shit. Got us up in this restaurant waitin' for his disrespectful ass, and now he got the nerve to cut his cell phone the fuck off on you? Girl, please. If I was you, I'd call the cell phone company and have them cut his shit off for real, since he like havin' it off so fuckin' . . ."

"Ay, yo, she don't need you to tell her what to-"

"Splash, I'm not talkin' the fuck to you, so mind ya fuckin' business."

"Mind yours, then."

"Boy, won't chu go out to the fuckin' parkin' lot and see if ya dick fit in ya car gas tank, 'cause you can forget about touchin' me tonight."

"I wasn't gon' touch you anyway . . . ya period still on."

Camay snickered at Splash's snide remark, as she wiped away her tears with the napkins that Tia had given her.

After rolling her eyes at Camay, Tia glared across their restaurant table at her husband. In response to her angry stare, he simply turned up the corner of his mouth and shrugged his shoulders. Their stare lasted for three seconds, before either of them spoke a word.

"All you need is some snakes in ya head, and you'd look just . . ."

"Splash, keep it the fuck up, and I swear on my fuckin' mom, I'm gon' embarrass ya ass up in this fuckin' restaurant."

"Tee, you already is wit' that boogey chillin' all in ya damn nose."

Splash, Tia, and Camay, were at Tastebuds. They were at the popular restaurant to celebrate Camay's twenty-fifth birthday. In the city of Philadelphia, Tastebuds was highly regarded for its delicious food, and its awesome variety of cheesecakes. To keep a relaxed atmosphere inside of the dining haven, its staff all wore pleasant expressions, while they catered to their customers. Overhead spotlights were purposely dimmed, while classic, R&B tunes floated moderately out of wall and floor speakers, giving anyone who stepped through the restaurant's doors an instant sense of comfortability. The floor space inside of Tastebuds was very impressive. Besides boasting a sea of restaurant tables, there were also cozy booths outlining the restaurant's exposed-brick walls.

"Man, I ain't sittin' here waitin' for this nigga," Splash quietly decided, pushing his chair away from the restaurant table. His stomach growled as he rose to his feet. "I knew I should've ate the other half of that mu'fuckin' hoagie earlier. I'm out. Plus, Tee ain't gon' do nothin' but draw when this nut ass nigga get here anyway. Fuck all-"

"And where you call ya self goin'?"

"Man, that nigga on some bullshit."

"So, you just gon' get up and leave? And don't try to lie and say you not fuckin' hungry, 'cause ya mother fuckin' stomach is over there soundin' like you hidin' a fuckin' baby lion in it."

Splash exhaled an impatient sigh and wiped his right hand over his wavy hair.

"And we here for fuckin' Camay, not Robbie. And you got one more time to cut ya eyes at that bitch over there, and I'ma-"

"Man, I was lookin' at her food."

"You 'bout to be lookin' at one of my shoes in 3-D, if you don't sit the fuck back down."

Tia narrowed her eyes when Splash glanced down at his Audemars watch. She had a personal rule of keeping him on a short leash, and it wasn't out of her own insecurities or that he had ever given her reasons to believe that he was unfaithful, she just preferred to keep her husband on his toes and thoroughly in check.

"Tia, I don't care if Splash leave."

"I do."

"Tee, you act like I gotta be here for you to eat."

"Splash, I swear, you really know how to get on my nerves."

"Now, you know how I feel when ya period be comin' on."

"It must be the same feelin' I be gettin' when I be layin' there and ya dumb ass dick can't get hard again, huh?"

Tia batted her eyelashes animatedly and waited for Splash to respond to her jazzy comeback. When he shook his head and looked away, she smirked and patted herself on the back. If life was actually a bitch, Tia would definitely be one of her best friends. She didn't bite her tongue for anyone. She was twenty-five, didn't have any children, and she owned the type of looks that would make a photographer reach for his camera. Having an Italian father, and a black mother blessed her with a blend of beautiful features. She had gray eyes, a buttery-tan complexion, and silky, auburn-colored hair that hung a few inches below her shoulders.

"Sike, Bay," Tia apologized sweetly, as she hung her oversized, black, Dooney & Burke pocketbook on the back of her restaurant chair with a smile. She knew that her husband was just as stubborn as she was, so she chose her next words manipulatively. "All of our neighbors know your name. Bay, you know what I was thinkin' about earlier, though? Instead of you havin' ya birthday party at ya club, you should have it out at the house. It supposed to be nice all next week, too. We can have a real decent pool party, Bay. We can do a Gucci, or something like a D&G theme at the house, and then you can tell everybody to switch it up and wear Louis Vuitton to ya club later on that night. I'm tellin' you, Bay, it'll be so nice and you know it."

Splash cracked a smile.

"Bay, can you just sit down and eat with me and Camay?"

Splash glanced down at his watch again.

"Please, Bay."

"Alright."

"Where you-"

"I'm gon' get my phone out my car real quick."

"Splash, don't be corny and leave."

"Tee, I'm grabbin' my phone, and I'm comin' right back."

While Tia was watching Splash swagger away from their restaurant table, Camay's eyes were resting on her red, BCBG clutch-purse that was down in her lap. Her nerves were sizzling beneath her brown skin, as she thought about her latest cell phone bill that was folded up inside of her purse.

"Cam?"

Different emotions fought for control of Camay's face as she slowly raised her eyes to look at Tia. Her heart was the victim of a level of pain that she had never experienced in her life. The awareness of her boyfriend cheating on her with her and Tia's other best friend was killing her softly. She had been keeping the secret to herself for weeks, and now that she possessed the proof of such an intimate betrayal, it was beginning to take a toll on her normal way of thinking.

"Stilettos for ya thoughts."

"Ya phone call stopped me from killin' myself this mornin'."

"What?"

Camay lowered her eyes down to her purse.

"Bitch, you playin' with me, right?"

"I had Robbie gun to my head when my phone started ringin'."

Camay's revelation left Tia speechless.

"Tia, I hate the person I see when I look in the mirror," Camay sadly confessed, becoming misty-eyed as the secret down in her chest screamed for freedom. As she sat there, she could feel the knife of betrayal as it slowly sliced down the middle of her soul and heart. "And I'm just so sick and tired of everybody always expecting me to be this nice person all the times. Tia, do you know what's so crazy? When I came back from college, I had this list of all this stuff I wanted to have done by my twenty-fifth birthday. I got the job I always wanted. Got my house. I helped my mom pay off hers. I even finally got my brother that appeal lawyer he been buggin' my mom about. I even got all the money you gave me to pay off my student loans."

5

"Camay, I know you not the fuck sittin' here tryna tell me that committin' suicide was one of ya fuckin' goals?"

"No."

"Cam, I can't even believe we havin' this conversation."

Camay lowered her head in shame. Her heart and soul were releasing screams that only her ears could hear.

"Girl, if you been accomplishin' all these things that mean so fuckin' much to you, I don't understand how you could even consider killin' ya fuckin' self."

Tia's words made the secret held hostage inside of Camay's chest scream even louder.

"And on your birthday at that."

Camay was truly the definition of a beautiful flower. She was soft-spoken, and she had a very subtle demeanor. Because of their remarkable resemblances, she was often mistaken for being the actress Taraji P. Henson.

"Cam, you-"

"Not lettin' people take advantage of me was on my list, too, Tia."

"Bitch, I know this shit not about Robbie, 'cause if it the fuck is, he the mother fucker you should've had that gun pointed at this mornin'."

"Here come our waitress."

"Watch me cuss you the fuck out when she leave."

"Whateva."

Out in the restaurant's parking lot, Splash felt like he was a small man inside of a gigantic microwave. It was the last week of July, and the summer weather was making a very hot statement in the city of Philadelphia. The humidity in the air had the unwelcoming feeling of a wool blanket, and the sun was up in the sky glowing like a thousand-watt light bulb.

After pocketing his cell phone, Splash glanced over his shoulder at his car as he headed back towards the restaurant's entrance. He was the proud owner of a cement-gray, 2010

Chevy Camaro. The car's 26-inch rims, customized moon roof, and suicide doors made the handsome vehicle the earner of many admiring stares. Tia's cranberry, 2010 CTS Cadillac wagon was parked directly beside it.

Tia's car was only two days old. Unlike Splash's car, her car didn't have any accessories, except for a Heckler & Koch,.40 caliber handgun, that was discreetly tucked beneath her driver's seat. The twin to the chrome piece of metal was hiding inside of Tia's pocketbook in the restaurant.

Splash and Tia had driven in separate cars, simply because Splash wouldn't let Tia drive his car to the restaurant .An hour earlier, the two of them had had a heated argument out in their driveway. A day never disappeared without them having some type of clash. Normalcy wasn't a part of their relationship. Nothing about how they lived was boring. They were outrageously competitive with each other over everything. If it was any couple that deserved to have a reality show, it was definitely them two.

Splash and Tia were hopelessly in love.

Helplessly.

A delicious breeze teased Splash's nostrils as soon as he reentered Tastebuds. His stomach growled instantly.

The aromas floating in the air inside of the restaurant could make a hungry stomach bite its own liver and kidneys.

For tonight's occasion, Splash was playing the 'I just got off of work' look. He prided himself in having a mean dress code. It was an everyday rule that he lived by. He had his powder-blue and canary-yellow tie dramatically unloosened around the open collar of his canary-yellow, D&G shirt. Purposely, he had the linen shirt untucked, concealing the twin Glock 45's on his waist, and he had his sleeves rolled up to his elbows, exposing his tattoo-covered forearms. His jeans were a pair of black, D&G denims that were precisely cuffed over his black, D&G sneakers. Besides his expensive Audemars watch on his left wrist, the only other jewelry he had on was his wedding band.

Splash was tall, handsome, and he had a snickers-brown complexion that covered his well-defined physique. He also had an ego the size of Disney World, but his charisma and sense of humor balanced out his personality, giving him a thorough character that caused people to gravitate to him wherever he went.

Splash made it back to the restaurant table just as the waitress was stepping away with the menus. As he pulled out his chair and sat back down, he winked his right eye at Tia.

"You took long enough."

"My dick got stuck in my car gas tank."

"Boy, shut-"

Camay's cell phone started to chime on the restaurant table. Three sets of eyes stared at it. The closest pair of eyes gave it a look that could have made bacon sizzle on a block of ice.

"Cam, you better cuss him the fuck out, too."

Splash kicked Tia's leg under their restaurant table.

"That ain't Robbie," Camay clarified, as she glared down at her ringing cell phone. She could feel the secret down in her chest trying to claw its way up her throat. "That's Jen."

Camay rolled her eyes at her cell phone when Tia snatched it up.

"I gotta pee," Tia announced, placing Camay's cell phone to her ear as she pushed her chair back and stood up. After pulling the strap of her pocketbook over her left shoulder, she spoke into Camay's cell phone. "Bitch, no the fuck you not.Illlll. Jen, Simon would cuss ya ass the fuck out, if he heard you singin' like that. What? What chu mean, why I'm answerin' her fuckin' phone? Bitch,what - eva. 'Cause I'm her secretary today, and?"

Splash flinched when Tia plucked him on his forehead.

"And that's for kickin' me."

"Yo, I'ma fuck you up."

Tia giggled girlishly when Splash tried to hit her back. When he missed, she stuck her tongue out her mouth at him and switched Camay's cell phone to her other ear. On her way to the restroom, she could feel Splash's eyes on her as she navigated her way through the sea of restaurant tables. For her husband's sake only, she began to strut more provocatively, while she continued her conversation on Camay's cell phone. Her Cesare Paciotti stilettos were stabbing invisible wounds in the restaurant's hardwood floors.

Women looked and hated.

Men stopped eating and stared.

Tia's body had more curves than a race track. Her body was wrapped in a black, mid-thigh, Maison Martin Margiela dress, and its silk material was hugging her figure like a scared child. Without heels, she stood 5'9" tall, and her measurements were 36-24-38. Like Splash, she heeded to a workout regimen that included miles of jogging, Pilates, and advanced cardio-exercises.

While Tia was pushing open the door to the ladies restroom, Camay was back at their restaurant table granting her secret freedom.

"Yo, what chu just say?"

"Robbie fuckin' Jen."

Splash's face balled up like a fist that had fifteen fingers.

"Can you kill them for me?"

"What?"

"Splash, I'll pay you."

"Cam, yo, what the-Ay, yo, who told you some nut ass shit like that?"

Camay unsnapped her purse, pulled out a page of her cell phone bill, and with fire blazing in her eyes, she tossed it across the restaurant table.

"They probably together right now," Camay assumed, watching Splash as he read her cell phone bill quietly. The idea of her boyfriend and best friend being together made her sick to her stomach, but at the very same time, it was influencing a real strong desire for revenge to develop in her heart. "They think I don't know, Splash. That bitch just called me to feel me out. Jen don't give a fuck about it being my birthday, Splash. Every time Robbie cut his cell phone off, she call-"

"Tia know?"

Camay shook her head.

"Why you ain't-"

" 'Cause all Tia gon' do is want me to fight Jen, and put Robbie out, and-"

"So, hold up, you tryna tell me that if Robbie would've showed up, you-"

"I was gon' sit here and act like nothin' was wrong, and keep playin' dumb."

"Cam, you trippin'."

"No, they trippin'."

Splash exhaled a deep sigh.

"I'm not lettin' people shit on me no more, Splash."

"Yo, would you feel like this if it wasn't Jen?"

"No."

"Cam, you-"

Splash tilted his head and looked up at the restaurant's ceiling when Camay dropped her face down into her hands, and began to cry again. His stomach growled for five seconds straight, but he felt no pity for it. He only felt pity for Camay. She was like a sister to him, and without question, he knew that she was the last person to deserve the type of pain that she was presently dealing with.

"Splash, please?"

Splash and Tia were professional killers, and only their very close friends knew this.

"I can pay you whatever-"

"Cam, I'll rock Robbie for free, but I ain't doin' shit to Jen."

"Why not?"

" 'Cause she like my sister, and if she ever asked me to do something to you, I'd tell her ass the same fuckin' thing."

Camay sighed and looked away. Her eyes rested on a young, white couple that were spoon-feeding each other cheesecake at a nearby restaurant table. Her heart envied their affection.

"Cam, if I rock Robbie, you know you gon' have to go to his funeral, right?"

"So."

"And what about his little sister?"

"What about her?"

"Cam, she live with ya'll."

"And?"

"Seein' her after I do this shit gon' eat you up, Cam."

"It won't if you kill her, too."

Fully unaware of the deep conversation that was being held in her absence, Tia was inside of the ladies restroom, pacing back and forth as she indulged in a heavy conversation of her very own.

"Jen, I understand that, but you never have Shateek, and maybe that's why-"

"Full fuckin' custody, though, Tia? Him and his fuckin' mom actin' like I don't . . ."

Tia switched Camay's cell phone to her other ear and exhaled a sigh of exasperation.

". . . love my fuckin' son."

"I know, Jen."

"Tia, did Splash know?"

"Did he know what?"

"That his aunt and Sabia was takin' me to court."

"Jen, don't chu think I would've told you some shit like that, if he knew that fuckin' shit?"

"So, he really ain't know then?"

"Jen, if you just got the fuckin' papers in the damn mail today, how the fuck would Splash-"

" 'Cause that's his fuckin' cousin, and you know how the two of them are."

The sound of Tia's stilettos paused when she stopped in front of the mirror and stared at her reflection. No one was in the ladies restroom with her. There was no one to witness the pain in her eyes, as she softly placed her left hand on her flat stomach. Just a month earlier, her stomach had been swollen with her unborn son. She had made it to five and a half months with him.

"Tia?"

Tia ignored Jen and continued to stare at her reflection until her eyes became so watery that she couldn't see herself anymore. For those first few seconds, she was happy that she couldn't see herself. Like Camay, she was dealing with her own issues that was burdening her soul. Having a miscarriage had reduced her to an emotional puzzle with far to many missing pieces to count. No one had any idea that she was so messed up from the experience, or that she was blaming herself for losing her son. Even Splash was unaware of how devastated she really was.

"Tia?"

Tia missed being pregnant. At the age of twenty-five, and in possession of all the material things a female could ever hope for, having her own child was her only true desire in life.

"Tia?"

"Jen, I'ma call you back, alright?"

"Girl, what chu-"

Tia thumbed the end-button on Camay's cell phone and dropped down into her purse.

"What a fuckin' day this turnin' out to be," Tia thought, sighing as she searched her pocketbook for her lip gloss and mascara. When the back of her hand touched the handle of her gun, it made her think about how close Camay had actually came to killing herself earlier that morning. "I know what Jen and Cam need. Tomorrow, I'ma take both of them to the mall ,and we gon' shop 'til we can't carry our bags. Some mall therapy would do us all some justice. I don't even remember the last time the three of us even spent some time to-"

"Tia?"

Tia turned around and faced Camay.

"Robbie here."

"Oh, his corny ass decided to finally show up, huh?"

"He proposed to me, Tia."

"And you told him to kiss ya mother fuckin' ass, right?"

"We flyin' to Vegas after Splash party next week."

For the second time that day, Camay had spoken words that had left Tia at a loss for words. However, as Tia looked at Camay with confusion and disappointment in her eyes, she had no idea that her best friend's decision to elope with her boyfriend was purely motivated by her ardent desire for revenge. Sadly, in days to come, Tia and Camay were both going to find out that their fates were inescapable, and that the issues they currently have are nothing in comparison to the obstacles they were about to encounter. Some toxic events were about to change their lives in ways neither of them could ever imagine possible.

Chapter Two

It was 8:24 a.m., and Splash and Tia were both enjoying an early morning, deep sleep. They were sprawled out on their California King, iron-canopy bed. The huge bed was in the center of their master bedroom, resting handsomely on top of an oval, three-stepped stage.

Splash was snoring.

Tia was drooling on Splash's chest. Her right hand was stuffed down inside of his maroon, Armani briefs.

Snookums, Tia's Pomeranian poodle, was busy chasing one of his plastic toys around Splash's and Tia's humongous bedroom. Every so often, he would yip excitedly when his yellow ball squeaked, and then he would look over and watch Splash or Tia, as they stirred in their sleep.

Splash and Tia were high school sweethearts. Hours after their senior graduation, they had both purchased airplane tickets to Las Vegas, and had eloped. The entire flight there, the two of them argued over which one of them dressed the best during the winter, and if the rapper Tupac was still alive, or not. Splash believed that he was; Tia didn't. Despite their immaturity, to the amazement of many people, Splash's and Tia's marriage had lasted much longer than anyone had ever expected. Trust was the key that had kept the two of them together. They loved each other unconditionally. However, on most days, the two of them couldn't stand to be in the same room with each other for longer than five minutes. Ironically, five minutes couldn't disappear without one of them thinking about the other in their absence.

Snookums' light barking stirred Tia awake. After blinking her eyes open, she raised her face from Splash's tattoo-decorated chest, and looked around her bedroom until Snookums appeared from the short hallway that led to Splash's walk-in closet. Tia's sleepy eyes zoomed in on the Dior Homme sneaker that Snookums was pulling by its shoestring. Sighing, Tia cut her eyes up to Splash's face, then she looked on in shock, as Snookums raised his hind leg and began to piss on Splash's four hundred and sixty dollar sneaker.

"Ohhh,God," Tia sighed, pulling her hand out of Splash's briefs slowly. With that same hand, she grabbed a fistful of her bed sheets and wiped her drool off of Splash's chest. "Ain't nobody tell his dumb behind to leave his closet door open any damn way. I really don't feel like they shit today. I'm not payin' for them sneakers, either."

When Snookums disappeared back into Splash's closet, Tia returned her face back to Splash's chest and closed her eyes. With a sigh, she stuffed her hand back down into Splash's briefs, wrapped her fingers back around his dick, and then listened to the sound of his heartbeat until she dozed back off.

Tia's full name was Tianna Paradise Bancroft. She was the result of a love affair shared between a young, black woman, and an unhappily ,married Italian man.

Carmen Masino, Tia's father, was an extremely wealthy man. The position he controlled as a loan shark for the Italian mafia, combined with his greenish-gray eyes, earned him the nickname, 'Money bags.' At the age of thirty-six, he was still boyishly handsome, very stylish, and he didn't have a want for anything. Everyone in his South Philadelphia neighborhood loved him. He was disliked by very few people.

Angelina Colletti, the mother of Carmen Masino's eleven-year- old son, was the only person that made up that few. Her and Carmen Masino shared a mutual hate for each other. It was a discord that had spawned from a night of drunken sex, where Carmen Masino's condom had gotten sabotaged by Angelina Colletti's clawing fingernails. Duty had influenced their marriage. At the altar, their vows had been nothing but empty promises that were attached to forced smiles, which were merely charitable expressions for their family members and friends in attendance. For a decade, love had only caught glimpses of freedom when it concerned their son. His existence served as their negotiation-bridge.

Heeding to his younger sister's demands, Carmen Masino began to date her best friend, Quintessa Bancroft. After one conversation over the phone, with neither of them sparing their true feelings on love and life, their hearts had become emotionally attached.

Voids in their lives had been filled with the presence of shared ideas and common aspirations.

Pain had been felt.

Sunshine had replaced rain.

For a few months, Carmen and Quintessa had remained discreet, carefully testing out their compatibility as a couple. Romantic trips were taken. Promises were believed, and a new life together was designed, with their unborn daughter's future highlighting the details. Sadly, none of their plans got the chance to see fruition, because the same individual who had joined their fates, turned out to be the same person who would destroy their destinies.

On one hot summer afternoon, a week after Quintessa had given birth to Tia, an envelope containing Carmen

Masino's secrets had arrived with the regular mail on his doorstep. The envelope had five pictures of him smiling happily with his new family. The manila envelope had been addressed to his wife in red ink. His wife had recognized the handwriting on the envelope immediately, and she knew that the pictures were sent by her sister-in-law with the intentions of humiliating her.

They did.

Each and every picture had stung like an open-handed slap to Angelina Colletti's face, and she snapped.

She.

Snapped.

Carmen Masino died in his sleep. He never once felt the steak knife that his wife had plunged into his heart, or even heard any of the cursed-accusations that had followed each blow. Over and over again, his wife had stabbed him until her arms would no longer rise and fall. Carmen Masino's wife stabbed him in the face, because he had a new family. She stabbed him in the throat, because she had always wanted to. She stabbed him because she finally could.

Angelina Colletti stabbed her husband's eyes out, wishing he was his sister.

Minutes later, Carmen Masino's wife wrote their son a suicide letter at their kitchen table. Her bloody hands had trembled with each written word. She knew that pain and confusion was going to suffocate her son's young mind when he returned home from football camp, so she explained the reasons behind her actions and left the blood-stained note beneath his pillow.

Angelina Colletti's recipe for death were twenty-four Percocets, and a warm glass of scotch. Her last breath was taken in bed beside her husband.

The death of Tia's father had crushed Quintessa Bancroft. Unable to attend the double-casket funeral, she had no choice but to mourn at home by herself. She had no idea that her best friend was behind the twist of fate that had set fire to her bright dreams.

Quintessa Bancroft owned the type of looks that would make Tyra Banks nod her head in approval. Unfortunately, like so many other smart and beautiful women all across the world, she had a poor sense of judgment when it came down to the men she chose to give her heart to. Her boyfriend before Tia's father wasn't just emotionally, and physically abusive, but he was also faithfully unfaithful. Her own sister had given birth to his son.

And his daughter.

His own cousin was the mother of his twins.

Carmen Masino was like a breath of fresh air for Tia's mother. She had inhaled him gratefully, and had exhaled him with much appreciation. As soon as she had realized that she was pregnant, he had quickly relocated her from her South Philadelphia apartment, and had moved her out into the luxurious suburbs of Chestnut Hill, Pennsylvania. Tia's father had purchased a mini-mansion for her, and had given her two refrigerator-sized safes, and then told her to plan for their wedding, which was why Tia's mother felt so distraught after his death, and why she felt so guilty when it came around to her touching any of the money that was inside of the safes. Each large safe held a million dollars in cash.

After four months of drowning in depression, Tia's mother had decided to pursue her dreams as an interior decorator. With 4,790 square feet to practice on, she chose to make her own home her very first project.

Tia was given anything that she asked for. Her mother had spoiled her rotten as a child, giving her a personality so colorful, none of the private schools in Chestnut Hill could tolerate her attitude. During her 11th grade year, she had gotten switched from private school to a North Philadelphia public school. On her first day there, she cussed out her advisory teacher, the school's principal, and a group of jealous-eyed girls, who had followed her from school to her car.

Tia's box cutter sent all of the girls running for safety. She met Camay and Jen the next day when she had joined their school's cheerleading squad. The three of them had clicked instantly, and became inseparable soon after.

While Tia was adjusting at her new school, her mother's career as a home decorator was taking off. After Tia's mother had posted a few pictures of what she had done to her own house on-line, people from all over the world began to seek out her expertise, forcing her to travel extensively. Horribly, she was having a meeting with a potential client inside of one of the World Trade Centers on September 11th, 2001.

Quintessa Bancroft's life and promising career had collapsed with the towers. Her body was never found.

Tia had cried enough tears to float Noah's Ark.

The irritation of a full bladder pulled Splash out of his deep sleep. The first thing he smelled when he opened his eyes was the Pink Oil Moisturizer that Tia had in her hair. Her Chanel scarfed-head was directly beneath his chin. Closing his eyes, he inhaled a deep breath through his nostrils, and slowly drifted off back to sleep. Had he just turned his head slightly to the left, he would have seen a small pile of some of his expensive footwear being baptized by Snookums' piss. Although Splash had ignored his full bladder, the very sight of Snookums pissing on his sneakers would have made him go ballistic.

Splash and Snookums had a long history of drama. They hated each other, and their beef was comical amongst family members and friends, because it was actually Splash, who had brung Snookums home to Tia as a wedding anniversary present. Snookums had turned on Splash as soon as he was placed in Tia's arms.

Sadly, like Tia, both of Splash's parents were dead as well. They died during the celebration of his 3rd birthday party.

In Philadelphia, Craig Barnes, Splash's father, was one of the most dangerous men to ever stand behind a gun; or knife. His handsome looks and contagious smile had helped him penetrate the circles of many of the men that he had been hired to kill. His main specialty was to shoot his targets in their faces. Splash's father wasn't a killer, he was a murderer. By himself, he had a total of thirty-three homicides.

Some of them were cops.

None of them were women.

Or children.

Sandra Bundy, Splash's mother, had once been considered to be one of the prettiest girls in her North Philadelphia neighborhood. Her ultimate dream had been to become a famous R&B singer. Her voice was extraordinary. She was elegant, beautiful, and she had a profound talent in writing songs that would capture untapped feelings in anyone that heard her sing them. Her only flaw was her weakness for Xanax pills. She worshipped them.

At recording studios, people in attendance would cry Sandra Bundy's tears when she recorded her tracks. The songs that she penned whenever she was riding a wave of intoxication were always captivating. They were her testimonies of how her father had a sick preference of sexually molesting her, and how breast cancer had stolen her mother's life from her when she was twelve-years-old. She wrote songs about Splash's father, and how he had rescued her from her father, who wasn't letting her go to school, because he wanted to rape her every day. Her pain was felt, therefore, many producers and engineers ignored her nodding-episodes, because Sandra Bundy often explained that whenever she did nod off, it was actually like a door was then opened for her to escape the demons that were constantly haunting her conscious.

After Splash's birth, his mother had suffered from post-natal depression. Her petite body had ballooned up to twice its normal size, and the stretch marks that were scribbled around her waist made her detest her own image. She hated the way she looked, but she hated being a mother even more.

In an upstairs bathroom, during Splash's birthday party, Sandra Bundy tried heroin for the very first time in her life. It was the worst mistake she could have ever made. She died as soon as the powerful drug mixed in with the blood in her veins.

Craig Barnes went crazy when he discovered Splash's mother's lifeless body. His screams made all of the party-goers silent. With tears spilling from his eyes, he stormed out of his parent's house hollering at the top of his lungs. He knew exactly where Splash's mother had gotten the heroin from. He was an enforcer for the Cubans that distributed the dope on a nearby corner. His mother and father had desperately tried to stop him, but nothing they said worked. His younger sister begged him not to go.

Rage had made Craig Barnes deaf.

Revenge made him blind.

When Splash's father had turned the corner of 4th and Jefferson Street, all of the Cubans quickly realized that something was terribly wrong. In open-mouthed shock, they all watched Splash's father shoot two of their drug dealers at point-blank range, then turn his guns on the Cuban bosses, who were sitting in their cars. Splash's father didn't have any picks that day. He didn't spare any of the dope fiends as they all desperately tried to run for cover, and his blazing temper had only intensified when the cops began to arrive.

Craig Barnes didn't have any plans of surrendering, and retreating was completely out of the question. It took a total of twenty-eight bullets to bring him to his knees. Pellets from a police officer's shotgun had flipped him onto his back, but his roars of revenge and hatred never ceased to stop flying from his lips. He had yelled until he began to choke on his own blood. Craig Barnes spent his last breath on a final prayer. He begged God to resurrect him on the pavement where he laid, and he had asked God not to separate the bond that he and his son had created.

Craig Barnes died looking up at the sky, hoping that his soul would catch up with Splash's mother's spirit.

It did.

Splash was raised by his father's parents. His real name was actually Rasool Barnes. At the age of nine, he had experienced an ethereal moment that had changed his life in a profound way. Miraculously, for reasons far too unexplainable for his young mind to comprehend, he had been blessed with the ability to talk to his father in his dreams. These visions of Splash's would only take place when he dozed off inside of his father's vintage, Nissan Pathfinder, which was parked in front of his grandparent's house, and had been there since his father's death.

The dreams were something that Splash couldn't get his grand parents to believe, so as he grew older, he became much more guarded about what he had chose to accept as being a very special gift of his. Splash's biggest disappointments were that nothing he said could convince his grandparents of what he was experiencing, and that his mother would never appear with his father in any of these visions. Splash's mother would send messages through his father, but she would never join them. Splash's father would often speak up for Splash's mother, and explain to Splash that it was very hard for his mother to see him, because she was ashamed to face him, but those sentiments were never enough for Splash. He yearned to see his mother. It was a hope that Splash had in his heart each time that he climbed into his father's jeep.

By Splash's senior year in high school, he had developed some phenomenal skills as a basketball player, and had drawn the attention of every top-seeded college in the Country. He was ambidextrous, and he could dribble a basketball with both of his eyes closed without missing a beat. He also could sink a jump shot from anywhere on the basketball court, and he was famously known at his school for dunking on anyone that challenged him when he came down the lane.

Besides Splash's grandparents, and his aunt, Tia was absolutely his biggest fan. She had the privilege of never missing any of his games, because she was the head cheerleader for their school's basketball team.

Tia was actually the only person who believed that Splash's surreal dreams were true. Even as teenagers, the two of them had shared a powerful chemistry together. By them both losing their parents, they had a common pain that both of them could identify with. Emphatically, they were very supportive of each other when it came to either of them facing any obstacles that life presented them with. Therefore, when Tia's mother passed away, Splash asked his grandparents for their permission to move into Tia's house with her. Since he spent most of his time there anyway, and because they both liked Tia so much, Splash's grandparents had granted his request, but their conditions were that him and Tia had to finish their last year of school, and that they do it without Tia getting pregnant in the process.

On the night that Splash and Tia eloped to Las Vegas, back in Philadelphia, Splash's grandfather died peacefully in his sleep. This sad news over the phone had stolen all of the joy and excitement out of Splash and Tia being newlyweds. They both flew back home in silence.

When Splash arrived at his grandmother's house, and he saw with his own eyes how distraught his grandmother was, he decided that he wasn't going to accept his scholarship to go play basketball at Duke University. This came as a surprise to everyone. Splash couldn't find the nerve to leave the only woman, who had been like a mother to him since the death of his parents. Splash's grandmother tried to get him to reconsider his decision, and she had even went so far as to ask Tia for her help, but Splash had stuck to what he felt was the honorable thing for him to do.

The true source and influence behind Splash's choice to stay home had been motivated by a compelling dream that had affected him deeply. His father had sunk down to his knees and had begged him to sacrifice his scholarship for the sake of staying close to his grandmother. Splash's grandfather had tearfully made the same request in that same dream.

Splash's grandfather had become part of an entity that he was unable to believe in while he was alive. On many occasions, Splash's grandfather had tried to send messages to Splash's grandmother through Splash, but when Splash would attempt to deliver them to her, his grandmother would react so emotional and irate, Splash never got the chance to finish any of them.

Splash's grandmother's faith in God was paramount, but her own personal doubts wouldn't let her accept that her grandson was in possession of such a sublime favor from her Creator. For her, it was simply unheard of.

From the age of seventeen on, Splash didn't mention nothing else about his dreams to his grandmother. The day that he had moved with Tia, he took his father's jeep with him, and put it in their two-car garage. It has been there since that day.

Splash began working for Tia's aunt, because of his pride. He didn't want to live off of Tia's money. In the beginning, Tia had found his independent attitude to be sort of cute. She adored the fact that Splash wanted to pave his own way. However, those sentiments vanished quickly when the hitman that had worked for Tia's aunt had retired, and Splash started vying for the open position. Splash had even offered to do his first job for free. Of course, Tia was completely against it. She stopped speaking to her aunt for two weeks straight. Tia tried to convince Splash that he was being irrational, but when he refused to change his plans, she stopped speaking to him as well.

Splash's first job had taken place in Baltimore, Maryland. His target was an embezzling, state senator, who had reneged on a deal that he had made with a corrupt District Attorney. By way of an e-mail, as was her business protocol, Tia's aunt had been provided with the senator's schedule, where he lived, along with the designation of where one hundred and twenty-five thousand dollars in cash could be picked up upon completion of the job. Splash's cut were seventy-five thousand dollars, and a free pass out of jail, if he was to ever get arrested while he was in Baltimore.

Tia had demanded that Splash allow her to be his driver, instead of his cousin Sabia. Her tears helped her win that argument. Tia didn't trust anyone else with her husband's life, especially while such an unpredictable set of circumstances were attached to it. So, on that cold winter night of November, seven years earlier, Tia unofficially became Splash's partner. In silence, while Splash handled his business inside of the senator's house, Tia sat outside in their rental car, and she was content with the sheer resolve that her husband's life was in good hands; hers.

She was him.

He was her.

They were Mr. and Mrs. Gunplay.

Chapter Three

"I just be feelin' real guilty about us doin' this shit," Jen admitted, as she struggled to pull her ashy-blue, Kira Platinina jeans up over her curvy hips. Rolling her eyes, she sucked in a deep breath, snapped the front of her jeans together, then looked over her right shoulder. "I sure as hell can't see how you don't. And I told you Splash got cameras all over his club, but you paid that no mind last night, didn't you? All fuckin' high 'n drunk, and you even had the nerve to try to kiss me while I was makin' somebody they fuckin' drink."

With an exasperated sigh, Jen knelt down and snatched up her bra, her plaid H&M shirt, and her pocketbook. Clutching all of those items against her stomach, she began to stalk around the huge, oval-shaped waterbed in search of her Ugg sandals. She wrinkled her nose in distaste as she stepped over a small pile of pink, anal beads.

"Jen, do your pretty little conscious bother you this much when you and Camay's man finish fuckin'?"

"Trixie, what the fuck that got to do with how you was actin' last night?"

"I'm just sayin'."

"Whateva . . . and for your fuckin' information, yes, it the fuck do."

"Jen, you-"

"And I guess you gon' call that your excuse for how you was actin' last night, huh?"

"Jen, I was trashed last night, "Trixie explained, propping herself up on her elbows. Her waterbed rippled beneath her naked body. "And Splash wasn't there last night anyway, so gimme a break. And lower your voice, too. These condos have thin walls, Jen."

Jen sucked her teeth and rolled her eyes, as she stepped into her sandals.

"They are, Jen."

"You sure wasn't worried about these walls being thin up in here last night."

"Well, I am now."

"Whateva, Trixie."

While Jen put on her bra and shirt, Trixie Masino gave her a scrutinizing stare from the middle of her waterbed. Within seconds, her pussy was moist, and her pierced-clit began to pulsate, quickly reminding her why she had gotten involved with her niece's best friend. Trixie loved men passionately. Some people would even say that she loved them obsessively, but her curiosity to experience how it felt to be with another female had sabotaged her senses completely. Without realizing it, Trixie had become infatuated with Jen's exotic features, and her shapely body. One uninhibited night back in June with the pretty Cambodian girl had stretched into a full month.

"I'm ready to go pick up my son."

Trixie pulled her bed sheets over her head and let out a loud groan.

"Trixie?"

"Lock the door on your way out."

"What?"

"You heard me."

"Oh, so now you gon' be petty and not take me to get my fuckin' son, Trixie?"

"Don't it look that way?"

Jen shot Trixie an icy stare and stormed out of her bedroom.

"And I wasn't the only one who was drunk last night, Jen!" Trixie shouted, snatching her mint-green, Christian Dior bed sheets off of her face. With one of her bed sheets still in her left hand, she climbed off of her water bed. "And for somebody who want me to fuckin' believe that she was so concerned with them cameras at Splash's club last night, you sure could've fuckin' fooled me!! I was drunk, but I wasn't as drunk as you think I was!"

Three Trixie's wrapped themselves with silk bed sheets as they marched down her condo's mirrored hallway. The one in the middle stepped out into her spacious living room by herself, and she had the look of a boxer just entering the boxing ring.

"Trixie, ya 'Kim Kardashian' lookin' ass crack me up."

"Jen, get the fuck out."

"Not a problem at all."

"And rip everything we did out of your memory, too."

"Done, "Jen quipped, as she picked her cell phone up off of Trixie's all-glass, coffee table. Her eyes rested on the double-headed dildo that was beneath the table laying inside of a big bowl of strawberries and whipped cream. "Not much of it was really worth all the mental space anyway. Now, as for all of them juicy ass secrets you told me, I-"

"All of them better go to your grave with you, Jen."

"And if they don't?"

Trixie sighed and bit down on her bottom lip. Her mind began to race. She had told Jen things that could get her lethal injection, if the wrong ears heard them.

"That's what I thought."

"Get the fuck out, Jen."

"Make me."

"Jen, leave."

"Bitch, you lucky I gotta pick up my fuckin' son."

"And you lucky that you're Tia's friend."

Jen blew Trixie a kiss and snickered as she sashayed over to Trixie's front door.

"Erase my number out of your phone."

"Trixie, how do you live with ya self, knowin' that your brother is dead because of you?"

Jen's question hit Trixie like a bag of bricks. Hugging her bed sheet-wrapped body tighter, Trixie blinked back tears.

"Huh, Trixie?"

Trixie hugged herself tighter, as teardrops started to spill from her eyes. She felt herself becoming nauseous ,and was surprised that her legs were still holding her up.

"Tia's mom was ya best friend, and you let her die not knowin' that it was you, who had sent them pictures to Tia's dad's house all that time."

"Jen, you no better a best fuckin' friend than I was!" Trixie snapped, glaring across her living room. Her entire body rattled with contempt, and as tear after tear fell from her eyes, she could feel the urge to kill Jen rising in her heart. "Who the fuck are you to judge anybody? I live with regrets everyday that I wake the fuck up!! Bitch, can you say that?! Huh, Jen?! Can you?! You been fuckin' Camay's boyfriend since high school ,and you got the nerve to still be fuckin' him! Bitch, you far from sinless! You got some juicy secrets, too!! Camay's boyfriend is your son's father, but I don't see you clearing your conscious of that! Why haven't you told Splash's cousin that ain't his son yet?! You know why, Jen?! 'Cause you a manipulating, snake ass bitch, and you better hope Splash cousin don't ask for a paternity test when y'all go to court, you-"

"If you cross me, I'ma cross you right back, Trixie."

"Bitch, worry about me putting a bullet in ya fuckin' head."

"Oh, that's how you feel, Trixie?"

"You the one that opened up this can of worms, not me."

"Trixie, you better-"

"And Splash far from slow, Jen."

"Meaning?"

"I saw you put the money from them bottles of Ace of Spades you sold last night in your pocketbook."

Jen glanced down at her pocketbook as she pulled Trixie's front door open.

"Trixie, I swear on my fuckin' son, if-"

"Jen, get the fuck out!!"

Jen slammed Trixie's door behind her, but as she walked down the hallway towards the elevators, her mind began to add up all the different ways that she could inject pain into Trixie Masino's life. A smile slowly grew on Jen's face when she thought of an individual, who would love to see Trixie grovel in pain.

Up in North Philadelphia, Splash and his grandmother were in his grandmother's bedroom. The two of them were engaged in a conversation that had both of them sticking stubbornly to their beliefs.

"Splash, God don't make mistakes."

"He did when he made Tia have that miscarriage."

"Did you hear what I just said?"

"Yeah, I heard you, Gran'mom, but-"

"God knows best, and until you accept that, you-"

"Gran'mom, how come you never believed my dreams, if you believe in God so much?"

"Splash, don't start that nonsense up in here today."

"How you gon' believe somethin' that some stranger tell you in church, but chu won't believe somethin' ya own gran'son been tryna tell you since he was little, though?"

"Boy, I ain't ask you to come by here so we can argue."

"I ain't tryna argue wit' chu, Gran'mom."

"Splash, can you please sit down for a second?"

Obeying his grandmother, Splash sat down on the edge of her bed and exhaled a heavy sigh. He shifted uncomfortably when the handle of his gun pinched the skin on his right hip.

"I see you still carrying them guns around, huh?"

"Gran'mom, I ain't got no-"

"Splash?"

"Huh?"

"Don't you dare sit there and lie to my face."

With a sigh, Splash broke his grandmother's stare and lowered his eyes down to his white, Kenneth Cole sneakers.

"You and your cousin Sabia-"

"Gran'mom, what chu wanted to talk to me about?"

Splash's grandmother reacted to Splash's reminder like her petite frame had been shocked by a voltage of anxiety. From her rocking chair, Splash's grandmother swept her eyes over to her closet door. A weary expression began to creep along the features of her face.

"What's wrong, Gran'mom?"

Barbara Barnes, Splash's grandmother, had lived to see seventy-five years of life vanish away. Before retiring, she had spent her years teaching math for the Philadelphia public school system. All of her Sundays were spent at church, and God's word meant so much to her spirit, that waking up some mornings a widow couldn't paralyze her with grief anymore, because her faith in God had become her spiritual wheelchair. Splash's grandmother was indeed lonely, but she wasn't without love. Her daughter and

31

grandchildren made sure that she was well taken care of, and although her husband and son were no longer in her life, she let her love and faith in God fill the voids their absences had left in her soul. It was her fear of God, and her undying devotion to her late husband, that had encouraged her to reveal a secret to her grandson, because for nearly twenty-two years, the dark secret had burdened her soul by hiding inside of her closet.

"Gran'mom?"

"Your grandfather loved you a lot, Splash."

"I know, Gran'mom."

"The night that your grandfather died, he had something that he wanted to give you."

Splash swallowed the lump in his throat. His eyes cut over to his grandmother's closet door.

"He was sitting right here," Splash's grandmother explained, as she slowly rose from her rocking chair. Clutching the front of her bathrobe, she sighed and stuffed her feet into her cotton slippers. "He was waiting for you and Tia to get back here from South street, but as we both know, the two of you were never even down South Street. Who would've known? Splash, I-I still feel like you made the wrong decision by not-"

"My dad and Gran'pop told me to stay with you."

"I told you I didn't want to hear-"

"They did, Gran'mom."

"Stop it!"

Splash's grandmother's back became blurry to him as he tearfully watched her crouch over and reach into her closet. He already knew what his grandmother was reaching for. Splash clinched his jaws as a collision of deep-seeded emotions made his chest tighten up around his heart. His eyes overflowed with tears because his grandmother's refusal to accept that his dreams were actually true was really the only barrier that had ever existed in their relationship. For Splash, it was something that always bothered him in the back of his mind.

"Splash, I'm sorry, but you know I don't like to hear that foolishness."

"She finally about to pass it off," Splash quietly realized, unable to take his eyes off of the faded-green, duffel bag that his grandmother was hefting out of her closet. His heart started to slam against his chest as he wiped his eyes, and quietly watched his grandmother bring the bag in his direction. "Yo, it'll fuck Gran'mom head up, if I tell her-"

"The day that your mother and father died, your-"

"You and Gran'pop had this real crazy argument, right?"

Splash's grandmother dropped the duffel bag down at his feet and gave him a strange look.

"Gran'mom, you and Gran'pop was up here in y'all room," Splash explained, speaking words that had been told to him in a dream four years earlier. Ignoring his cell phone that had just begun to ring down in the side pocket of his brown, Banana Republic cargo- shorts was easy, because his grandmother was watching his lips like each word that he spoke was unhatching a whirlwind of powerful memories for her. "Y'all started arguin' 'cause you caught him gettin' the gun my dad gave him from under his pillow. Gran'mom, you kept blockin' the door so Gran'pop couldn't get by you. Right, Gran'mom? And when Gran'pop came back, he had this bag with him. You was in here gradin' some test papers, and Aunt Steph was downstairs feedin' me and Sabia some of my birthday cake. Gran'pop kept tryna talk to you, but you wouldn't answer him. Now, how could I know all that, Gran'mom? I was only three back then? Gran'mom, you know Aunt Steph ain't tell me,'cause she don't even know nothin' about this bag. So, if you ain't tell me, who you think did?"

Splash's cell phone started ringing again, and it still went ignored.

"Gran'mom, Gran'pop told me all that in one of my dreams."

Splash's grandmother placed her left hand over her heart ,and slowly began to backpedal to her rocking chair.

"Gran'pop told me killed one of them Cuban dudes that ran the corner where my dad died at, and he took that bag from him."

Splash's grandmother's eyes cut down to the duffel bag, then back up to him.

"It's four kilos of heroin, and the gun Gran'pop used to kill that Cuban dude with in this bag, Gran'mom."

"Get that bag out of my house, Splash."

"Gran'mom?"

"Now!"

When Splash stood up and grabbed the duffel bag by its two straps, his grandmother stared at it like a thousand snakes was inside of it .Splash stood there and waited for his grandmother to raise her eyes and look at him, but she wouldn't, which hit him with a lot of pain.

"Gran'mom, you still don't believe me, do you?"

The tears leaving Splash's grandmother's eyes matched his.

"Gran'pop told me to tell you he-"

"Stop it!!"

"That's crazy, Gran'mom."

"Get that bag out of my house, and don't come back here, until you-"

"It's cool, Gran'mom. I'm leavin'."

"Click."

"Salvatore, after them guards fucked main man up, my cousin gave him ya sister info."

"And your sure of this?"

"Him and my cousin was cellies."

"Where?"

"In the hole at the 'F'."

"State Road?"

"Yup."

"Click."

"And this cousin of yours . . . how does he know my sister?"

"He used to fuck her back in the day."

Salvatore Masino nodded his head thoughtfully and lowered his eyes down to the old newspaper that was folded on his lap. With a sigh, he unfolded the newspaper with his beefy fingers, and for a second time, with a little more interest, he began to read the article that was being discussed. The newspaper article receiving attention was about three prison guards, who were all murdered back in June. The article went on to explain how the investigating detectives, and Internal Affairs, both believed that the motives behind all three deaths were all connected. All three prison officials were employed at a Philadelphia County prison, and allegedly, the three of them had used excessive force on an inmate, who had been caught with two cell phones in his jail cell. The inmate, whose name wasn't given, was a convicted drug dealer from the Grays Ferry section of Philadelphia. It was believed that the inmate had put contracts out on the lives of all three prison guards. While waiting at a red light in his car, just blocks away from the long strip of County prisons, the first guard to die was shot twice in his face. Two days later, the second guard was stabbed in his throat outside of an Olde City nightclub. The third prison guard had been found inside of a Center City hotel elevator, with one gunshot wound to his right eye. No one had witnessed any of the slayings.

"Click."

Salvatore Masino looked up from the newspaper and glanced at the two sets of hands that were engaged in sign language behind the wide, office desk in front of him.

"Click . . . Click."

Out of the corner of his left eye, Salvatore Masino spied on a third set of Hennessy-brown hands that were deftly assembling two machine guns at the very same time.

"Click."

Salvatore Masino returned his attention back to the two sets of hands that were engaged in sign language. Opposite him, sitting behind her kidney-shaped, ivory, office desk, was Yasmeen Bey. She owned a pair of the talking-hands. Her oldest son, Malcolm, who was standing closely at her side, owned the other set of hands.

Kenyatta,Yasmeen Bey's youngest son, owned the pair of hands that were simultaneously putting together the machine guns on the other side of his mother's office.

Yasmeen Bey was forty-seven. She was born deaf, and she looked at the world through inquisitive, brown eyes. As she aged, beauty continued to submit to her physical features, but because she practiced Islam, and wore black over-garments on a daily basis, it was impossible for her looks to be admired by anyone. Only Yasmeen Bey's eyes were visible for the public to see, and nothing else. She was a business woman with some strong aspirations. She owned twenty-three Daycare centers that stretched from Philadelphia, up to South Boston, and they ended down in Orlando, Florida. Her worth was rumored to be in the low millions.

The rumors were true.

Sufyan Bey, Yasmeen Bey's father, was an intricate member of the South Philadelphia, Black mafia. His purpose was to make sure that his organization kept an ample supply of heroin and cocaine. His relationship as a close friend to Salvatore Masino made this an easy responsibility for him. Sufyan Bey was currently serving a life sentence at a Minnesota Federal prison, because of the huge seizure of nine hundred and thirty-five kilos of heroin, that were found in the basement of one of his stash houses.

The Federal task-force had celebrated triumphantly at the success of the major bust. Ignorantly, they were unaware that the South Philadelphia stash house only sheltered Sufyan Bey's smaller shipments, and that one of his other houses directly across the street held twice the amount of what was in the house that had gotten raided.

At the age of fourteen, Yasmeen Bey killed her mother, who at that time had had a gun aimed at her father's head. She had no idea why her mother had suddenly pulled the gun out of her purse, while three of them were eating breakfast at their kitchen table. However, had Yasmeen Bey known the reason behind her mother's actions, she still would have reacted in the same manner. For Yasmeen Bey, the decision to kill her mother was made with less time that it took to blink an eye. Since she was born deaf, her mother had adopted an unloving, and callous attitude towards her.

Her father didn't.

Sufyan Bey had quickly made it his priority to learn sign language to establish a communication-bridge between him and his daughter.

His wife didn't.

If Yasmeen Bey's mother would have just taken the time to learn sign language, she would have known that her husband had sent their daughter out to his car to retrieve his gun. Because her mother was so uncaring and insensitive, it had created an intense amount of animosity and hatred inside of Yasmeen Bey. Which is why, upon her swift return from her father's car, instead of handing her father his gun, she crept quietly up behind her mother and blew the back of her head off.

Despite the representation of two, respected lawyers hired by her father, Yasmeen Bey was sentenced to juvenile life. The very next day, her father's stash house was raided.

After she turned twenty-one, Yasmeen Bey was released from the all-female, juvenile facility, that was located in Bristol, Pennsylvania. A limousine had escorted her back to South Philadelphia. All of her father's money, power, and respect was waiting for her. Her father had more than enough of all three influences, so her lucrative plans to start her own chain of Daycare centers immediately flourished, without any obstacles ever hindering her progress. She was loved and admired by her entire staff. All of her employees had been personally hand-picked by her alone. Most of them were women, who had all learned sign language, and they all kept Yasmeen Bey thoroughly informed from their various sites, by communicating with her through e-mails and text-messages.

Unable to hear, Yasmeen Bey was more inclined to study the eyes of people, and their body language. She made her judgments of a person by the emotions that reflected in their eyes, instead of the words that parted their lips. This gave her the ability to detect a deceitful person within minutes of being in their presence. If a person's handshake didn't match their smile, she made it known right away. Yasmeen Bey's judgment of an individual was never questioned by anyone.

Malcolm and Kenyatta Bey, Yasmeen Bey's two sons, were her ears and voices. They were her killers too. She named them after two South Philadelphia legends, and the Bey brothers lived up to their names ruthlessly. They were fearless in the face of danger, and far more deadlier than the swine-flu.

And A.I.D.S.

Put together.

Malcolm Bey was twenty-six, and older than his brother by seven years. Both siblings were tall, and in visibly good shape, and both of them had dreadlocks that reached down to their shoulders. Their only contrast was that Malcolm had green eyes, and Kenyatta had brown eyes like his mother.

"Click . . . Click."

Salvatore Masino shifted uncomfortably in his chair.

The talking-hands stopped moving.

"My mom want chu to know that she appreciate you stopping by her office this mornin'."

"Your grandfather was a very good friend of mine, and I'm sure your mother knows that my services will always be available to her."

"That's ya word, Salvatore?"

"Absolutely."

"Well, I need you to get ya sister Trixie on the phone, 'cause my mom want me and my brother to rock that nigga that work for her."

"Click . . . Click."

Salvatore Masino looked across Yasmeen Bey's office desk into her eyes. The black material covering her head and face made her brown eyes appear more penetrating.

"That prison guard sittin' at that red light was the husband of one of my mom's favorite employees," Malcolm revealed, stepping from behind his mother's desk. He walked over to a nearby rain-streaked window that overlooked the busy intersection of 21st and Passyunk Avenue. "My mom paid for they wedding, Salvatore. They was only married for two weeks."

"I'm sorry to hear that."

The sound of a toddler wailing out in the Daycare center seeped beneath Yasmeen Bey's office door.

"Click."

"Salvatore, I'm startin' to think that ya services not really available to my fuckin' mom."

"And what would give you that impression?"

"I asked you to call Trixie, and you still ain't pull out ya mu' fuckin' cell phone yet."

"Kid, take it easy with the curse words."

"What the fuck you just say?!"

Kenyatta looked up for the first time since Salvatore had arrived. He looked at his brother, then turned his attention to Salvatore. With a sigh, he went back to assembling his A-R 15's, after his mother made eye contact with him and shook her head.

"Salvatore, you tryna fuckin' tell me what words I can say outta my fuckin' mouth?"

"Of course not. I just prefer a little re-"

Yasmeen Bey slapped the surface of her office desk with her right hand. A few pictures and knick-knacks rattled, but nothing fell.

Normally, Salvatore Masino wasn't intimidated by anyone. He was sixty-four, and had a head full of gray hair, but beneath the linen fabric of his blue, Emporio Armani suit, his old bones were still wrapped with solid muscles. He was a self-made millionaire, who preferred to be feared than loved. At the moment, Yasmeen Bey and her two sons, the oldest one especially, were completely unnerving his composure.

"Click . . . Click."

Salvatore Masino couldn't use his cell phone, because making an outgoing call would no longer allow his two bodyguards access to overhear what was being said inside of Yasmeen Bey's office.

Malcolm Bey sighed impatiently and stuffed his hands down into the pockets of his Akoo jeans. He looked out his mother's office window at Salvatore Masino's white, Ford Excursion, and he quietly wondered if the rumors about the SUV being bulletproof were actually true, as the gray skies rained on it.

"Can you answer a question for me, Malcolm?"

"What's up?"

"Why isn't your cousin to blame for this mess?" Salvatore asked, trying to make some sense out of a situation that was making his Tuesday morning a frustrating one. After glancing down at his Jagler Lecoutier watch, he crossed his legs and laced his thick fingers over his lap. "I mean, 'cause it's clear that my sister's involvement in all of this wasn't personal. I'm also for certain that had she known one of those prison guards was closely related to your mother, out of respect, she wouldn't 've agreed to taking those jobs in the first place. You understand what I'm saying? Kid, I don't know if you're aware of this, but Trixie and your mother used to be very good friends when they were younger."

"Yeah, I heard."

"Click."

"Well, how about we use this little misunderstanding as an avenue to patch up their-"

"My mom ain't tryna fix no old fuckin' friendships, Salvatore."

"Click . . . Click."

"She want revenge for her employee, and me and my brother gon' make sure she get what the fuck she want."

"And we ain't got no fuckin' picks."

Salvatore Masino looked over his shoulder at Kenyatta Bey.

"Yatta, chill."

"Fuck old head."

"Excuse me?"

"Yatta?"

"Tell him what the law is, and get him the fuck outta Mommy office then."

Smirking, Malcolm backed away from his mother's office window. He turned around and calmly walked over to the front of his mother's desk and sat on the corner of it. Only three feet separated him and Salvatore Masino.

"We payin' my cousin bail this afternoon, after the rain slow up."

Salvatore Masino jutted out his bottom lip and nodded his head.

"Me and my brother gon' rock his nut ass right after we pick him up."

"Click."

"Salvatore, my mom know Trixie about her business."

"And for her, that's all it was, Malcolm."

"And that's exactly why we just want the nigga that work for her, and we gon' leave it at that."

"I don't understand."

"It's just business for us, too."

"And how is that so?"

"Because if it wasn't, we would've rocked Trixie, then got at chu next."

"Kid, take it easy with the threats."

"I ain't cha mu' fuckin' kid, and I don't make threats."

Salvatore Masino uncrossed his legs and inhaled the citric aroma of a plug-in, lemon scented air freshener that was in an outlet on the other side of Yasmeen Bey's office. The comfort of knowing that he had two bodyguards, who would hastily exit his SUV outside, and slaughter everyone inside of Yasmeen Bey's Daycare center appeased Salvatore Masino enough to keep him semi-relaxed. He knew that his bodyguards were at attention, and prepared to make an entrance at the drop of a dime.

"Salvatore, man, you makin' this shit deeper than it gotta be. We just want Trixie to give up the nigga that-"

"She won't even consider it."

"Why you say that?"

"Trust me, it's not even an option."

"At all?"

"At all."

"Well, how 'bout this then, Salvatore, "Malcolm reasoned, brushing one of his dreadlocks out of his face. He glanced over his shoulder at his mother, then returned his attention back to Salvatore. "How 'bout me and my brother rock Angelo and Mikey for you? We'll do that shit for free, and we can have it done before the sun go down. That hundred stacks you got on they heads can stay in ya pockets, Salvatore. Real talk. I heard Trixie don't want it done 'cause they y'all nephews 'n all that, but I'm sayin', if you get me dude info, that shit a done deal, Salvatore. Favor for a favor."

"Click . . . Click."

Salvatore Masino exhaled a deep sigh and lowered his head. Malcolm Bey's offer was tempting, but Salvatore Masino knew that if he did choose to accept the conditions that went along with it, he was certain that he would be crossing a line that would leave a dark spot on his heart forever. His thirst to exact retribution on his two nephews for robbing and raping his niece was indeed a top priority of his, but in exchange, he would be committing an act that would strip his own character of the basic morals that made him the man that he was.

"We ain't got all day, Salvatore."

"My niece and her husband work for Trixie."

"Ya niece?"

Salvatore Masino nodded his head slowly. He envisioned his bodyguards exiting his SUV. He cleared his throat.

"Click."

"I never met her, "Salvatore admitted, staring past Malcolm Bey. He held Yasmeen Bey's intent stare and continued to talk, hoping to God that his bodyguards were on their way inside of the Daycare center. "She's Angelo's sister. Her name is Tia. Her and Angelo know about each other, but the two of them have never met. Actually, Trixie's the only person from my family that's ever had anything to do with her. You see, it's been almost twenty-six years, and we've all been still blaming her existence for why my sister-in-law killed my brother Car-"

"Yo, I don't want no fuckin' history lesson on ya family."

"Malcolm, before you were born, your mother, my sister Trixie, and Tia's mother, used to be very good-"

Yasmeen Bey slapped her office desk and stood up with fire in her eyes.

"Angelo and Tia is your brother and sister."

Malcolm Bey looked over his shoulder at his mother.

Kenyatta Bey stood up with one of his machine guns.

"My brother Carmen was foolin' around with your mom and Tia's mother at the same time."

"What?!"

Salvatore Masino dove to the floor when Yasmeen Bey's office door crashed open.

"Doom! Doom! Blat... Blat-Doom! Pop, Pop, pop, pop-Blat... Blat... Pop, pop-Doom! Doom! Doom! Doom!"

Chapter Four

Philadelphia teardrops.

Pennsylvania scars.

As the clouds cried, the dark skies cracked and continued to produce some powerful noises, causing the heavens to sound like they were being snapped into thousands of invisible pieces. The raindrops were the size of nickels. Once in awhile, lightning would join the mild storm and scribble its flashing-signature across the canvas of the late night sky. Since its arrival earlier in the afternoon, the heavy rainfall had remained consistent, and it was still descending with no visible signs of easing up any time soon.

It was a little past midnight when Splash pulled into his wet driveway. He stopped a few inches behind the rear of Tia's Cadillac wagon, killed the engine on his car, then exhaled a heavy sigh. After pulling his car keys out of the ignition, he tilted his head back against his headrest and exhaled another heavy sigh. His heart was shedding tears that his eyes wouldn't. Earlier, after he left his grandmother's house, he had went to his Olde City nightclub, where he had stayed in his office and drowned his feelings with a bottle of Jose Cuervo. Instead of numbing his emotions, the gold liquor had caused Splash to become introspective about how him and Tia were living their lives, and he left his office with the decision that him and Tia were no longer working for her aunt.

From behind a rain-streaked window, Tia stared down at her husband's car. She was having a funny conversation with Camay on her cell phone, as she stood at the far-end of her huge walk-in closet. Snookums was down at her bare feet licking her left ankle.

"Tia, you lyin'."

"Cam, I can call my fuckin' cousin right now, and she-"

"Crabs in his beard, though."

"Bitch, he had crabs all up in his mother fuckin' beard."

Tia and Camay erupted into giggles.

"Oh, my-Oh, my God. Tia, that is sooooo nasty."

"And he had one of them real big beards, so you can imagine how many of them nasty little mother fuckers was crawlin' all on his face."

"Illll."

"All in his mustache and everything."

"And he married?"

"Camay, his triflin' ass got two wives, and the nigga still had the nerve to cheat on both of them."

"Niggaz ain't never satisfied."

"Girl, you gon' die when I tell you how his wives found out."

"What happened?"

Tia sunk down to the floor and started to laugh hysterically. Her shrieks and giggles echoed up and down her dark, walk-in closet.

Tia's walk-in closet was once a small bedroom that had adjoined her master bedroom. Back during her mother's stylish-renovation of their house, Tia's mother had turned the small bedroom into a spacious shelter for all of her clothes. There was a center aisle of peach carpet that separated a total of four, smaller, walk-in closets. On both sides of the carpeted-walkway, there were two closets behind all-glass doors, but there was one closet in particular that was far more unique than the other three. The closet where Tia's expensive shoes lived could swivel itself into a room-sized vault. This option was only accessible if a switch was pressed beneath the shelf that displayed Tia's Christian Louboutin shoes. It was there, where Tia' s mother hid the two huge safes that Tia's father had left her with. Now, the secret-room also hid Splash's and Tia's arsenal of guns, and all of the money that the two, refrigerator-sized safes couldn't hide.

"Tia?!"

"H-Hold-Hold up. W-Wait."

"Girl, you stupid."

Tia started to laugh louder.

"Tia, it can't be that-"

"His-Camay, his-His daughter-"

"He got them from his daughter?!"

"Girl, no."

"Well, will you stop laughin' and tell me what happened, so I can laugh, too."

"Oh, my God," Tia laughed, wiping the tears that were running down her cheeks. Switching her cell phone to her other ear, she rose to her feet and laughed again. "Bitch, I-I swear, I almost peed on my fuckin' self. Camay, he was-Oh, my God. Girl, my fuckin' stomach hurt. Cam, his nasty ass was sleep on his couch, and his daughter saw one of the crabs on his face and she got real scared, right. So, she ran to her mom and was like, 'Mommy? Mommy? Daddy got all these baby roaches in his beard'."

Camay's explosion of laughter was so contagious, Tia broke out into another fit of giggles and slid back down to the floor with her cell phone pressed against her ear. When Snookums started to bounce around, and began to lick her face, Tia curled up into a fetal position and laughed louder.

Five minutes later, Tia and Camay were sharing an awkward silence on their cell phones. Their laughs and high-spirits had gotten killed by the arrival of Camay's boyfriend. His presence in Camay's bedroom had created such an air of strained tension, Tia could feel it thriving on the other end of her cell phone.

"Tia, I'ma call you tomorrow on my lunch-"

"Beep."

Tia looked at the screen of her cell phone when it alerted her that she was receiving an incoming call. Her heart belonged to the second caller.

"Cam, hold on."

"If that's Splash, I'm hangin' up."

"Why?"

"'Cause you gon' have me holdin' on forever, and-"

"Well, bye."

"Bye."

"Camay?"

"What?"

"You better make sure Robbie ain't got no baby roaches in-"

"Bitch, shut the-"

Tia thumbed the screen of her cell phone and placed it back to her ear.

"Bay, what's wrong?"

When Splash didn't say anything, Tia sighed and stared helplessly out at his car. With her index finger, she traced a trickle of rain as it slid down the outside of her closet window. Sadness began to hum a melody inside of her heart, causing both of her eyes to grant several teardrops their freedom. She was emphatically aware that the loss of her husband's parents bothered him the most when his birthday came around.

"My heart gon' always be the sponge for ya pain, Bay."

The dark skies cracked into invisible pieces.

48

"No matter how deep it is, you can always share it with me."

"I'm home."

"I know."

"You don't miss a beat, huh?"

"Not when it come to you."

"Where you at?"

"My closet."

"Oh."

"I gotta surprise for you, Bay."

"You got Snookums euthanized?"

"Stop bein' smart."

"Yo, I'm dead serious."

"Boy, shut up."

"Is ya surprise gon' make me feel better?"

"Yup."

"Fancy face?"

"Huh?"

"My heart gon' always be a sponge for ya pain, too."

"I know, Bay."

A few seconds ticked by without Splash or Tia saying anything else.

"I love you, Bay."

"I love you more."

"Now, can you hurry up?"

"Roger that."

When Splash ended their call and stepped out of his car, Tia turned from her closet window and took off in a sprint. She could feel the wings of butterflies tickling the inside of her stomach as she ran. Biting her bottom lip anxiously, she did a hurdle over Snookums, and raced out of her walk-in closet into her master bedroom. While running, Tia wiped what was left of her tears from her cheeks.

Snookums was right on Tia's heels. He chased her fast-moving feet across the Brazilian, hardwood floors, did half a lap with them around Tia's staged-bed, and continued his foot-pursuit over to Tia's silver, perfume stand.

After giving her countless perfume bottles a quick once-over, Tia chose her 'Halle' perfume. She sprayed the enticing fragrance a few inches away from herself, and giggled girlishly when her skin tingled from its aromatic-kisses, as she did a pirouette in its falling mist. Leaving her cell phone on her perfume stand, Tia stepped over to her wall-sized mirror that separated Splash's walk-in closet from their master bathroom.

"Now, it's time to get unwrapped," Tia thought, looking at her naked reflection, as she stepped into her red, peep-toe, Guisseppe Zanotti stilettos. Done with appraising herself, she looked down at Snookums. "See you tomorrow, Snookums. Don't be up here bein' bad, either. Now, Mommy gotta go."

Tia rushed over to her bedroom door and quickly pulled it shut behind her. The further she walked down her long, dark, hallway, the less she could hear Snookums' whimpering escaping beneath her bedroom door. In haste, she quickened her steps as she tried to make it to her designated spot before Splash entered their house.

Unfortunately, as Tia immediately noticed, Splash was already standing down in their Roman-styled foyer. He was finger-jabbing their alarm panel that was embedded on the wall beside the arched entrance that led to their dining room.

"Bay, you feel like opening one of your birthday presents early?"

"What's wrong wit' the alarm system?"

Splash's and Tia's entire mini-mansion was computerized. From various stations in their house, touch-screen panels were available, offering them a choice of system controls that included security, lighting, music, and it also listed indoor and outdoor zones of their house.

"The motion-lights ain't come on when I pulled up, either."

"Probably the rain."

"Where you at?"

"Up here."

"Oh, I ain't . . . even . . . see . . . you."

When Splash looked up, he couldn't believe that his own eyes were being honest with him. His wife was completely naked, except for a gigantic, red, gift ribbon that was wrapped around her waist. Splash was mesmerized by what he saw. His lips parted in amazement. Once again, Tia had done something that left him astounded, and her timing was perfect. She was standing up on their second floor landing, where their hallway opened out gracefully into a black, marbled-terrace. Her back was against their aquarium that was built inside of their hallway's wall, giving her naked, gift- wrapped body a pinkish-silhouette.

Splash's and Tia's handsome fish tank was 20 feet wide, and it boasted a variety of colorful, freshwater fish. Upon closer inspection of the magnificent aquarium, Splash's first wedding band could be spotted resting on the pink gravel, nestled between a white castle, and a treasure chest, that was back in the far right corner.

"For me?"

"Yup," Tia blushed, placing her hands on her hips as she assumed a sexy pigeon-toed stance. The look of hunger in Splash's eyes made her pussy wetter than the weather outside. "All for you, Bay. Unless you wanna wait for your birthday, or something."

Beyonce's song, 'Halo' was floating in the darkness throughout Splash's and Tia's entire house. Wall speakers were emitting the soft melody everywhere, giving their small castle a sense of warmth and comfort just like Tia wanted it to.

"Ya period went off?"

"It sure did."

"Solid."

Tia smiled. For her, being a wife was one of the highlights of her life. She treasured the relationship that she shared with her husband. It was the core of her strength. With no mother for guidance, Tia had learned how to be a good wife from reading self-help books on marriage, and by listening to her T.V.-mother; Oprah. She knew that she was a handful, and that she worked her husband's nerves, but when it came to his happiness, she never had a problem bending over backwards for him.

"What's goin' on in the theater?"

"Go look."

Splash stepped further into his dark foyer. His sneakers left six, wet footprints on the black, Pergo floors behind him. When he reached the entrance of his Home Theater, he glanced inside, then looked up at Tia with appreciation dancing in his eyes. She had his favorite porn-DVD playing on their movie screen.

"What chu thinkin' about right now, Bay?"

"Honestly?"

"Honestly."

"A lot of shit."

"Like?"

Splash lowered his head and sighed. His eyes rested on the duffel bag in his right hand.

"Bay, if-"

"Tee, what's on my mind gon' fuck the mood up."

"Can it wait 'til tomorrow?"

"Yea."

"Good, 'cause I'm tryna go half on a baby."

"I got my half."

"You better."

Splash met Tia at the rear of their foyer, where their leather-padded spiral staircase flowed down from their terrace. He sat his duffel bag down by his feet and caught Tia when she jumped in his arms.

"You smell good."

"And you smell like you been drinkin'."

"Cuervo."

"Figures."

For the space of a couple of heartbeats, Splash and Tia gazed at each other and spoke no words. Amazingly, with nearly seven years invested into their marriage, and countless obstacles behind them, they were both still madly in love with each other and they both knew it.

He was her.

She was him.

They were Mr. and Mrs. Gunplay.

"I'd kill God for you, Fancy face."

"Kiss me, Bay."

My halo.

"Where?"

"Anywhere you want."

When Splash bent his head and softly kissed her on her lips, Tia felt her insides melt like plastic inside of a microwave. She let out a guttural moan as Splash's hands slowly slid down the center of her back. His touch felt so good. Heat started to radiate where his hands palmed her ass cheeks, sending waves of liquid fire up and down the back of her thighs. She had only meant for her and Splash's kiss to be brief, but as he began to kiss her more greedily, Tia couldn't stop herself from matching his lust by licking back into his mouth with pleasure. She sighed at the prickly sensation of her nipples hardening, as they responded to the dampness of Splash's shirt. Tia parted her legs and welcomed Splash's fingers as they inched closer to her pussy.

My halo.

Splash pulled Tia's bottom lip into his mouth and sucked on it, as he slid his middle finger inside of her pussy. She was wetter than the bottom of a boat out in the middle of the ocean, and the fact that she was so turned on, turned Splash on. His dick grew to its full length of ten inches. Tia's fists grabbed two handfuls of the front of his white, short-sleeved, Kenneth Cole shirt.

"Squeeze it."

Splash's voice in Tia's right ear sent chills through her entire body. Like he had commanded, she tightened the walls of her pussy around his finger. She closed her eyes and imagined that his finger was actually his dick.

"You ready for another one?"

Tia sighed and nodded her head.

My halo.

Splash placed another finger inside of Tia in a slow and deliberate motion. Slowly, he began to move his fingers in and out of her. The urge to taste Tia's pussy made him kiss her harder. Her tongue danced with his. He could feel the walls of Tia's pussy squeezing his fingers every time he pushed them back inside of her.

"You gon' fuck me all night, Bay?"

Splash nodded his head.

"Promise?"

"Promise."

"Can I ride it?"

Splash nodded his head again.

"Can I suck it?"

Splash didn't nod his head, and he didn't answer Tia, because he couldn't. Visions of Tia riding his dick had stolen his voice. A second later, visions of her sucking his dick as she stared in his eyes gave his voice back.

"Squeeze them."

Tia sighed with pleasure and did as she was told. Behind her closed her eyelids, visions of Splash fucking her from the back were intoxicating her with lust and extreme pleasure. She could feel the thickness of his dick gliding along her pussy walls. She felt the fat head of his dick touching the back of her sugar tunnel.

My halo.

Splash knew that Tia was about to explode, because her body started to vibrate against his. Her moans began to grow louder. She wrapped her arms around him tighter and leaned her forehead against his shoulder. Splash finger-fucked Tia harder and faster. He pushed his two fingers inside of her as deep as he could get them.

"Squeeze them."

"Bay?"

"Go 'head."

"Oh, my God."

"Squeeze them again."

"Unnnnnn."

"Yea, like that."

"Bay?"

"What?"

"I'm-"

"Let it go, Fancy face."

Tia could feel all of the juices in her body rushing for her pussy. It felt like her lungs weren't getting enough oxygen. Her heart felt like it was beating a thousand times a minute. Her legs were trembling. Her stilettos suddenly felt like stilts. Tia could feel her orgasm reaching its apex, and it felt so good.

"Cum all over my fingers."

"I am-I-I-I'm-Oh, my-Unnnnnnnnnnn."

Tia's moans were like music to Splash's ears. He held onto her limp body with pride. He held his wife's body with nothing but undying love in his heart for her.

My halo.

"Wow."

"You cool?"

Tia exhaled a deep sigh and nodded her head with a satisfied smile on her face. She looked up into her husband's eyes and shook her head.

"I should get my fingers bronzed."

"Boy, shut up."

"I'ma get some insurance on these mu'fuckers."

"Alright, Bay," Tia sighed, stepping away from Splash with unsteady legs. Her heart was still doing backflips in her chest. "I'm ready to get unwrapped. Take that wet stuff off and come in the theater, so we can finish part 2 of this."

With that said, Tia turned her back to Splash and started strutting sexily down their foyer towards their theater. Her stilettos clicked all the way there.

Splash pulled his gun off of his waist and started to undress like his clothes were on fire. His hard dick slapped his stomach when he pulled off his Polo boxers and shucked them to floor.

"Ay, Tee, I'm gon' for a record to-"

"Ahhhhhhhhhhhhh!!!"

Tia's scream had so much fear attached to it, Splash's heart skipped two beats. His blood curdled in his veins as his legs took him forward with speed. When he reached the arched-entrance of his theater, the lights were suddenly cut on, momentarily blinding him in his tracks. Once his eyes adjusted to the flood of light, his dick got soft, and his heart dropped down to the heels of his feet. Splash dreadfully realized that the storm had nothing to do with his alarm system not working.

"If your black ass move one more fuckin' inch, I will blow her goddamn head off!"

With clenched fists, and his heart slamming wildly inside of his chest, Splash glared across his theater into the white man's eyes, who had two guns aimed at Tia's head. His eyes then flicked to the other white man, who was slowly approaching him with a shotgun. Splash had the slightest idea who the two white men were, or what they wanted, but from the looks in their eyes, they meant business, which made it obvious to Splash that him and Tia didn't have too much longer to live.

Splash and Tia locked eyes.

My halo.

Chapter Five

A single teardrop escaped Tia's eye, and slowly trickled its way down her right cheek.

"Bitch, you better stay still."

Tia swallowed nervously and lowered her hand back down to her side. Her entire body began to tremble in fear as she dared herself to raise her eyes, and look at the face of the white man standing beside her. She quickly noticed that the color of his eyes matched hers. Tia's eyes stretched open in disbelief when her suspicion of who the man was rang true.

"Do I still need to introduce myself?"

Tia stayed silent as her eyes studied her brother's face. His skin was pale, and his mustache and beard was so scraggly, it looked more like a disguise than anything else. He didn't resemble the person that she saw in the photo albums at her aunt's house. In person, her brother looked like the ghost of the man she had seen in the pictures. He was much thinner, and he smelled like he hadn't taken a shower in months.

"Yo, what the fuck ya'll want?!"

The white man with the shotgun stopped a few feet in front of Splash and smirked.

"Pussy, what the fuck-"

"Click-Clack."

Splash gave the white man with the shotgun a defiant stare to let him know that racking his shotgun didn't intimidate him one bit.

"You wanna be a hero?"

"Fuck you."

"Fuck with me."

"Mikey?!"

"Angelo, this-"

"Yo, ya'll in the wrong fuckin' house!!"

Tia looked at Splash with sad eyes. She wanted to tell him who the two intruders were, but shock had kidnapped her voice. It was still hard for her to accept the fact that her brother was standing inside of her house. With each passing second, her fear rose to another level.

"Listen, dog, ya'll mu' fuckers in the wrong spot."

"Ya name Splash, right?"

"Man, how the-"

"G-G-G-G-G-unit!!"

Angelo and Mikey spun on their heels with wide eyes. They both aimed their guns at the huge birdcage next to Splash's and Tia's concession stand.

"Holy shit."

"Angelo, it's one of them fuckin' talkin' birds."

The charming bird preening his feathers inside of the huge birdcage was an African gray parrot. His name was Gunna. He was an old birthday present that Tia gave to Splash. Gunna could mimic songs, movies, people, and just about anything that he overheard. Since Splash and Tia entertained a lot of their guests in their theater, Gunna's vocabulary was very extensive, and he was comically known for blurting out some of the craziest stuff at the oddest times.

"Eat that cake, Anna Mae."

"What he say?"

"Hey, Mikey, Fuck the bird and concentrate!"

Splash and Tia stared at each other, both wondering what the other one was thinking.

"Your Splash, right?"

"Who the fuck is you?"

Tia looked at her brother when he chuckled.

"Ask your wife."

Splash looked at Tia with confusion in his eyes. Her facial expression told him many things and nothing at the same time.

"I'm Angelo, and my cousin Mikey is the one with the shotgun pointed at ya dick."

"We here for the fuckin' safes."

Angelo looked over at Gunna's birdcage and shook his head.

"We been in here ten minutes, Angelo."

Like Tia, Splash was wondering how Tia's brother and cousin had discovered where they lived. He recalled a conversation a week earlier, where Tia's aunt Trixie was telling him and Tia how her nephews had raped and murdered one of their own female cousins.

"Bring his ass over here, Mikey."

"I don't know who lied to ya'll, but them safes not here no-"

"Bitch, shut the fuck up!"

Tia melted to the floor when her brother smacked her in the face with one of his guns. As she fell, her right ankle twisted in her stiletto, causing her to reach for it in agony.

"Mother fucker, you want some, too."

Splash never knew what it felt like to be a coward, but he did at that very moment. Humiliation introduced itself to his heart as he crouched down beside his wife and covered her body protectively with his own.

"They gon' kill us, Bay."

Tia's whisper entered Splash's left ear and placed a strong grip around the throat of his soul. His wife's fears unnerved him. He had to do something.

"Put your hands behind your fuckin' back!"

"Man, I ain't-"

"Do it, or I'ma shoot through you just to kill her!"

Angelo's threat made Splash hold Tia tighter.

"Oh, you think-"

"Alright!" Splash barked, letting Tia go slowly. His adrenaline was racing through his veins. "Ya'll mu ' fuckers doin' this shit for nothin', 'cause we ain't got no fuckin' safes in here!"

"Shut the fuck up, and put your goddamn hands behind your back!"

"He tellin' ya'll the truth!"

"Bitch, say somethin' else."

"Tee, chill!"

"But they not here no more!" Tia screamed, ignoring Splash. Her emotions were getting the best of her as she watched Mikey handcuff Splash's hands behind his back. "Somebody lied to ya'll. My mom been moved-"

"Fuck your mom!"

Tia stared into her brother's soulless eyes. His statement about her mother had struck a nerve.

"Fifteen minutes ,Angelo."

"We on schedule?"

"Sort of."

"Okay, gimme that chloroform shit, and keep your eyes on her."

Mikey dug his hands into the front of his windbreaker jacket and pulled out a small jar, and a torn piece of an orange, dirty towel.

"Oh, naw," Splash protested, as he tried to rise back to his feet. A knee to the center of his back from Angelo sent him crashing back to his carpeted-theater floor. "Pussy, get off me! Yo, ya'll ain't-Arggh. Get-Arrghhh."

"Leave him the fuck alone!"

Angelo had a psychotic look in his eyes as he viciously pistol-whipped Splash with his guns. The sight of blood pouring out of the back of Splash's head fed his frenzy. Even when Splash's body went limp beneath him, he continued to rain down blows.

"Splash?!"

"Mikey, get-Get this bitch off-"

Mikey dropped his shotgun, the jar of chloroform, and the small piece of towel, and ran up behind Tia. He grabbed a handful of her and yanked her off of Angelo, but his only mistake was that he had let Tia go. Luckily for him, Angelo had been given enough time to recuperate from Tia's sudden attack and was able to stop Tia from reaching his shotgun.

A blind-sided kick from Angelo left Tia dizzy. Her face nose-dived down to her carpet with a thud. She twisted her face in pain when her brother kicked her again. Mikey's shotgun became blurry to her as tears drowned her eyes. She couldn't believe that her and Splash were so helpless inside of their own house.

"Looks like we won't be needing' the chloroform after all."

"She almost got to your fuckin' gun, Mikey."

"My bad."

"Just go get-"

"Flavorrrrr Flaaave!!"

Angelo's neck whip-lashed in the direction of Gunna's birdcage. He let out a heavy exhale in relief when his eyes rested on the colorful bird.

"Can I bring it with us?"

"Fuck no."

"Why not?"

"Mikey, we not takin' the fuckin' bird."

Tia turned on her side and looked over at Splash's motionless body. The blood from his head was making a stain in the carpet all around him.

"Mikey, go get Aunt Trixie, and hurry up."

Angelo's orders to Mikey answered all of the questions that were floating around in Tia's mind. A new pain joined the agony she was already feeling. With great disappointment, Tia closed her eyes and as she started to sob quietly, she vowed to herself that her brother and cousin would have to kill her first, because by no means was she going to let them rape her as long as she had a single breath inside of her lungs.

Outside, on Splash's and Tia's rear-patio, Trixie Masino was slowly regaining consciousness. Both of her eyes were swollen shut. She was hog-tied, and had on nothing but a pink, Hollister sweater. Her nephews had sodomized her with a gun and had used a tire iron to break her collar bone. Not slipping back into an unconscious state of mind for Trixie was a struggle; mind, body, and soul. She fought the urge to blackout with every aching fiber in her body. The inner battle was so difficult, that for ten seconds, she had forgotten to exhale. Her nephews had beaten her unmercifully, until a sobbing confession of where Tia lived had escaped her bloody lips.

Trixie Masino was willing to bet her life that Jen had told Angelo and Mikey where her condo was. Her nephews had arrived not even an hour after Jen had left her house. Angelo and Mikey had gained entry to her building by pulling a fire alarm.

The sound of Splash's and Tia's patio door being slid open immediately made Trixie's body tense. She hadn't the slightest idea where she was.

"Your presence is finally needed, Aunt Trixie."

"Take . . . me . . . to . . . a . . . hospital."

"Not on your life."

Trixie Masino hissed in pain when she felt a handful of her hair get grabbed roughly. As she was pulled by it, her shattered collarbone punctured through her skin, making her howl out in agony. Every raindrop that hit her body felt like bullets as they landed on her skin.

When Mikey reappeared dragging her aunt by her hair, Tia gasped at the sight of her.

"We did a nice job on her, didn't we?"

Tia rolled her eyes at her brother, then looked back at her aunt unsympathetically. Had their roles been reversed, she would have chosen death over giving up her aunt's whereabouts to anyone, let alone, her brother and cousin, so, with knowing this, Tia had a newfound disgust in her heart for her aunt as she looked at her hog-tied body.

"Aunt Trixie, this bitch here is tryna fool me into believin' my dad's safes aren't here any-"

"Why you bring these mother fuckers to my house, Aunt Trixie?!" Tia screamed, glaring at her aunt's swollen and bruised face. She could feel the fear in her heart becoming a different type of emotion, and she welcomed it, because it was transforming into anger, and she knew that if she became extremely upset, she was capable of doing anything. "How could you do this shit to me and Splash of all fuckin' people?! How could you do this to us?! Huh?! After all the shit we did for you! Aunt Trixie, you ain't shit! I fuckin' hate chu! Look what they did to my fuckin' husband!"

"Cuff her, Mikey."

"Who?"

"Who the fuck do you think?"

"Her?"

"Who the fuck else?"

Tia felt the temptation to claw her cousin's eyes out when he approached her brandishing a second set of handcuffs. When he placed them on her wrists in front of her, instead of behind her back, she bit down on her lower lip anxiously, because he had just made a grave mistake.

"Mikey, if those safes are as big as we heard, I'll find them my fuckin' self."

"What about them?"

"Keep an eye on him and Aunt Trixie for me."

"And her?"

"She's comin' with me."

Tia's eyes flicked from Mikey to Angelo.

"Why not kill him and Aunt Trixie, and get it over with right now?"

" 'Cause all the fuckin' shootin' gon' wake up their neighbors, and I wanna get the money before-"

"Angelo, if you ask me, I think the storm will drown out anything that we do in-"

"Mikey, just do what the fuck I said!"

"Okay, I'll wait 'til you come back."

"Tia, it gotta be now, or never," Tia quietly encouraged herself, frowning in pain as she shifted her weight to her right ankle. Her eyes cut over to the small stack of fashion magazines that were laying on the carpet ten feet away from her. "You can do it. Just go 'head. If you don't, they gon' kill you and Splash. Tia, you gotta hurry-"

"King Kong, ain't got . . . nothin' . . . on . . . me!!"

The sound of the actor Denzel Washington's voice startled Angelo and Mikey. With wild eyes, both of them dove to the floor, and aimed their guns in the direction of Gunna's birdcage.

"Jesus fuckin' Christ!"

"Mikey, I fuckin' swear, I'm gonna kill that dumb ass bird, if it says one more-"

Tia bolted into action.

"Mikey, get her!"

"Boom!!"

Mikey's shotgun roared like twenty lions.

"Bocka! Bocka! Bocka! Bocka!"

Angelo shot at Tia's fast-moving, naked body like he was trying to set her bones on fire. He kept his Kahr 45's fixed on Tia's last row of theater seats, because she was using the furniture for cover as she ducked and continued to run. The recoil from Angelo's guns shook his thin arms, causing his bullets to fly high over Tia's head.

Tia thought of her mother as she ran beside the backs of her theater seats. Tears were streaming from her eyes. Bullets were violating everything around her, and as one of them grazed the back of her right arm, she went down on one knee and flipped over her Vogue magazine. After taking a deep breath, Tia let out a loud scream, because as her index finger married the trigger of her pistol-gripped, 357 automatic, she could feel the intense rush of vindication swelling inside of her veins.

"Boom!!"

Tia disregarded the threat of Mikey's shotgun and rose from behind her theater seats with vengeance glowing in her eyes. The Sig Sauer in her hands had been accessorized with a sound suppressor, so as she pumped its trigger, the blue metal simply jerked and coughed.

"Pfft, Pfft, Pfft, Pfft, Pfft."

Horror painted a dark expression on Angelo's face as his eyes watched five of Tia's hot bullets kiss his cousin's face. Fearing the same fate, he ran frantically through an entrance of Splash's and Tia's theater that led to their kitchen.

"Don't run now!" Tia screamed, shooting Mikey three more times as she stepped over his lifeless body. She was tempted to shoot her aunt as she jogged by her. "Ya'll mother fuckers wanted to come up in here, and kill me and my fuckin' husband tonight?! You was gon' try to rape me, Angelo?! Huh?! Aunt Trixie ain't tell you and Mikey that we kill people for a livin' in this mother fuckin' house?! Me and my fuckin' husband gone bury you and Mikey in our backyard!!"

Tia stepped around the hexagon-shaped island in her kitchen with slow and deliberate steps. Her heart was up in her throat, but she was far from scared. She felt braver than she had ever felt in her life. Cold air danced around her ankles as she slowly, and cautiously approached her patio doors. Small puddles of rain and shards of glass were at her feet.

The sound of car tires screeching in the distance met Tia's ears when she stepped out onto her rear-patio. There was no doubt in Tia's mind that the driver of the fast-moving car was none other than her brother. She let out a soft whimper, and buckled down to her rain-wet, patio floors. Releasing her gun, she began to cry like a baby, because even though a strong sense of relief was stroking her heart, she was inwardly struggling with the hard and cold fact that she had to walk back into her house, and put a bullet inside of her aunt's head.

Chapter Six

Rain.

On.

Me.

The thunderstorm taking place only appeared to be incomplete and lacking all of its qualities, because there wasn't any sort of dazzling, lightning display to go along with it. However, ever present as it was, the thunder sounded like a gigantic, bowling ball was being rolled across the late night skies, while a steady downpour of raindrops fell to the earth like every angel up in heaven was shedding tears.

Beneath those same crying skies, Tia stood fixated on the middle of her rear-patio with her eyes staring blankly at the darkness of her backyard. Her hair was plastered against her face. She was still crying. Her gun was back in her hands. Down at her feet, raindrops were beating at the surface of her patio floors, creating a rhythmic sound that was reminiscent to a tribe of Indians beating on their drums.

Simply as a precaution, Tia looked over her shoulder one last time, before she turned her back on her rear-patio and backyard, and stepped back inside of her house. Suddenly, a frightening and horrific thought crossed Tia's mind. She took off for her home theater in a hurry. Fear stabbed at her a thousand and one times when she realized that her brother could have possibly made it back into her house through her front door. Tia's worries were highlighted when she heard her aunt release a shrill cry. In haste, she quickened her steps with her gun leading the way.

Time seemed to slow down for Tia as she reentered her home theater. The feeling of fear unhanded her heart, and the voice in her mind told her that everything was okay, but she still didn't lower her gun. She wasn't convinced that the worst was over. Besides her eyes, the only thing moving on Tia's body were the raindrops that were dripping from her skin.

Tia's home theater was just another reminder of the creative talent that was lost with the untimely death of her mother. It was one of her finest projects. Plush, white carpet covered the floors. Facing the 14-foot wide movie screen, were five rows of tomato red, leather seats. There were four seats in each row, with two-step drops at the start of each one. Up above them, a plexi-glass ceiling provided an amazing view of Splash's and Tia's office, and their guest bedroom. It was a feature of the home theater that always left people impressed. Adding the sports-bar and concession stand were Splash's ideas.

Eerily, the sound of thunder sent chills through Tia's body. She shivered like a tongue made of ice had licked her spine.

Tia's home theater looked like the end of an intense, drama-influenced, movie set. A connect-the-dots trail of bullet holes was peppered across her movie screen. The big holes rose and dove like an earthquake's seismic chart. The huge dots ended on the opposite side of Tia's home theater, three feet shy of Gunna's tall, Bamboo birdcage. On the carpet, spent shell casings were plain to see. Red cartridges from Mikey's shotgun matched the blood that stained the white carpet, where his head and face had vomited his brains and left eye.

After Tia looked around at everything, and everyone, she knew that some type of miracle had unfolded inside of her house, and although she wasn't a spiritual person, she felt truly grateful for the favor that God had given her and her husband. Taking a deep breath, she realized just how emotionally unstable she actually was. She felt like a butterfly in a tornado. It was sheer will power that was keeping her legs from turning into jelly. Even as she reluctantly accepted that all of the madness was finally done and over with, her nerves were still going berserk. Her heart was banging against her chest like a wild animal inside of a small cage. She could see, but just barely, because of the new tears that were drowning her green eyes. Her gun no longer held significance as the sight of her husband pinched her heart.

"Tia?"

The sound of Tia's gun falling to the floor reached Trixie's ears.

"Tia, is-Tia, is that you?"

Tia looked down at the gun at her feet.

"Tia?"

Just as Tia was about to reach down and pick up her gun, her peripheral vision caught Splash making a slight movement, which inspired her to ignore her aunt, and focus all of her attention on her husband. She forced her unstable legs to start moving. The pain exploding in her right ankle forced her to limp.

"Tee?"

"I'm right here, Bay."

"What-"

Splash groaned in pain as Tia helped him turn over onto his side. His shoulders felt like they were about to pop.

"Bay, you-"

"Tee, get these fuckin' cuffs off me."

"Okay."

"What happened?"

Splash shut his eyes when a series of sharp pains began to stab the back of his head. He clenched his jaws and waited for them to end, but when they became more intense, he kept his eyes closed and suffered in silence.

"Bay, Aunt Trixie brung them here."

Splash opened his eyes.

"I killed one of 'em, but the other one got away."

Splash closed his eyes again. He flinched when some raindrops from Tia's wet hair landed on his ribcage and raced across his stomach. The handcuffs on his wrists were so tight, his fingertips were numb. What Tia had just told him about her aunt provided a numbing sensation to the excruciating pain living in the back of his head, and as he opened his eyes to look at Tia, the look on her face confirmed what he didn't want to be true.

"She right over there."

Tia moved her left knee so that Splash could see her aunt. In doing so, he got to see Mikey's lifeless body as well.

"She dead?"

"She alive . . . for now."

"Go see if he got keys for-"

A shock of pain prohibited Splash from completing the rest of his sentence.

"Don't we got handcuff keys upstairs, if he don't?"

Splash nodded his head painfully.

"Is ours Smith & Wesson?"

Splash grimaced and nodded his head again.

"These is, too."

"Tee, hurry up."

Tia stood back up and paused. She looked back down at the deep gashes in the back of Splash's head and sighed. His pain was hers. She was him. Her next pattern of moves were fueled by her husband's dire need for some medical attention.

"Call Sabia, Tee."

An hour and thirty-seven minutes later, Splash and Tia were joined by five more people. After calling Splash's cousin Sabia, Tia had also called her best friend Camay, who had arrived shortly after Splash's cousin. The other three people were Salvatore Masino, and his three bodyguards. They had showed up while Splash and Tia were upstairs in their bedroom putting on some clothes.

In Splash's and Tia's absence, Trixie Masino had convinced Splash's cousin that her brother could help dispose of Mikey's body. His phone call to Salvatore had Tia extremely upset with him.

Splash's porno-DVD was still playing on the movie screen, but no one made mention of it.

"Tia, I was tryna help ya'll the fuck out!"

"By callin' some mother fuckin' strangers to my goddamn house, Sabia?!"

"Ay, yo, ya aunt know 'em, and stop fuckin' hollerin' at me, too!"

"Sabia, that bitch you untying is the reason why me and ya fuckin' cousin almost died to-"

"She ya fuckin' aunt!"

"That bitch ain't shit to me!"

"That bitch ain't shit to me!"

"Gunna, shut the fuck up!"

Splash wanted to speak, but he had a splitting headache. His eyes were on Salvatore and his two bodyguards. He wasn't paying Tia and his cousin any attention. His hands were wrapped around the Glock 45 and extra clip that were concealed in the pockets of his black, Ralph Lauren bathrobe. He was sitting two barstools away from Camay, who was also watching Salvatore and his bodyguards, as they talked in a huddle over Mikey's dead body.

"Splash, tell Tia to get outta my way."

Tia looked at Sabia in disgust as he scooped her aunt's body off of the floor.

"Tee, come here."

"Bay, she-"

"Come here."

Tia reluctantly stepped aside and let Sabia walk by with her aunt. She was mad at Splash's cousin, because she wanted him to have hatred in his heart for her aunt, but by him showing her different, she looked at him like he was traitor too. She didn't want to cry, but her aunt's disloyalty had cut her deep, and to see her get carried away cut her even deeper, so as she slowly walked over to her husband and stepped into his embrace, she unshamefully let all of her emotions run free.

"I know, Fancy face, "Splash whispered, as his own eyes became cloudy. His wife seldom cried openly, so he knew that she was really hurting inside. "But fuck it, though. Tee, you not fuckin' with her gon' kill her ghost. This our mu'fuckin' reason to be done. We can live regular now. You hear me?"

Tia nodded her head against Splash's chest.

"We got a second chance at life, and we gon' make the most of every fuckin' day we wake up to."

"Bay, I wanna kill her."

"I do, too."

Splash and Tia shot Camay a surprised look when she made a gagging sound and began to vomit. Both of them watched her as she sprinted out of their home theater in the direction of one their downstairs bathrooms. The sight of Mikey's face had been too much for Camay's stomach.

"You ain't gon' holla at him, before he leave?"

"I ain't got nothin' to say to him."

"That's ya uncle, Tee."

"And that was my fuckin' aunt that ya cousin carried out of here."

Splash understood how Tia felt, but as her uncle got closer, he felt compelled to say something. Her uncle's eyes showed concern, so as his bodyguards passed by with Mikey's body, Splash fell in stride and walked with him.

"Good lookin' out."

"I wish I could've prevented this from happening."

Splash followed Salvatore and his bodyguards into his foyer. When they reached his front door, he stepped around them and opened it for them with a heavy sigh.

"That was a family member of yours that left with my sister?"

"Yea, that was my cousin."

"He's a good kid."

"Yea, he cool."

"I didn't mean any disrespect by coming to your house unannounced, or anything."

With his bodyguards on their way to his SUV with Mikey, Salvatore appeared to have something that he wanted to get off his chest, and Splash noticed it right away.

"Your sister was the only one from her dad side of the family that she ever had."

Salvatore pushed Splash's front door closed and placed his back against it. He let out an exhausted sigh and looked down at his left arm that was in a new cast.

"What chu got shot?"

Salvatore raised his eyebrows and nodded his head.

"When?"

"This morning."

"You know where ya nephew Angelo be at?"

"When I find out, I promise to call you first."

"You a man of ya word?"

When Salvatore smiled, Splash smiled too. An unspoken bond had been formed between them. In the darkness of

Splash's foyer, standing beside one of the many pillars that soared to the ceiling, Splash and Salvatore shook hands.

"You think you can arrange for me to talk to your wife?"

"Not tonight."

Splash looked over his shoulder when he heard Tia clear her throat.

"Tia, can I speak to you for a second?"

Splash shook his head when Tia ignored her uncle and disappeared back into their home theater. A flicker of shame lived in Salvatore's eyes for a couple of seconds, so Splash avoided his eye contact purposely.

"I'm willing to hear any advice that'll help me out."

"Be thorough, and just start actin' like her uncle."

"What's your cousin's name?"

"Who?"

"The one that took Trixie to the hospital?"

"His name Sabia."

"Is this his number?"

Splash looked at the screen on Salvatore's cell phone. His eyes stared at the only number that he recognized.

"Is it okay for me to get your number from him?"

"Splash, why is you still fuckin' talkin' to him?"

"Tee, chill."

Salvatore pulled Splash's and Tia's front door open and stepped out into the rain. He lowered his head and followed their pebbled-walkway that stretched over to their driveway, where his bulletproof SUV was waiting. He knew that Splash and Tia were both watching him, because he didn't hear their front door shut behind him.

"Hey, Uncle Salvatore?"

Salvatore turned around and looked at his brother's only daughter with hope in his eyes.

"Tell Aunt Trixie we quit, and that I hope she die in her own spit up."

Chapter Seven

"A million fuckin' dollars, Gary?"

"Dog, we do this shit, we'll be up like Viagra."

"You gotta ratchet for me?"

"No question."

"What we gon' do it in?"

"My bitch from Nicetown gon' let me use her wheel."

"Not that fat bitch you told me you met on the party-line?"

"Yup."

"You trippin'."

"She think I gotta fuckin' job interview out near that mall where ya cousin Camay live."

"It be that much money in them Super Markets?"

"Just think ... this truck be on some shit, pickin' up like, fifty, sometimes, sixty thousand, from like thirty different mu' fuckin' Super Markets 'n shit, Prep."

"Damn."

"That's what I'm sayin', and the last jawn they stop at down South Philly, on Oregon-"

"Yo, them guards that be on them trucks ain't sweet, though, Gary."

"These mu'fuckers drivin' this truck look like some 'Grumpy old men' type of mu'fuckers, Prep."

"That's crazy."

"And the fuckin' e-way only three blocks away."

"And you tryna do this shit this Saturday?"

"They only do this shit on the first Saturday of every month, so we-"

"You 'bout to have me in my fuckin' bag, and I ain't been out of jail for six hours yet."

"Ay, man, you tryna win, right?"

From behind his mother's screen door, Prep stared past his childhood friend, and looked at an empty potato chip bag resting out in the middle of Diamond street.

"How it feel to finally be home?"

"After I get some pussy, I'll tell you."

Prep was excited that he was out of jail, but when his son's mother unexpectedly pulled into an empty parking space in front of his mother's house, nothing about being free felt good to him anymore. His thick eyebrows knitted themselves together over his angry eyes. For the thirteen months that he sat inside of a Philadelphia County prison, his son's mother had refused to bring their son to visit him. She never accepted any of his phone calls, and she had never sent him a single picture of his son's first birthday party. Ignoring the house arrest monitor fastened around his right ankle, Prep pushed his mother's screen door into Gary's chest and stepped outside.

The humid, summer air grabbed Prep immediately.

So did Gary.

"Nigga, get the fuck off me!" Prep growled, snatching his arm free of Gary's grip. After giving Gary a mean stare, he stalked down his steps, until his black, hiking Timberlands met the pavement. "Then she gon' drive this pussy shit around here?! Yo, this bitch really got the game fucked up, if- Yo, her dizzy ass ain't even got my fuckin' son with her!"

"Yo, Prep?"

Prep ignored Gary and kept walking to the curb. With each step, he was gathering spit in his mouth. He glared at his son's mother's side profile as she laughed and continued to talk on her cell phone, while she parked her new boyfriend's black, SUV.

Gary's cousin was her new boyfriend.

The rumor was that they were engaged.

Prep was enraged.

Rihanna's sultry singing, and a cool, air-conditioned breeze, softly peppered Prep's scowling face with kisses when his son's mother lowered her window. Prep's angry eyes slid down to his reflection on the Nissan Armada's driver's side door. He looked at his clenched fists, wishing they held guns.

"Welcome home, Pr-"

Prep released his mouthful of saliva.

"Fuck outta here, you smut ass bitch!!"

"Scuuurrrrrr!!!"

"I hope ya nut ass bang the fuck out!" Prep hollered, stepping back as his son's mother pulled away from the sidewalk erratically. He watched her as she disregarded a red light, and sped recklessly across the 29th and Diamond Street intersection. "I told my mom not to tell her I was fuckin' home! Her dumb ass should've had my fuckin' son with her! I should've smacked her-"

"Yo, ya phone ringin'!"

"Ohhh, shit! That fuck around and be them house arrest mu' fuckers!"

Gary held Prep's screen door open for him, as he rushed up the steps and ran into his house.

Five minutes later, Prep was standing back at his screen door again. He was staring at the plume of smoke that was rising from the cigarette in Gary's left hand. He wrinkled his nose in distaste at the smell of nicotine.

"I got something for ya bitch ass," Prep silently vowed, glaring down at the back of Gary's curly-haired head. Thoughtfully, he shook his head and smiled devilishly.

"Nigga, my fuckin' mom told me ya snake ass put cha cousin on Ashley. Tryna act like you don't know what's goin' the fuck on. It's cool, though, 'cause soon as we take that paper, I'ma blow ya mu'fuckin' top off. The gloves is off, and the love is lost. I'ma slide right out Camay house, and lay low, then I'ma rock Ashley and take my fuckin' son. I'ma show my ass this fuckin' time, watch."

As Prep stared outside at Gary, he had no idea that Gary had intentions of killing him after their heist too.

Hours later, many miles away from North Philadelphia, Splash and Tia were sitting inside of Tia's car in their driveway, and they were having a conversation that was tickling Tia's heart.

"Well, what would you do, if I got diagnosed with skin cancer, and all of my hair started falling out?"

"Rock a baldy with you."

"You mean that, Bay?"

"Yup."

"What if I went blind?"

"I'd describe everything in detail, so you could imagine it in ya mind."

"Awww, Bay."

"Tee, I ain't sayin' that shit 'cause it sound thorough."

"I know, Bay."

Splash opened his eyes and watched Tia as she touched up her lip gloss in the mirror of her sunshade.

"Bay, you mad at me for snappin' on Sabia last night?"

"Naw."

"I just felt like-"

"Tee, you ain't gotta explain ya self."

"So, you don't think I was wrong?"

Splash sighed and looked out Tia's passenger window at the line of manicured trees on his far right. The tall trees stood ten feet away. Side by side, the conifer trees acted as property dividers, separating Splash's and Tia's two-lane driveway from their neighbors' own. The tall trees also performed the same job in the rear for the two, large properties, where both of their expansive backyards met. Similar landscaping could be seen throughout the entire private community of mostly doctors, judges, and lawyers.

Splash and Tia were the only killers, who resided amongst their upscale residents.

A pro-life activist would insist that Splash's and Tia's neighbor be included.

She was an abortion doctor.

"Tee, we could've died last night, "Splash reminded Tia, grabbing her hand. After swallowing, he stared into his wife's eyes and let his heart have control of his tongue. "Yo, my gran'mom would've been plannin' my fuckin' funeral today, if it wasn't for you. You my wife, and if I ever think you was right, or wrong, about anything, that shit ain't gon' stop me from holdin' you down. You my fuckin' heart, Tee. I wouldn't give a fuck who you snapped on, 'cause last night was some crazy shit, and we had mu'fuckers in our house we didn't know. Even when you wrong, you gon' always be right in my eyes, Fancy face."

"Boy, I love you so much."

"You better."

"Since I'm right about everything in your eyes, why I can't bring Snookums with us?"

"No comment."

Tia rolled her eyes when Splash released her hand and pulled out his cell phone.

"You ready?"

"Bay, we ain't gotta go, if you don't really want to."

Splash and Tia were headed to their timeshare cabin located in the Poconos. It was Tia's idea. Their luggage was right behind them in Tia's backseat.

"You worried about Sabia, ain't you?"

"I just need somebody to run my fuckin' club, if we gon' be out there for-"

"Just leave it closed."

"I ain't leavin'-"

"Sabia and Jen ain't gon' get along anyway."

Splash sighed and reclined Tia's passenger seat all the way back.

"So, are you ready to leave, or not?"

"Give me another Motrin."

"They in my pocketbook."

"Get 'em for me."

"You want 'em, you get 'em."

Splash closed his eyes and smirked.

"What?"

"It sound like we back to normal."

Tia smiled and reversed her car out of her and Splash's driveway. With her right hand, she dug into her pocketbook for the bottle of Motrin. She was looking forward to her and Splash's getaway, even if it was just for three days. They were going to return home a day before Splash's birthday.

"Bay, here."

"What?"

"The Motrin."

"I 'on't want 'em now."

"Yeah, we back to normal."

Seventeen miles later, Splash was asleep, and Tia was talking on her cell phone to Camay as she weaved her Cadillac wagon in and out of traffic on the headlight-speckled I-95 expressway. The traffic was moving quickly in both directions.

"I'm just happy none of our neighbors heard all of that shit."

"Thank God for thunder and rain."

"Tell me about it."

"Splash still ain't talk to Sabia?"

"Nope."

"You think he okay?"

Tia glanced over at Splash.

"I hope they ain't lock him up, thinking he did all that shit to your aunt."

"That's what I was thinkin' earlier, "Tia admitted, glancing over at Splash again. Shaking her head, she let out a long sigh. "I just ain't wanna tell Splash that. Knowing Sabia, him and my aunt Trixie came up with some type of story to tell-"

"You know the doctors gotta report that she got raped, Tia."

"As long as the cops don't come to my fuckin' house, I don't care what she decide to-"

"Hold on, Tia."

Tia switched her cell phone to her left hand and grabbed her steering wheel with her right hand. She had a lot on her mind, and since Splash had dozed off on her, she was trying to preoccupy herself by talking to Camay, because she wasn't ready to be alone with her thoughts yet.

"Tia?"

"Who was that?"

"Guess?"

"Nope."

"Which one of my cousins gotta crush on you, and cried when I told him you and Splash got married?"

"Prep?"

"Yup."

"He home?"

"Sure is, with his crazy behind."

"Cam, did you talk to Jen today?"

Tia removed her cell phone from her ear and gave the screen a strange look when Camay didn't say anything.

"Camay?"

"What?"

"Is it something you not tellin' me about Jen, 'cause I'm startin' to think it is."

Splash opened his eyes and sat up. He had been woke the entire time, replaying in his mind everything that happened the previous night, and wondering how it all could have been prevented. He had thought up some solutions.

"What's wrong, Bay?"

"Tell Camay to call you back."

Tia ended her call with Camay and gave her husband her full attention, because a look in his eyes told her that he was about to say something important. The seriousness in his eyes was similar to how he looked after he had spent some time in his father's jeep.

"Tee, besides what we got in the bank, and not countin' our credit cards, how much money you think we workin' with?"

Tia sighed and stared through her windshield thoughtfully. She thought about all of the cash that her and Splash had in the safes in their small vault.

"You think we got more than a mill?"

"I think we got more than that, Bay."

"So, how come our alarm system ain't protect us like we some millionaires?"

Tia shrugged her shoulders.

"You feel what I'm sayin', though, Tee?"

"Kinda, but-"

"We supposed to have some shit like dude house was in that Bruce Willis movie."

"Like when his house shut down, and them shutters came down on his windows?"

"Exactly."

"That's what you wanna do to the house?"

"And I wanna get some shit, where our doors won't open unless we say our names-"

"I got my iPad in my suitcase."

"We can check online when we get to the cabin."

"Your headache went away yet?"

"All this fuckin' gauze you wrapped around my head got my shit feelin' like my brain got a condom on."

"No it don't."

Splash sat back and closed his eyes again. This time he had plans on going to sleep for real.

"We should be there in like thirty minutes, Bay."

"Wake me up when-"

"No, Bay, finish talkin' to me."

"Yo, Gunna my fuckin' man, Tee."

"I know, right."

"So, you think I should still have my party at the house?"

"I don't see why not."

"For some reason, I got this fuckin' feelin' some nut shit gon' happen, Tee."

Chapter Eight

"You can think whatever you want, but that ain't gon' stop you from needin' stitches."

"At least I don't need a casket."

It was 3:21 in the morning, and Splash and Tia were both laying in bed pillow-talking.

"Bay, you need stitches."

"Tee, I heard you."

Splash was irritable, because he was exhausted and sleepy. His eyelids were too heavy to keep open. He was regretting that he had promised Tia that he would stay awake and talk to her, until she fell asleep.

"Bay?"

"I'm up."

"Well, open your eyes."

"Tee, my eyes ain't gotta be open for me to talk to-"

"Wanna go down to the lake and watch the sun come up?"

"Nope."

"Why?"

" 'Cause it's too dark, and I ain't tryna get bit by no fuckin' snake."

"We can take a flashlight."

"We need to go to sleep."

"Bay, you believe in God?"

"Sometimes."

"When don't chu?"

Splash's eyes flipped open. He sighed and stared blankly up at the spinning ceiling fan above him. Tia's question made him recall a painful memory. With that memory came the need to hold his wife in his arms, so he turned on his side and pulled her close.

"I hated God the day you lost the baby," Splash whispered, after clearing his throat. The emotions reflecting in his wife's eyes matched what he felt in his heart. "Yo, I was crying so hard, I almost crashed on my way to the fuckin' hospital. I prayed alway there, Tee. Man, when I got there, and they told me- Tee, I'm tellin' you, if I had wings, yo, I would've flew up to fuckin' heaven and snapped. I would've snapped, Tee."

"Bay, you think we cursed?"

"Cursed?"

"One time, my cousin Jamillah told me that God curse people when he mad at them."

"We ain't cursed, Tee."

"But we done did a lot of stuff, Bay."

"And you think that shit happened last night, 'cause we cursed, or something?"

"It crossed my mind."

"Tee, we got blessed last night, if anything."

"After I lost the baby, I felt cursed, too."

Tia closed her eyes when Splash wrapped his arms around her tighter.

"Wanna know when I believe in God the most?"

"When you in ya dad truck?"

"How you know?"

"'Cause that's when I would believe in him the most, too."

"You know what I always wanted to ask you ,Tee?"

"What?"

"What made you believe me?"

"The look in ya eyes," Tia admitted, stroking Splash's left cheek tenderly. She smiled when her husband's right eyelash brushed hers. "I even felt jealous, Bay. I mean, like, you know how much I miss my mom. I would give everything I got to talk to her just one time. Bay, if you told me it was rainin' berries outside, I'd go and get some buckets. I trust you with my life. I know I get on your nerves, and I can be a handful at times, but I know my place as your wife, and I'll always have your back, Bay."

"Us against them."

"Yup."

"You still not tired?"

"Nope."

"Wanna get it in?"

"You think you can hang?"

"I can hang like a noose."

"Can you hang 'til the sun come up?"

"I can hang 'til that mu'fucker go back down."

"I hear you talkin'."

Twenty-two minutes later, small pieces of fire were dancing on top of the scented candles that were decoratively positioned around the cabin's master bedroom. Exotic language and soft moans were filtering with the cool central air, and drifting above to the spinning ceiling fan.

A half empty bottle of Moet was responsible for the lustful sounds coming from the waterbed.

"Ummmmmmm, Bay," Tia moaned, as she squirmed with pleasure. She dug the back of her head into the satin bed sheets that were slowly unpeeling their way off of the bed beneath her. "That feel sooo good. Ummmmmm, right there. Umm hmm. Oh, my God. Sssssssss . . . yes, yes, yes. Yyyyeeeaaaahhhhh, Bay. Right th-Oh, shit. Oh, my fuckin' God. Bay, please don't stop. If you do, I'ma kill you. Oh, my God, I'ma-Ummmmm."

Tia loved when her husband performed oral sex on her, because he always ignited a fire between her legs, and left her feeling like she was floating on a cloud somewhere. His tongue was phenomenal. It was never in one spot for too long, then there were moments, where it seemed like it was everywhere all at once. Every lick of his was magical. His thick tongue was dipping into her wetness, snaking up and down her pussy lips, teasing circles all around her clit, and then like a deep sea diver, he dove hungrily back inside of her like he was searching her pussy for some hidden treasure.

"Get it, Bay."

"I got it."

Tia grabbed two handfuls of her own hair when the euphoric sensation of her first orgasm came to life. Biting her bottom lip, she raised her hips to feed Splash her goodies. Her clit was swollen and pulsating like a tiny heart, and with the licks that her husband were giving her, she was about to become the first female to ever experience having a heart attack inside of her pussy.

Splash pulled Tia's clit into his mouth, and as he sucked on it, he moved his head from side to side.

Dying at that very moment would have been the sweetest death for Tia. She could feel all of the stress and tension in her body escaping through her pores. A teardrop left her eye as her first orgasm came to an end, and a second one introduced itself to her husband's probing tongue.

With a wide smile, Splash climbed off of the bed and raised his hands like he was a boxer that had just been crowned champion.

"You so silly."

"And I did that with no fingers this time."

"Come step back in the ring."

"Oh, what chu want a shot at the title?"

"If you scared, say you scared."

"Get it wet for me."

"You want me to play with it?"

Squeezing his hard dick, Splash nodded his head.

"Put it in my mouth, Bay."

Splash's hesitancy, combined with the insatiable look in his eyes, influenced Tia to start her act all alone. Being nasty for her husband was something that she loved to do. After moving some pillows out of her way, she positioned herself so that Splash would have a real nice view of what she wanted him to see. Her gray eyes never left his. Licking her lips seductively, she started her show. First, she began by teasing both of her nipples with the tips of her middle fingers. Watching Splash stroke the length of his dick was exciting her. She felt the juices in her wet pussy creating small waves, as she slowly lowered her right hand down across her stomach. Her body trembled when she patted her clit with the tips of her four fingers.

"Can I suck it, while I play with it, Bay?"

Splash walked over to the edge of the waterbed and stared down at his wife's naked body. Her clean-shaven pussy was decorated with tattoos of colorful fruit. Her titties were full and round, and as she looked him in the eyes and pleasured herself with two of her fingers, his adoration for her beauty made him proud to be her husband.

Losing their virginity together was just another invisible pillar that held Splash's and Tia's marriage up.

The sensation of a thousand soft kisses peppered the inside of Splash's chest when Tia slowly trailed the length of his dick with her wet tongue. When she did the same thing again, his knees got weak. When she did it again, he closed his eyes and clenched his jaws.

"Damn, Tee, "Splash groaned, sighing as Tia licked slow circles around the head of his dick. Her slurping sounds, hums, and warm mouth, was too much for him. "Turn around, so I can hit it from the back, Tee."

After flipping over to her stomach, Tia looked over her shoulder at Splash as she arched her back and raised her hips. The moment that she was impatiently waiting for had finally come. She sighed when her husband grabbed her hips and positioned himself behind her. The tip of his hardness pushed against the opening of her wetness, and she shivered in anticipation. His first stroke was like a hot knife slicing butter. When he penetrated her, he stabbed her slow. His thickness brung to life every nerve in her pussy. Her softness contracted around his hardness.

"Make ya pussy wetter for me."

Tia reached back between her legs, and began to stimulate herself by rubbing small circles around her clit.

"Yea, make that shit gushy."

"I'ma cum all over ya dick, okay."

"Not yet."

"Please?"

"No."

Tia's throaty moans encouraged Splash to provide her with deeper strokes. He raised his left leg and put his foot on the bed beside Tia, and then stepped in closer.

"Harder, Bay."

"Like that?"

"And deeper."

"That dick feel good, don't it?"

"Yeah, it-Oh, my-Bay, smack my ass."

"Smack!"

"Mmmmmmmmmmm."

"You better not cum yet."

"Bay, I-I-didn't, but-"

"Turn over."

Splash and Tia fucked from the bed, down to the floor, over to the wall, and back to the bed.

"This dick belong to me?"

"Yup."

"Say it."

"This ya dick," Splash whispered into Tia's hair, stirring her with circular motions as he laid between her legs. The warm moistness of her pussy made him want to stay in that position for the rest of his life. "You know this belong. . . to . . . you, Fancy face. I'm just carryin' it around for you. You ready to cum with me?"

"I been ready."

Splash put Tia's legs over his shoulders and raised up into a push up position.

"Get it, Bay."

"Aaarggghhhh."

"Don't-Don't-Don't stop!"

"Ahhh, sshhiiitt"

"Bay, I'm-"

"Ahhh, shit, Tee!"

"I'm cumin all over-Bay, I'm-I'm-Oh! My God!!!"

Chapter Nine

At 11:27 a.m., Tia blinked her eyes open and turned on her side. She quickly noticed how well rested her body felt as she stretched and gazed through a window at the picturesque view of all of the mountains, trees, and beautiful, blue sky. Being away at the cabin had always provided her with a soothing sense of relaxation. Without awakening Splash, Tia crawled off of the waterbed with a smile on her face. After she got out of the shower, she dried off, lotioned, and slipped on a paisley, Forever 21 sundress. With her iPod and cell phone in hand, Tia headed down to the kitchen to make her and Splash some breakfast. Once she was done eating, she had plans on taking care of some important business on the internet, and over the phone.

Splash and Tia shared their cabin with an old, Israeli couple, who lived in Rochester, New York. The husband was an International arms dealer, and the wife was an Investment banker. The Israeli couple felt indebted to Tia, because while Tia's mother was redesigning their house back in 1999, she had witnessed the murder of one of their house staff in their wine closet, and she never mentioned anything about it to anyone. For her obvious display of loyalty, the rich Israelis had made Tia's mother a silent partner in all of their commercial properties, and they also let her share their cabin with them.

One sight of the bi-level cabin would inspire romance in anyone. On the inside, a person could easily forget that they were surrounded by a massive wilderness. The cabin was stuffed with two bedrooms, three and a half baths, a spa, and a game room that had six video games, a pool table, and a two-lane bowling alley. All of the bathrooms had marble sinks, gold fixtures, heated tile floors, and one of them also included a Jacuzzi that could fit five people.

Behind the handsome cabin, thousands of fragrant plants and flowers surrounded a gazebo that had a hammock, and instead of cutting down any of the forest, the landscapers had placed a swimming pool in a clearing in the woods. Of course, those amenities could only be enjoyed during the summer.

As for any fans of the snowy weather, there were six snow mobiles and a bunch of ski equipment inside of a small barn that was sitting off to the left of the long, gravel driveway. Beneath the floor of the cabin, there were forty-three metal footlockers full of guns and explosives that Splash and Tia knew nothing about.

The closest house to Splash's and Tia's timeshare cabin was an even nicer cabin that was on the opposite side of Locust lake. The property was owned by a female, Supreme Court judge, who was under the impression that Splash was some type of music executive, and that Tia owned her own line of hair products. In a passing conversation, Tia had casually revealed those lies to the judge's daughter when the two of them had crossed paths as they both jogged on a trail two summers earlier.

Back in the present moment, Splash was awakened by the smell of turkey bacon, cheese eggs, grits, and pancakes. He sat up in bed just as Tia was entering the bedroom with a plate of food in one hand, and a glass of orange juice in her other.

"Hey, handsome."

"How long you been up?"

"Like two hours."

Splash accepted the plate of food and glass of orange juice from Tia, and wasted no time in making the cheese eggs and turkey bacon disappear. Tia sat down beside him and picked up a piece of toast off of his plate.

"So, what's on our agenda today?"

Tia shrugged her shoulders and a bit off a small piece of Splash's toast.

"Where my phone at?"

"Still downstairs on the charger."

"Can you get it for me?"

"Ya head don't hurt no more?"

"Not like that shit did yesterday."

"Good, "Tia said, smiling as she stood up. She pulled up her sundress to show Splash that she had no panties on. " 'Cause some more of this is on the agenda this afternoon. I took care of all the alarm system stuff already, too. I found this place in Delaware on the internet. I sent them an e-mail, and they said they can do all the stuff we want in one day. I made the appointment for Friday at 10:00, so we gotta go home a day early. This cleaning company gon' come out and take care of the theater, too. After they leave, I got another company comin' by to put down some new carpet. Everything gon' be ready in time for ya party. I'ma be waitin' for you down at the lake. Oh, and ya phone gon' be on the bed when you get out the shower."

After Tia left, Splash finished off the rest of his breakfast, then made his way to the bathroom. Instead of meeting Tia at the lake, he made a pit-stop at the gazebo, because after he got out of the shower, he had received a phone call from Salvatore Masino.

"So, my cousin cool, though?"

"Yeah, he's okay."

"What's up with his phone?"

"I'm not sure, but he did mention that he was going to see you on your birthday Saturday."

Splash waved away a big mosquito and sighed, as he stared up at the line of mountains that stood behind the tall trees. He switched his cell phone to his other ear and sat down on the hammock. He was relieved to hear that his cousin Sabia was safe, but something was telling him that Salvatore Masino was keeping something from him.

"So, what else is up?"

"What do you mean?"

Splash waved away another mosquito.

"So, you tryna tell me that you got my number from my cousin just to tell me that he was cool?"

Salvatore was silent for three seconds. His silence confirmed Splash's suspicions.

"We really need to talk."

"Ain't we doin' that right now?"

"Not over the phone."

"I ain't in-"

Splash cut his sentence short and looked at his cell phone when it alerted him that he was receiving another phone call. He stood back up as he placed his cell phone back to his ear.

". . . e-mail address, and I can give you the information-"

"Ay, Salvatore I'ma call you-"

"Do you have an e-mail address?"

"Yea, I'ma text it to you, after I get off the- This my cousin mom on my other line, and I know she probably trippin' about where he at."

"I understand, but just make sure you-"

"Yo, I'ma get right at chu."

Splash ended his call with Salvatore Masino and accepted his aunt's phone call.

"Splash?"

"What's up, Aunt Steph?"

"Do you know why your cousin didn't show up for Shateek's custody hearing this morning?"

"That was this mornin'?"

"It sure was, and Jennifer almost walked out of there with two black eyes, because she was in there rolling her eyes at me every time I said something to the judge."

"Aunt Steph, they would've locked you up, too."

"I had bail money in my pocketbook."

"You crazy, Aunt Steph."

"Now, where is my son, and why is his phone off?"

"I ain't-"

Before Splash could finish the rest of his lie, his cell phone alerted him that he was getting another call. He sighed and looked up at the sky when he looked at the screen of his cell phone and saw who the caller was.

"Aunt Steph, can I call you back real back?"

"Umm hmm."

Splash thumbed the screen of his iPhone and placed it back to his ear.

"Splash?"

"What's up, Jen?"

"You tell me."

"So, you fuckin' Robbie, huh?"

"Ain't nobody- Who the fuck said some . . ."

Splash lowered his cell phone down to his side and clenched his jaws. He was disappointed in Jen. He loved her like a sister, and for that reason, he raised his cell phone back up to his ear and spoke to her like an upset brother.

"Ay, yo, Jen, you be makin' it real fuckin' hard for me to defend you some-"

"Splash, I-"

"Man, listen to me!" Splash growled into his cell phone, as he stepped out of the gazebo. He could feel his headache returning. "I already know, 'cause Cam showed me her fuckin' cell phone bill, so stop tryna deny that shit. Yo, you outta pocket, Jen. Niggaz be on ya top at the fuckin' club every night, and you gon' choose Robbie of all mu' fuckers? Like, how you be thinkin', Jen? That nigga a fuckin' creep. Plus, Cam like ya fuckin' sister."

"I know."

"And what's up with you and my aunt?"

"She tryna get full custody of Sha-"

"Man, so what."

Splash hated how Jen and his cousin dealt with their son. They used him like he was a rope in a tug-of-war match. Since their relationship failed, it appeared like their idea of being parents just flew out of the window. Luckily for them, Splash's aunt was there to catch their responsibility.

"Miss Stephany always so quick to point out all my mistakes, but she never speak on all the bullshit Sabia be into."

"Ya'll both outta pocket, Jen."

"Splash, that's ya family, so you gon' be on they side no matter what."

Jen's comment made Splash frown. He was paying her a thousand dollars a week to be a bartender at his club, and she only worked on the weekends. He never asked her for any money that she borrowed from him. When his grandmother and aunt told him not to hire Jen, he did anyway, and when his cousin Sabia told him to fire her, he didn't. The number of times that he spoke up in her defense was countless, so what she said had hurt his feelings.

"Did Cam tell Tia about me and Robbie?"

"Naw."

"You think she is?"

"Won't chu call her and ask her."

"You openin' the club tonight?"

"Tryna change the subject, huh?"

"No."

"Yea, you is."

"So, are you?"

"Stop fuckin' with Robbie, Jen."

"Alright."

"Jen, I'm dead fuckin' serious."

"I am, too."

"And call my aunt and apologize to her when we hang up."

"Apologize for what?"

Splash looked at his cell phone when it alerted him that he was getting another call. It was Camay.

"Ay, Jen, hold on."

"Alright."

Splash accepted Camay's phone call.

"What's up, Cam?"

"Just checkin' on you."

"You talk to Tee?"

"I just got off the phone with her."

"What's up with nut ass Snookums?"

"He out in the yard with Robbie little sister."

"If you give him away, I'll cop you ten Gucci pocketbooks."

"And Tia will have a fit."

"So."

"Splash, I changed my mind about what we talked about last week."

"I figured you would."

"What I saw at ya'll house-"

"Cam, hold on real quick."

Splash touched the screen of his cell phone and switched back to Jen.

"Ay, Jen?"

"Splash, hold on."

When Jen clicked over to her other line, Splash switched back to Camay. He had no idea that Tia was Jen's second caller.

"Cam?"

"Splash, I got Robbie on the other-"

"Just call me back."

"Somebody just kidnapped his cousin Devon."

"For real?"

"I'll call- Splash, I gotta go."

"Alright, Cam."

Down at the lake, Tia was sitting at the end of the pier with her legs dangling over the edge. Her cell phone was laying beside her right thigh. She ended her phone call with Jen, because she had wanted to call Splash to see what was taking him so long, but when she looked over her shoulder as she was about to call his cell phone, Splash had appeared from behind a big tree.

The weather was beautiful. Up in the sky, a dozen clouds looked like big pieces of white, cotton candy, and all of them were taking turns at hiding the sun from the earth.

Splash walked up beside Tia and sat down on the pier beside her.

"I was just about to call you."

Tia giggled when Splash tickled her side.

"Bay, remember the first summer we came out here?"

"Yup."

"It rained that whole week."

"We still had fun, though."

"I know, right."

"Ay, Tee, we should get married again."

"And we should go somewhere nice for our honeymoon, "Tia added, smiling as she stared out at the lake. Visions of Paris flashed in her mind. "Bay, I just want us to start all over this time. We was already talkin' about slowin' down anyway. It ain't like we need for anything. We never did. I just want us to live normal now, Bay. I know you got the club, but you should start that basketball camp that you always talk about, Bay. You would be a decent mentor, Bay. And all that money we got, I was sittin' here thinkin' how we should donate some of it, or just leave a bag of money on somebody steps, or something. Sometimes, I be wantin' to give all that shit away."

"Robbie might need a donation."

"Robbie?"

"Cam, said his cousin Devon got kidnapped."

"She ain't tell me that."

"It must've just happened, 'cause she called me after she got off the phone with you."

"You can do what chu want, but Robbie ain't gettin' nothin' from me."

"You know he gon' ask Cam, Tee."

Tia sighed and picked up her cell phone.

"Tee, Robbie got mu' fuckers really thinkin' that he gettin' to a dollar."

"He sure got Cam fooled."

"That nigga gettin' fronted work from some Dominicans, Tee."

"He probably got people thinkin Cam car his."

"That ain't even half of it."

"That ain't half of what?"

"That ain't half of that nigga lies, "Splash revealed, raising his eyebrows. He chuckled because some of things that he knew about Camay's boyfriend were comical. "Tee, he got mu' fuckers in Philly thinkin' he copped that house for Cam, 'n all that. I'm sayin', like, he got Frankford on smash, but niggaz be on his top. If it wasn't for Devon, he would've been got gripped up by somebody, Tee. Come on, you know that nigga don't rock. So, like, he better hope Devon cool, 'cause if they rock him, he done. Tee, I guarantee you, he askin' Cam to help him pay that ransom."

"Why can't he get it from them fuckin' Dominicans, or whoever the fuck they is?"

"Tee, them mu' fuckers wouldn't even put up no bread, if he got snatched."

Tia couldn't believe what she was hearing. None of it made any sense to her.

"It can get worse, Tee."

"How?"

"If Robbie burn them Dominicans to get his cousin back, he gon' owe them for the work they be frontin' him."

"That's on his dumb ass."

"They probably know where he live, though, Tee."

"Camay ain't got nothin' to do with his bullshit."

"Tee, in the game, mu' fuckers be makin' they own rules."

"I'm callin' Cam."

"Hold up, I got something else to tell you."

"Is it bad?"

Splash nodded his head.

"How bad?"

Splash handed Tia his cell phone. He wanted her to read the e-mail that he had received from Salvatore for herself.

"Check my last e-mail."

"I know it ain't from my Aunt Trixie?"

"Naw, it's from ya uncle."

"How he get ya-"

"Sabia."

"Oh."

"You see it?"

"Yeah, I see it."

Two hours later, Splash and Tia were back inside of the cabin lost in their own private thoughts. Splash was downstairs in the game room playing pool by himself, and Tia was upstairs in the bathroom with the door locked.

Salvatore's e-mail had put both of them in different mental spaces.

Outside, the moon had started his shift, and the sound of nature was echoing all around the forest.

"This shit is unbelievable," Tia thought, as she sunk lower into the Jacuzzi. She couldn't believe that she had another brother, and that him, his brother, and mother, wanted to kill her and Splash. "Maybe Splash was right. It ain't like they know where we live, and-"

Tia reached for her cell phone when it started to ring. She placed it to her ear without looking to see who the caller was.

"Hello?"

"Tia, it's me."

The sound of her aunt's voice made Tia stand up in the Jacuzzi. Her heart started to bang against her chest. She wanted her aunt dead.

"What the fuck do you want, Aunt Trixie?"

"Tia, I'm sorry."

"And you know me well enough to know that I don't give a fuck, right?"

"If I could change what happened that night, I-"

"Do me and Splash a favor and die, Aunt Trixie."

"Tia, what do I have to do for you to forgive me?"

"You have to stop breathin'."

"Tia, don't-"

Tia pressed the screen on her cell phone and placed it back on a towel that she had laying on the marble border of the Jacuzzi, where she had her glass of 99 Bananas sitting. A knock on the bathroom door made her look over her shoulder, as she sat back in the Jacuzzi. She had the bathroom door locked for a reason. It wasn't that she didn't want to be bothered with Splash, but after reading the e-mail that her uncle had sent to his cell phone, she just wanted to be alone long enough, so that she could wrap her mind around the entire situation. Knowing that she had another brother was a shock in itself, but to think that their fates were going to join them as enemies gave her a melancholy feeling in her heart.

On the opposite side of the bathroom door, Splash was picking at a scab on the back of his head. The gashes in his head were starting to heal, and they were irritating him, because they kept itching.

"Ay, Tee, I gotta take a dump!"

"You do not!"

"Yo, I do so!"

"Well, use the other bathroom, then!"

"Why you got the door locked?!"

"Why you hollerin'?!"

"No more locked doors!!"

Tia snatched the bathroom door open and blocked the entrance with her arm, but Splash pushed his way into the bathroom anyway.

"Bay, why-"

"What's goin' on up in here?"

"I was in the Jacuzzi."

"Oh, so what Splash not allowed?"

"Bay, I just wanted to be alone for-"

"First the Roc break up, now this."

"Now what?"

"Now this."

"I thought you had to use the bathroom?"

Splash flashed Tia a smile and picked up her glass of 99 Bananas. With his free hand, he pulled down his blue JC de Castelbajac shorts, and stepped out of them with a grin, because he didn't have any underwear on.

"You was freeballin', huh?"

"I think one of my balls got bit by a fuckin' mosquito."

"You stupid."

After Splash took a sip of her drink, Tia took her glass from him and climbed back into the Jacuzzi.

"So, you still wanna be alone?"

"Do I have a choice?"

"Nope."

"Well, why you ask me, then?"

" 'Cause, I got manners."

"Boy, please."

"My manners better than yours."

Tia moved over when Splash joined her in the Jacuzzi. When her cell phone chimed, alerting her that she had received a text message, she moved to reach for it, but Splash picked it up and handed it to her.

"Thanks, Bay."

Splash took a deep breath and ducked his head under the water. He made it to the count of eleven when Tia started to shake his leg under the water, so he sat back up.

"They killed Robbie cousin."

"Damn."

"Cam said they set his body on fire."

"What she say about Robbie?"

"They took everything he owed them Dominicans from Devon, so now he-"

"They gon' kill that nigga, Tee."

"Bay, I wanna go home."

"Right now?"

Tia nodded her head and sighed. In her text-message, Camay had expressed that she was scared, and Tia was slowly beginning to feel scared for her.

"It don't look like our lives gon' get to be normal no time soon, huh?"

"I guess not."

"Ay, didn't you give Cam and Jen them twin Rugers?"

"Bay, Cam ain't touch that gun since I gave it to her."

"Robbie got a gun, 'cause I let that nigga bring that shit in the club one night."

"That's probably the same gun Cam was gon' use to kill herself."

"What?"

When Tia stood up in the Jacuzzi, Splash stood up too.

"Last week, when we was at the restaurant, she told me that she was about to kill herself, but I had called her when she had Robbie gun to her head, so she decided not to do it."

"Yo, you serious?"

"Why I'ma lie about something like that, Bay?"

"Yo, Tee, I gotta tell you somethin'."

"What?"

Before Splash could tell Tia about Jen and Robbie, and how what they were doing probably inspired Camay to consider committing suicide, his cell phone started to ring in the pocket of his shorts. He stepped out of the Jacuzzi behind Tia and picked up his shorts with a frown on his face.

"I'ma be in the room gettin' our stuff ready, Bay."

"Here I come."

Splash raised his cell phone to his ear and followed Tia out of the bathroom.

"What's up, Salvatore?"

"I just gotta call from somebody that has an idea where my nephew Angelo might be."

"That's the best news I heard all day."

Chapter Ten

"Hello?"

"Yo, Prep?"

"Yo?"

"What chu was sleep?"

"Yeah."

"Ay, yo, come to the door real quick."

"What?"

"Come to the door."

"Man, for what?"

"'Cause, I gotta surprise for you, dog."

"What time is it?"

"Nine o'clock."

"Yo, Gary, you outta fuckin' pocket."

"That's what you sayin' now, but-"

"My mom car out there?"

"Naw, I 'on't think she got home from work yet."

Prep let out a heavy sigh and sat up in bed. He looked around his small bedroom in disgust, because everything in it reminded him of how immature his standards were before he had gotten arrested. His dreams were much bigger now, and after him and Gary pulled off their heist, living his young life to the fullest was at the top of his agenda.

"Here I come."

"Alright."

Prep reached over to his nightstand and laid his cordless phone on its base. It took him four minutes to reach his front door, because he had put on a pair of his basketball shorts, but once he opened it and his eyes saw the surprise that Gary had for him, he had second thoughts on killing his best friend.

"You gon' let us in, or what?"

"We not gon' bite."

"Girl, speak for yourself."

Gary chuckled and pulled Prep's screen door open. After ushering the two strippers that he had with him into Prep's vestibule, he elbowed Prep in his side and gave him a toothy-grin.

"Where ya room at?"

Prep looked into the eyes of the stripper closest to him, but instead of answering her, he openly admired what he saw.

"If you take a picture, it'll last longer."

"Yo, where you from?"

"Why?"

"Don't chu gotta twin sister?"

"No."

"Terez, stop lyin' to my man."

"Well, won't chu tell him that me and Daisy here to have a threesome, and that we not here for interviews, then."

"Yo, his room upstairs at the end of the hallway."

"Now, was that so hard?"

"Man, shut up and go 'head."

"Come on, Daisy."

Prep and Gary stared at the asses of the two strippers as the two of them climbed Prep's stairs. Once the girls were out of sight, and after they heard Prep's door shut a few seconds later, they both faced each other with wide smiles on their faces.

"Yo, that Rican bitch bad as shit, ain't she?"

"Her ass fat as shit."

"She a freak, too."

"What's up with the other one?"

"That's Tyrin sister."

"Tyrin from Ms. Clark class?"

"Yup."

"So, she the fuckin' one that tried to poison Tyrin with-"

"Anti-freeze."

"I should get her nut ass back for Tyrin."

"You crazy."

"This nigga that was on my block had some flicks of Tyrin," Prep explained, as he moved past Gary and pushed his screen door open. He looked up and down the street for his mother's car, but he didn't see it. "Ay, yo, she still bad as shit. My mom must be doin' a double, or something. So, where the fuck you meet-"

The gun in Gary's hand stole Prep's voice when he turned around.

"They dance at this new spot on 2nd and Cambria."

"Yea?"

"Yea."

"I trust you wit' my life, Prep," Gary confided, offering Prep the gun in his hand. After Prep accepted the gun from him, he sighed and lowered his eyes. "Dog, we been tight since we was ten. When I first moved around here, ain't nobody show me love, but chu. Like, I know a lot of shit ain't been goin' ya way, but I'm rockin' with chu, Prep. That's on everything. Yo, before my fuckin' cousin Boobie got locked up, I snapped on that nigga for fuckin' wit' Ashley. Ask her."

"Gary, it's cool."

"In three days, we gon' be up, Prep."

"I know."

"Yo, you got condoms?"

"Yea."

"You straight?"

"Why you ask me that?"

"You just had this real crazy ass look on ya face like you-"

"What's ya name again?"

Prep looked up at the top of his stairs. The two strippers, to his surprise, were standing there completely naked.

"Gary, what's his name?"

"Prep."

"Daisy talkin' 'bout it's Shrek."

"Well, that's what it sounded like he said in the car."

"Shrek, though, Daisy?"

"It's people out here with crazier names than that."

"Yo, my name Prep."

"Daisy, go put Gary out and bring Prep upstairs."

"That's how you feel, Terez?"

"Yup."

"Ya'll better take care of my man, too."

"We took care of you, didn't we?"

"Oh, so that couple of dollars wasn't no motivation, huh?"

"Prep, bring me something to drink when you come upstairs, and hurry up, 'cause talkin' to Gary makin' my pussy dry."

"Ay, Terez?"

"What, Gary?"

"Don't forget to tell my man that shit you told me about Robbie."

"I'm not."

Before Daisy could reach him, Gary pushed Prep's screen door open and stepped outside. He turned around and looked back inside of Prep's vestibule with a smile on his face. Prep waited until after the two strippers had returned to his bedroom, before he joined Gary at his screen door. The gun in his hand was sending evil messages to the demons in his heart, and as he forced himself to smile, he became impatient for the moment when he would finally get to put a bullet in his best friend's face. He wanted Gary to have a closed casket funeral.

"Yo, I'm out, Prep."

"Gary, you know you like my brother from another mother?"

"That's why I put chu on this sting wit' me."

"Ay, yo, this jawn got shells in it?"

"Yea, and it's one in the top, too."

"Yo, what shorty supposed to tell me about Robbie?"

"Oh, naw, she said she overheard some niggaz talkin' 'bout they heard his cousin Devon got kidnapped at the club the other night, or some shit like that."

"Yea?"

"You ain't talk to Camay yet?"

"Naw, but I'ma call her after I put these bitches out, and see what's up, though."

"Alright, I'ma call you later on."

"Yo, if you see my pop, tell that nigga I said come the fuck around here, too."

"I got chu."

"Alright."

After Prep closed his front door and locked it, he walked into his kitchen and grabbed a sharp knife out of the sink. He couldn't wait to cut the house arrest monitor off of his ankle. His mother noticing that it was missing was the only thing that worried him. Prep was the only child. His father was a neighborhood drunk, and his mother worked at a West Philadelphia library as a librarian. Up until his parents had gotten divorced, Prep had been a good student in school, and his behavior had always been respectful around the house. Once his father moved out, his attitude took a drastic turn for the worse. Seeing his father drunk on any given street corner on his way home from school had been some of his most embarrassing experiences in life. However, during his time away in jail, his father had visited him more than anyone, and he had never missed any of his court dates.

Once, Prep's father had seen him shoot a man in an alleyway. A day later, Prep's father came by his house sober with some sage advice that Prep committed to his memory.

At his bedroom door, Prep popped the clip out of the Glock 40 that Gary had given him to make sure that it was indeed loaded. A frown appeared on his face, because not only was the clip empty, but there wasn't a bullet in the chamber of the gun either. As he stood there, he had his first idea that Gary might possibly be up to something crafty on their heist like he was. Him lying to Gary about not talking to his cousin Camay had been a harmless lie, but for Gary to tell him that the Glock was loaded three days before their dangerous robbery was just plain suspect in Prep's eyes.

"I gotta surprise for his nut ass," Prep thought, smirking as he pushed the empty clip back inside of the Glock. With the hand that held the knife, he twisted his doorknob and stepped into his bedroom door with his right shoulder. "I still got all them mu' fuckin' 40 shells in my-"

"About time."

"Come-Come fuck me- Come fuck me in my ass!"

Prep closed his bedroom door and started moving like his lease on life was almost up. He felt like he was the luckiest man alive. On his bed, the two strippers were doing something that made his dick grow to its full length and width. They were in the 69 position going at it, and Terez was on top with her ass facing Prep.

"Prep, hurry, hurry up."

"Hold up."

Prep cut his house arrest monitor off and completely forgot about his need for a condom.

"Put it in my ass, Prep."

"Poppy, let me make it sloppy wet first."

Prep closed his eyes and experienced the best of both sexual worlds. His first stroke went into Daisy's mouth. His second stroke went into Terez's ass. He was so far gone that he didn't hear his mother when she knocked on his bedroom door, or when she had pushed it open.

"Boy, you must've lost your mother fuckin' mind!!!"

Chapter Eleven

"How do you feel, Trix?"

"How do I look?"

"I hate to say it, but you look pretty bad."

"Well, that's exactly how I feel, Sal."

Salvatore unbuttoned his suit jacket and sat beside Trixie on her oval-shaped waterbed. He knew that his visit was unwelcomed. Him and his younger sister had a troubled past. When he reached out for her hand, she snatched it away and exhaled an annoyed sigh of frustration.

"It's times like this when we supposed to have each other to lean on, Trix."

"Where was your shoulder when I was a teenager?"

"Am I-"

"Why are you here, Sal?"

"I'll get to that in a second, "Salvatore responded, removing his stare from Trixie's bruised face. Her suffering made his heart feel heavy in his chest. "I know that you and Carmen were a lot closer than you and I are, Trix. I'm still your brother, though. At some point, your gonna have to- It's nothing wrong with askin' for help. Trix, ever since that shit happened with Uncle Vito, you've treated me like-"

"You didn't believe me when I told you he raped me, Sal."

"It wasn't that I-"

"I only had to tell Carmen once."

"Uncle Vito was like a father to me, Trix."

"To me, he was the devil."

"Trix, if I could, I'd resurrect him and kill him again."

"What happened to your arm?"

Salvatore told Trixie all about his visit at Yasmeen Bey's office, and he also explained to her that Malcolm Bey was their nephew.

"Aren't you and her father still okay?"

"Trix, this not one of those situations where a sit down can prevent a war."

Trixie sighed and closed her eyes.

"I'm here to help, Trix."

"I'm for hire."

Salvatore and Trixie looked at Splash's cousin Sabia as he entered Trixie's master bedroom. He had been listening to their entire conversation.

"I don't think that's a good idea."

"What chu think, Trixie?"

"Kid, can you give me and my sister some-"

"Sit down, Sabia," Trixie interrupted, following Sabia with her eyes as he circled her waterbed. His presence made her spirits rise. "Sal, if it wasn't for him, I'd be dead. He hasn't left my side yet. That says a lot to me. Now, I'm not disagreein' with you and sayin' that hirin' him is a good idea, but I don't have Tia and Splash any-"

"Trix, Yasmeen Bey's sons have cemeteries under their fuckin' belts."

"Does hearin' that make you wanna change your mind, Sabia?"

"Even if them niggaz was ghosts, I wouldn't change my fuckin' mind."

"That's all I wanted to hear."

"And I still don't think this is a good idea, Trix."

"Sal, well, what do you suggest I do?"

"Come to my house in Miami with me, until we figure this out."

"Yo, I'ma be out in the living room, Trixie."

"Okay."

After Sabia left Trixie's bedroom, Salvatore moved closer to Trixie and grabbed her hand.

"So, you're really worried about this thing with Yasmeen Bey, huh?"

"Trix, she knows too much about our family to deal with her like a regular enemy, and you know that."

Trixie closed her eyes and nodded her head in agreement. Just like Tia's mother Quintessa,Yasmeen Bey had once been one of her best friends as well. Actually, the three of them were all extremely close at one point in their lives, but that all changed when she played matchmaker between her brother Carmen and Quintessa.

"Sal, why you never told me about her and Carmen?"

"He made me promise."

"To keep it from me?"

"Carmen didn't want anybody to know, Trix," Salvatore explained as he rose to his feet slowly. His pain medication was beginning to leave his system, and the pain from his gunshot wound was gradually returning. "I think he felt embarrassed. You know how he was, Trix. Anyway, he had me drop him off at her house a few times over there on Jackson Street, and I just kept quiet about it. Shit, I was worried about what her father was gon' think more than anything, Trix. That shit could've started a big war, and fucked up a lot of business for me, but when I saw how happy Carmen was, none of that shit even mattered. You know what I'm startin' to think? It makes sense now, Trix. I think that deaf bitch sent those goddamn pictures to Angelina. It was her, Trix. It was her all this fuckin' time."

"It wasn't her."

"Trix, she had-"

"I sent those pictures to Angelina, Sal."

"What?"

"I sent them."

Salvatore felt himself getting light-headed, so he backed away from Trixie's waterbed, until his back touched her bedroom wall. He leaned against her armoire for support as he stared at her in disbelief. He wanted to believe that she was lying to him, but her sobs made those hopes disappear.

"I didn't- Sal, I didn't think she was going to kill-"

"What did Carmen fuckin' do to you to deserve that, Trix?"

The disappointment in her older brother's voice tore through Trixie's soul like metal claws. Revealing her painful secret came with the instant regret that she had even revealed it at all.

"What did Carmen do?"

"Nothin'."

"Trix, what did he do to you?"

"He didn't do anything, Sal."

"And I sincerely hope that your conscious will never let you fuckin' forget that our brother died for fuckin' nothin'."

Trixie let out a gut-wrenching scream when Salvatore walked out of her bedroom, which caused Sabia to rush to her side with concern in his eyes. He had been a secret admirer of hers since the first time he had laid eyes on her.

"What's wrong?"

"I don't- Sabia, I- I don't have no- I don't have nobody now."

"You do so."

"My whole fuckin' life is fallin' apart, Sabia."

"Trixie, all you gotta do is add me to ya life, and I'll help you put it back together."

The cemetery was as wide as the eyes could see. It was a resting place for the dead, and because it was, it put a sense of dread in Splash's soul every single time he was there. Something about walking over the graves of dead people spooked him. There were mausoleums and ranks of tombstones that seemed to never end.

"Everybody has to taste death one day, Splash."

Splash looked from his father to his grandfather. Both of them were sitting on the grass with their backs leaning against their own tombstones. It was an eerie sight to see. It was either here at the cemetery, or at a man-made shooting range inside of some large factory, where Splash's dreams took place whenever he fell asleep inside of his father's jeep.

"Dad, I ain't scared to die."

"Splash, if you would've been lookin' in the mirror when you just said that, you wouldn't 've even believed what you said."

"I'm not, though."

"How's your grandmother?"

Splash looked at his grandfather and sighed. The last time he saw his grandmother was when she gave him the small duffel bag. He hadn't spoken to her since.

"Gran' pop, she finally gave me that bag, but-"

"You told her you knew about it already, didn't you?"

"I 'on't even wanna talk about it, Gran' pop."

"Ay, Pops, me and Splash gon' take a walk for a minute."

"Take ya'll time."

Splash grabbed his father's hand and helped him up to his feet. Together, the two of them walked in silence, until they reached the steps of a mausoleum that was the size of a small bedroom. Splash's father sat down, but Splash remained standing.

"So, what's goin' on with you?"

"Remember how you told me that time to always be the flame, and to never be the moth?"

"Of course."

Splash sighed and sat down beside his father. "Somethin' tells me you about to drop somethin' heavy on me."

"Dad, I'm startin' to feel like the moth."

"What's changed since the last time we talked?"

"Everything."

"I'm listenin'."

Splash took a deep breath and then began to tell his father all about everything that had taken place in the last two weeks. At one point, he rose to his feet and started to pace back and forth, because telling his father how Angelo and Mikey got over on him and Tia set his nerves on fire.

"When the last time you spoke to your grandmother?"

"That day."

"Do that guy that got away know where she live, too?"

"Un-uh."

"Do Tia aunt know where she live?"

"Yeah."

"Do you see where I'm goin' with this?"

"Dad, dude ain't-"

"Hold on, before you say anything else, how can you tell me that your grandmother even okay, if you haven't talked to her in a week, Splash?"

" 'Cause, I talked to Aunt Steph, and-"

"Rasool, don't let nothin' happen to your grandmother."

"Dad, ain't nobody gon' do nothin' to Gran'-"

Splash snatched his eyes open to see Tia tapping on the passenger side window of his father's jeep. Her eyes flashed an apology when he gave her an agitated stare and pushed the driver's side door open.

"Bay, I'm so sorry, but the people from the alarm company need ya handprint, and you gotta say ya name into this voice recorder, too."

With Tia leading the way, Splash left their two-car garage and walked back into their house. He followed Tia through their kitchen, into their theater, and out into their foyer.

"I think he out front, Bay."

"Who?"

"The supervisor from the alarm place."

"It's like a hundred mu' fuckers in here."

"It is not."

"I counted eleven in the kitchen."

"Where the other eighty-nine at, then?"

"It was seven in the theater, and there go two more goin' upstairs."

"You still missin' eighty people."

"Damn, dude head big as shit."

"That's the supervisor."

"Yo, Tee look, his shit givin' his whole body shade."

"Shut up."

"Yo, this nigga count for that other eighty."

"So, you're the man of the house?"

Splash smiled and shook hands with the big-headed supervisor, who was standing in the middle of his lawn.

"This is a real nice house you two have."

"Thanks."

"We shouldn't take too long," the supervisor explained, squinting up at the sun as he wiped the perspiration from his enormous forehead. "My crew is pretty fast. It's usually the windows that slow us down, because we normally do factories, and really big commercial properties, so this'll be a breeze. Okay, so, this is what I need you to go ahead and do for me. It's all pretty simple. I just need you to say your name into this little device loud and as clear as you can, then after that, I'm gonna have you place the palm of whichever hand you use to open your front door onto this inkpad here, and after that, we're all set."

One by one, Splash did as he had been asked with Tia standing right beside him. A car with tinted windows pulling into their driveway got his attention, so he elbowed Tia, so that the car would have her attention as well.

"That's Rhonda."

"I'm gon' wash this ink off my hand."

"Alright."

"Ay, Tee, tell Rhonda she ain't gettin' her allowance, if she ain't got no present for me."

Later that night, as Splash did laps in their swimming pool, Tia and her cousin Rhonda relaxed in two beach chairs with drinks in their hands.

"I think I'm pregnant, Tia."

"Don't play with me, Rhonda."

"I'm serious."

"Swear on both our moms, then."

"I swear on both our moms that I think I'm pregnant."

Tia sat up in her beach chair and looked at her cousin.

"If, I am, I wanna keep it, Tia."

"Rhonda, you only seventeen."

"I'ma be eighteen next month."

After rolling her eyes at her cousin, Tia stood up and snatched her cousin's drink out of her hand. On her mother's side of her family, Rhonda was a cousin of hers that stayed in some type of trouble, which was the main reason why most of their other family members treated her like an outcast. Tia was actually the only person that she respected and listened to.

"Girl, come on."

"Where?"

"Rhonda, don't make me fuckin' choke you with ya bikini top out here."

"Well, tell me-"

"We goin' in the house, so you can take a fuckin' pregnancy test."

"I already got one in my pocketbook."

"Well, go get it and meet me in the bathroom."

"Which one?"

"Mines."

"Tia?"

"What?"

"If, I am, you gon' be mad at me?"

Tia looked over her shoulder at her cousin as they both walked up her rear patio steps. The shame in her cousin's eyes saddened her.

"Hopefully, I won't have a reason to be mad at you."

"Tia, can I wait 'til tomorrow to take it?"

"You sure can't."

"Why not?"

"Why should you?"

" 'Cause, I'm scared."

"Ya ass should've been fuckin' scared to let somebody stick they dick in you without a condom on."

Fifteen minutes later, Tia returned to her backyard by herself. Without saying a word, she sat back down in her beach chair and picked up her drink. She had an attitude. When Splash walked up to her, she rolled her eyes at him.

"What's wrong wit' chu?"

"Nothin'."

"You ain't just roll ya eyes at me for nothin', Tee."

"I ain't roll my eyes at chu."

"You trippin'."

"I am not, so get out my face."

"Done."

"Bay, Rhonda pregnant."

"Yea, alright."

"I'm dead serious."

"Where she at?"

Tia took two gulps of her drink and sat it down in the grass beside her Chanel sandals.

"She left?"

"Come here, Bay."

"Yo, you just told me to get outta ya face."

"Well, now, I want you back in it, so come back over here."

"Yea, alright."

"Come here, Bay."

After Splash was done drying himself off with his towel, he hung it around his neck and looked at Tia and shook his head. Instead of going over to where she was sitting, he sat down in a beach chair that was a few feet away from the one she was sitting in.

"So, Rock 'n Roll Rhonda pregnant for real, huh?"

"Didn't I tell you to stop callin' her that?"

"Man, she like it."

"Well, I fuckin' don't, so stop callin' her that, before I give you a nickname you definitely won't like."

"Ay, Tee, I ain't tryna be fuckin' beefin' wit' chu on my birthday."

"We not," Tia assured Splash, as she stood up and slid on her sandals. While finger-combing her hair, she walked over to where Splash was sitting and sat down beside him. "I'm sorry, Bay. Rhonda just got me stressed out right now, that's all. She stayin' the night, so when Cam get here in the mornin', she can help us decorate out here, and set up all the tables and everything, so once the caterers get here, they can just set all the food out and leave."

As Tia went on and explained to Splash how his D&G-themed birthday party was going to be a big hit, Splash tilted his head back and silently gazed up at the stars in the dark sky. He wasn't too excited about his party anymore. He still had a gut feeling that having so many different people at his house all at once wasn't such a good idea, and unfortunately for him, he was absolutely right, because his birthday party was going to be a total disaster.

Chapter Twelve

"Bocka! Bocka! Bocka! Pop, pop, pop, pop, pop-Boom! !Bocka! Doom! Doom! Bocka! Bocka! Pop, pop, pop-Boom!! Bocka! Bocka!"

The early afternoon shootout sounded like a competitive gun-recital. Although some of the guns were louder than others, each owner standing behind their weapon was squeezing their trigger with every malicious hope of dropping the target in their sights. In just fifty-three seconds, enough bullets to stop a small herd of elephants had been discharged, and as the wailing sound of police sirens grew louder and louder off in the distance, the intensity of the drama was beginning to put anxiety in the hearts of every shooter involved in the chaos.

The madness was unfolding in the huge parking lot of a shopping plaza located on 4th and Oregon Avenue.

"Yo, Prep, go 'head!!"

At that very moment, Prep felt like everything that he had done up until that point had been one colossal mistake, and the thought of him going back to jail for the rest of his life was starting to make him feel dizzy. For support, he leaned his shoulder against the mail truck that him and Gary were hiding behind. The big bag of money in his right hand was weighing him down like an anchor.

"Dog, what the fuck you waitin' for?!"

Prep gave Gary a blank stare and took a deep breath. As he exhaled, his courage slowly began to return. He was beginning to feel like himself again.

"Prep?!"

"Gary, shoot back at them mu'fuckers!"

"I ain't got no more fuckin' shells!"

"Here!"

As Prep handed his gun to Gary, a string of cop cars, followed by two unmarked cars, raced their way through the shopping plaza's parking lot entrance. After their vehicles all came to screeching stops, the armored truck guards rushed over to greet them all with their fingers pointing in the area where the three of them had last saw Prep and Gary, before they had ducked out of sight. A few feet away from them, their armored truck sat idling quietly beside the Shopping plaza's big, Super Market, with both of its rear doors still ajar.

Every single store in the shopping plaza had small crowds of people staring out at the dramatic scene.

"Damn."

"Yo, they gon' surround us."

"They gon' kill us, if we don't give-"

"Prep, look out for my mom, dog."

"What?"

The mail truck that Prep and Gary were kneeling beside was peppered with bullet holes on its driver's side. The cars parked in front of it, next to it, and behind it, were also riddled with bullets as well.

"Give my half to my mom, alright?"

"Gary, we-Dog, yo, this shit over, man."

"I'ma distract them, so you can-"

"Ain't no-"

"Prep, yo, just shut the fuck up and listen to me!!"

Prep let out a frustrated sigh and looked down at the bag of money at his feet. As he listened to what Gary had to say, he shook his head at their predicament. They were surrounded by five, long ranks of parked cars, but at any second, the cops would be coming to find them.

"You ready?"

Prep's eyes were blurry, because his childhood friend had decided to make the ultimate sacrifice.

"Gary, you-"

"Dog, is you fuckin' ready, or what?"

"Alright."

Prep and Gary rose to their feet at the same time. Teardrops fell from both of their eyes as they looked at each other.

"Gary, this shit wasn't even worth it."

"It will be, if you get the fuck away."

"I'ma make sure you got the best lawyer-"

"Dog, where I'm goin', I ain't gon' need one."

"Gary, we can just-"

Gary shoved Prep real hard and took off running. He wanted to be seen by all of the cops, so he held his head up high as he began to weave his way around all of the parked cars. At the top of his lungs, he was screaming obscenities, but the gun down at his side remained silent. Because Gary didn't want to die alone, he chose not to shoot the gun in his right hand, until he was close enough to the cops and armored truck guards to achieve that goal. Bravely, as they all began to fire their weapons at him, he lowered his shoulders and ran harder. Once he felt comfortable with his position, he jumped on the hood of a parked car and let the Glock in his hand roar like a pack of lions.

In the opposite direction, almost forty cars away, Prep was crouched down in between two parked cars with his eyes glued to an unpaved trail that separated a fabric store from a Chinese buffet. He could feel his heart beating in his throat as numerous sets of eyes watched him from behind the glass-fronts of both businesses. As he bolted forward, his concern for Gary's fate forced him to steal a glance over his shoulder, but when he spotted a police helicopter up in the sky, he returned his attention back to the dirt path that could possibly lead to his freedom.

The loud gunshots were echoing off the walls, following Prep to the end of the trail that stopped on Marshall and Packer Avenue. Twice, he had stumbled, because the bag of money was so heavy, that when it had banged against his left thigh, the weight of it had knocked him off balance as he ran. Every breath that he took felt like he was inhaling fire into his lungs. The thought of stopping entered his mind a hundred times, but the sight of Gary's getaway car kept giving him the energy that he needed to keep his legs moving.

Meanwhile, in Chestnut Hill, many, many miles away, Splash's and Tia's mini-mansion was buzzing with excitement. The celebration of Splash's birthday party was turning out exactly the way Tia had said it would. A real party planner would have been impressed, because Tia's preparations for the special event had all of her and Splash's party guests smiling and enjoying themselves. While a six-person team of caterers were moving around the party with trays that held glasses of champagne, bottled water, and colorful jello shots, another private company that Tia had hired was out front, acting as a valet service for the party guests as they arrived.

It was a beautiful, Saturday afternoon. The sky was clear of clouds, and the sun was fulfilling its job description by shining with the brightness of a million and one light bulbs.

Tia was playing hostess, and she was loving every minute of it. Many of the party guests had never been to her and Splash's house, so most of them were just walking around admiring their home like it was a small museum, which Tia loved, because it reminded her of how talented her mother had been.

"Bay, ya gran' mom and aunt just got here."

"Alright, here I come."

Without raising his head from his pillow, Splash tossed his cell phone over to Tia's side of their bed and let out a long sigh. That was the twelfth time that Tia had called him. In so many words, she was just trying to get him to come downstairs to join in with the festivities. He was fully dressed, but he wasn't in the mood to socialize with anyone, and he had no intentions on leaving his bedroom anytime soon. The celebration of his birthday had always given him a melancholy attitude, because it also marked the death of both of his parents.

"Cousin Splash?"

Splash uncrossed his legs and propped himself up on his elbows. The sight of his five-year-old cousin standing in his bedroom doorway brung an instant smile to his face.

"Cousin Splash, your birthday cake bigger than me."

"For real?"

"Yup. It's this, this big."

Splash chuckled and sat up in his bed when his little cousin opened his arms real wide to show him how big his birthday cake was. His cousin Shateek was adorable. He looked like his mother, but he had his father's mannerisms.

"Teek, where ya mom at?"

"Swimmin' in the pool."

"Yo, come over here, so I can tie ya sneaker."

"I know how to tie my own sneaker."

"Since when?"

"Since yesterday."

"Alright, let me see."

"Watch, 'cause Mom-Mom said I'm five, and I'm 'pose to . . . tie . . . my own-See."

Splash grinned proudly when his little cousin poked out his tiny, red, D&G sneaker. His lace wasn't tied perfectly, but as far as Splash was concerned, it was perfect enough. He loved his cousin Sabia's son like he was his very own.

"So, this where you hidin' at, huh?"

In Splash's bedroom doorway stood a man that Splash had a lot of love and respect for. His name was Tuna. He was the manager of Splash's nightclub, but he was also Tia's uncle. He was Tia's mother's younger brother. Because of Tuna's dark complexion, large stature, and deep voice, many people were intimidated by his presence. His thick beard and bald head added to the perception that he was a no-nonsense type of individual, but in all actuality, he was really the exact opposite.

"What's up, Tuna fish?"

"You tell me?"

"Tia sent chu up here, didn't she?"

"Actually, I wanted to introduce you to-"

"Mr. Tuna, can I get on your back?"

"Can I have some of them curls in ya hair?"

"You can have this."

Splash and Tuna looked at each other and laughed when Shateek dug in the back pocket of his shorts and pulled out a party wing.

"Teek, man what chu doin' wit' a chicken wing in ya pocket?"

"'Cause-'Cause-'Cause, Cousin Tia said I can give it to Snookums."

"I sure did," Tia confirmed, as she stepped around her uncle's huge frame and entered her bedroom. Pursing her lips together, she grabbed Shateek by his hand, then she walked over to her bed and pulled Splash to his feet by his.'Ya'll gran' mom wanna see both of ya'll. Uncle Tuna, I advise you to have a side-bar, or somethin' with ya date,' cause if it's left up to me, I'ma start off by tellin' her ass they invented deodorant for that smell she got under her damn arms. Like, really, I just wanna know where you found her? What's her name again?"

"Victoria."

"Oh, you finally brung Victoria out in public, huh?"

"Bay, she smell like oodles 'n noodles."

Splash smirked and elbowed Tia's uncle in his side as they followed Tia out of their bedroom, and began to walk down their second-floor hallway.

"Cousin Tia, can I have some oodles 'n noodles?"

Tia, Splash, and Tia's uncle erupted into laughter.

"Huh, Cousin Tia?"

"Boy, no."

"Why?"

" 'Cause, I said so."

"But I want some oodles 'n-"

"There she go right there, Bay."

Splash scooped his little 'cousin off of his feet and stepped between Tia and her uncle. He smiled down at his Roman-styled foyer, and waved back when a few people spotted him staring down at them from his terrace. Some faces were familiar, and some weren't. All of them appeared to be having a good time, except for an attractive, older lady that Tia was pointing her finger at.

"Okay, Tuna."

Tia rolled her eyes when her uncle smiled at Splash's compliment. Not only did her uncle's date stink, but she also had a real negative vibe about her, and she kept studying everyone at the party like she was hiding from someone, or really didn't want to be seen.

"Bay, come see how nice the backyard-"

"Cousin Splash, I wanna see the fish."

Splash switched his little cousin to his left arm and spun around, so that both of them faced the humongous aquarium in his hallway's wall.

"I'll see ya'll out in the backyard."

Tia gave her uncle a hug, and she kept her eyes on him as he slowly began to move his big frame down her spiral steps to her crowded foyer. She wondered what was it about his date that he found intriguing, because he was famously known for dealing with only white girls, and to Tia's knowledge, her uncle had never been romantically involved with a black woman in all of his forty-two years.

"Cousin Tia, can I feed Snookums, now?"

"He in his cage in the guest room."

Splash's little cousin hit the floor running when Splash put him down.

"Bay, you moved ya car this mornin'?"

"Rhonda got it."

"Excuse me?"

"Her car wouldn't start up."

"And you just felt perfectly fine with givin' her yours, huh?"

Shrugging his shoulders, Splash twisted the doorknob on his and Tia's office door and pushed it open. Tia followed him inside, and over to the large window behind their office desk that provided a view of their entire backyard.

"So, I'm guessin' that chu ain't see the passenger side of her car, 'cause it look like she was playin' bumpin' cars with mailboxes some fuckin'-"

"Tee, check nut ass Robbie out."

Tia stepped closer to her office window and looked down at her backyard. There were people everywhere. It was easy to spot Camay's boyfriend, because he was dancing in the middle of a small crowd with two drinks in each hand. His behavior was odd for someone who was about to attend his cousin's funeral in three days.

"Cousin Tia, I'm finish."

Splash scooped his little cousin back up and tossed him up in the air. His cousin's giggles put a smile on his face.

"I love you, Cousin Splash."

"I love you too, Teek."

As Tia ushered him out of their office and back out to their hallway, Splash felt like he was finally ready to enjoy his birthday party. Him and Tia held hands as they walked down to the other end of their hallway. Before taking the spiral steps that spilled down to their kitchen, they shared a brief kiss, which ended in a fit of laughter, because Splash's little cousin had thought their open affection in front of him was just simply hilarious.

Once Splash and Tia made it outside to their rear patio, they kissed once more, then went their separate ways. Splash took his little cousin over to where his grandmother and aunt were, and Tia went back into their house, because she didn't see Camay anywhere in her backyard.

After searching her entire house, Tia went to the last possible place that she thought Camay would be. Without knocking, she pulled her downstairs bathroom open and peeked inside.

"Cam, why you not outside?" Tia asked, pulling her bathroom door closed behind her. After glancing at the reflection of her face in the mirror, she stepped out of her gray, peep-toe, D&G stilettos, and let out a long sigh of relief. "Girl, these three inch heels is killin' my-Cam? Bitch, ain't no way in the fuckin' world you drunk already. Camay?"

Camay raised her face from her hands. She was crying. Her tears had caused her mascara to run down her face. She opened her mouth to speak as she raised her eyes to look at Tia, but no words left her trembling lips.

"Cam, what's-"

"Tia, my period late."

Those words hit Tia like a ton of bricks. A month earlier, her, Camay and Splash had experienced a disastrous threesome, which left them all privately regretful for different reasons. Those regrets were born during the late night hours, after the grand opening of Splash's nightclub. Throughout the entire overcrowded venue, Splash and Tia had been humorously approving, and disapproving each other's choices, when it came to what females they would include in their threesome, if they were to ever have one. While they around the club, the two of them had used their cell phones to send each other text-messages and photos of their picks, but they couldn't agree on the same female, because, either Tia didn't like who Splash had picked, or she just didn't particularly like all of his enthusiasm about the whole idea. It had ended with them both not speaking to each other.

Camay had arrived just as the last of the party-goers were being escorted out of the doors by Splash's bouncers, and Tia's uncle. She was furious that night, because her boyfriend had come home with passion marks on his face and neck.

In an attempt to douse the flames that was in her best friend's chest, Tia had treated Camay to her own bottle of Ace of Spades. After an animated-toast, the two of them had clinked their glasses together, and then they went out on the empty dance floor, and had begun to dance to the music that was still playing.

Back on that infamous night, Splash left his office, and had joined Tia and Camay out on his nightclub's spacious dance floor. His motives were harmless, but the man in him, helped by the silver Patron that was swimming in his blood, had influenced him to appraise Camay's attractive qualities as her and Tia smiled and danced circles around him.

A whisper from Splash had caused Tia to look at Camay sexually for the first time in her many years of knowing her. An intimate kiss, followed by a whispered-response had made Splash's dick stiffen, causing it to push against his Fendi jeans.

Camay's pussy had betrayed her by moistening when Tia's whisper had tickled her left ear. Like Tia, she wasn't bi-sexual, but she had smiled shyly and nodded her head to answer the question that had been asked of her.

That night, three whispers had ignited an unextinguishable fire.

Tia was so drunk, that everything that had taken place from that point on was vague to her memory. She had no recollection of how kissing Camay had made her sick to her stomach, or that she had vomited on the front of Camay's Prada dress, and had passed out in the private bathroom in Splash's office. The very next morning, Splash had filled in the blanks for Tia as she laid in their bed. Her hangover became a migraine headache when he told her that him and Camay still had sex, but when Splash had got to the part of telling her that his condom had slipped off inside of Camay, she could have sworn that she had felt the earth stand still.

"I got an appointment to see my doctor tomorrow mornin'."

"Want me to go with you?"

"Tia, I can't believe this shit happenin' to me."

"You sure it's not Robbie's?"

Camay nodded her head sadly.

After wiping away a falling teardrop with the back of her hand, Tia sighed and shook her head.

"I wasn't going to tell you, because I wanted to be sure that-Tia, I can't have Splash's baby."

A sensation of dizziness suddenly came over Tia as she moved over to where Camay was sitting on the toilet seat. Her legs felt like jelly, so she used Camay's knee for support as she lowered herself down to her bathroom floor.

"Tia?"

Tia grabbed her chest.

"Tia, what's wrong?"

"Call-Cam, call . . . an . . . ambulance."

"Oh, my God."

At that very moment, on the opposite side of the bathroom door, something special was happening. Splash was escorting his grandmother by the arm down the short hallway that led to his and Tia's two-car garage. His grandmother had surprised him by telling him that she wanted to spend some time alone in his father's jeep. If Splash and his grandmother were walking just a little bit slower, the two of them would have crossed paths with Splash's cousin Sabia, but it was Camay, who had pushed Splash's and Tia's bathroom door open in his face as he was marching by.

"Sa-Sabia, get Splash!"

"What?! Yo, where the fuck Jen at?!"

"Sabia, Tia need-"

"I'ma kill that bitch, watch!"

"Something wrong with Tia!"

"And somethin' 'bout to be fuckin' wrong with Jen, too!"

When Sabia snatched a gun off of his waist and stormed off, Camay ran back into the bathroom to check on Tia.

"Cam, who was that?"

"Girl, you just scared the-"

"I think I had an anxiety attack."

"You okay?"

"Help me up."

"Tia, Sabia gotta-"

A gunshot loud enough to wake up the dead made Tia and Camay flinch. Together, they scrambled out of the bathroom and bumped into Splash, who had heard the gunshot also.

"Splash, Sabia-"

Camay's words were stolen by another loud gunshot.

"Tee, what the fuck goin' on?!"

"I don't-"

With a third gunshot, a small stampede of party guests came running into Splash's and Tia's house from their backyard.

It took Splash thirty-seven seconds to make it out onto his rear patio, but to him, it had felt like forever. His aunt met him there screaming at the top of her lungs. She had his little cousin's limp body in her arms. Half of his little cousin's cute face had been torn off by two bullets.

Another loud gunshot rang out from Splash's swimming pool.

"Yo, Splash, get ya cousin, man!!"

Robbie's loud plea for help was almost louder than the gunshot that had snatched Splash out of his trance. His screams and shouts after that were drowned out by the water that had filled his mouth and lungs when Sabia wrestled him back under the water. Robbie was kicking and flailing his limbs like a wild animal, and once Splash dove in his swimming pool and rescued him from certain death, he still continued to swing and holler, because he had his eyes closed, and he didn't realize that it was Splash, and not Sabia, who was pulling him to the edge of the swimming pool.

The loud sirens of an ambulance and police cars pierced the summer air.

Splash watched his cousin as he escaped through the tall trees that separated his neighbor's property from his. The urge to run after his cousin vanished when Splash spotted his grandmother among the throngs of people, who were spilling their way out of his house back onto his rear patio, and down into his backyard. His grandmother looked disoriented, which Splash assumed could only mean one thing. Her eyes locked on his as he climbed out of his swimming pool.

"God, please save Shateek," Splash silently prayed, as he fell to his knees. Remembering the blessing his father had received so many years ago, he turned over on his back and stared at the sky through watery eyes. "He only a baby. He don't even know what a sin is. Exchange my life for his, if anything. God, please don't stain my birthday with this type of pain again."

"Bay?"

Splash opened his eyes and looked up at Tia. The deep sadness in her eyes mirrored the anguish he was feeling in his soul.

"Tee, what the fuck happened?"

"They said Sabia and Robbie was tusslin' over the gun, and it went off. Shateek was right next to them."

"What the fuck was they-"

"They said Sabia said that Shateek wasn't his son, and that he was lookin' for Jen at first, but he saw Robbie-"

"What?"

"Bay, Sha-Shateek dead."

Splash closed his eyes. His heart felt like it was being kicked inside of his chest, and as Tia began to sob uncontrollably, he made a promise to himself that he would never ask God for any help, even if his own life depended on it.

Chapter Thirteen

Several days later, Tia found herself at odds with her own conscious as she drove north up the I-95 expressway to Camay's house. It was hard for her to accept that Shateek was actually dead. It was even more difficult for her to come to terms with the fact that her best friend was pregnant by her husband. She was experiencing a low point in her life, and no matter how far, or how deep she searched her troubled soul, she was still unable to find any answers that would help her cope with her problems. She was overwhelmed with enough pain to make a giant beg for mercy.

Tia took exit 46b, and followed it, until a red light stopped her at Oxford Valley Road. There, she closed her eyes for a second and leaned the back of her head against her headrest. Her eyes blinked at the cold blast of air that was coming from a vent in her dashboard. When Tia opened her eyes, the traffic light was green, so she made a left onto Oxford Valley Road, and drove a half a mile to the affluent community of Melissa Circle, where Camay lived in Yardley, Pennsylvania.

A light drizzle chased Tia from her car to Camay's front door.

"What's up, Tia?"

"Hey, Prep."

It was no secret to Tia that Camay's cousin Prep had a crush on her. However, his infatuation for her was the furthest thing from her mind as she stepped into Camay's foyer and gave him a warm hug.

"Where Cam at?"

"Upstairs in her room."

"So, how long you gon' stay home this time?"

"How long you gon' stay married?"

For the first time in three days, a slight trace of a smile appeared on Tia's face.

"What's up, Tia?"

Tia paused in the middle of Camay's staircase and looked over her shoulder at Robbie, who was sitting in Camay's livingroom. His audacity to speak to her had caught her totally off guard, and had paralyzed her legs.

"Robbie, I understand that you just got back from your cousin's funeral, "Tia said, as the temptation to pull her gun out of her pocketbook slowly subsided. So badly, she wanted Robbie to meet her stare, but he wouldn't. "But honestly, as I'm sure you already know, I can care less. I refuse to feel sorry for you. And you wanna know why, Robbie? 'Cause, you don't fuckin' deserve pity. You or Jen. Y'all deserve closed caskets like Shateek gotta have, because it was y'all slimy shit that cost him his fuckin' life. Robbie, Shateek was only five. Five fuckin' years-old. I swear, I hope when them Dominicans catch up to you, they fuckin'-"

"Tia?"

Tia looked up at Camay. She was standing at the top of her stairs hugging herself with one of the saddest looks on her face that she had ever seen.

"I thought chu was puttin' him out?" Tia asked, once her and Camay were in Camay's bedroom. The chill from the central-air made her rub her hands over her arms.

"Cam, how much shit that mother fucker gotta put chu through, before-"

"I gave him a week to find somewhere else to-"

"Ay, y'all cool?"

Tia and Camay cut their conversation short and looked at Prep.

"Damn, it feel like Alaska in this jawn, Cam."

Camay's master bedroom was fit for a queen. She had high ceilings, white, marble floors, and imported bedroom furniture that had been cut from a tree in Africa. Her house was an enormous piece of beautiful property that she had worked extremely hard for. Growing up in the White Hall projects in the Frankford section of Philadelphia had instilled a drive in her to want the best that life had to offer, and her house was visual proof of how determined she was to achieve that goal.

"Y'all wanna go shoppin' to get y'all mind off of everything, and get away from Robbie?"

"Prep?"

"Huh?"

"Where you get money from?"

"I had some money stashed, before I got locked up."

"Do Aunt Janice know you out here?"

"Dag, man, why you keep askin' me that shit?"

"Prep, this only my second time askin' you that, and if I find out you got into some trouble, I'ma-"

"Ay, Cam, let me holla at chu for a minute."

After Camay left her bedroom to see what Robbie wanted with her out in the hallway, Tia reached into her pocketbook and pulled out her cell phone. She felt Prep's eyes on her, but she didn't pay him any attention. Her mind was on her husband, so she wanted to call him to get a feel of what type of mood he was in. As she sat back down in the chaise lounge-chair beside Camay's bed, she put her cell phone to her ear and waited for Splash to answer her call.

"What's up, Fancy face?"

"Hey, Bay."

"You still at the house?"

"Un-uh, I'm at Camay's."

"Oh."

"You still at the club?"

"Naw, I'm at my gran' mom's now."

"They had Sabia on the news again."

"I seen that shit. They got his picture on the front page of the paper, too."

"I know. Rhonda called me and told me."

"Mu'fuckers been callin' me all fuckin' day."

Tia sighed and switched her cell phone to her other ear.

"So, you okay?"

"Man, I ain't gon' be okay for a long-Ay, Tee, hold on real quick. This that lady from the funeral home returning my call."

"Just call me back."

"Alright."

Sighing, Tia thumbed the screen of her cell phone and placed it in the lap of her peach, Polo sundress. She shook her head and crossed her legs. As she stared blankly at the back of her white, Polo sneaker, she began to think about Shateek's funeral, which was two days away. She was certain that her soul was going to tear itself into pieces, once she laid her eyes on his tiny casket.

"Tia, if Camay feel like goin' tomorrow, you'll go with us?"

Tia looked up and stared at Prep without answering him. Instead, she gave him an annoyed glance and dropped her eyes back on her sneakers. She completely had forgotten that Prep was still in Camay's bedroom with her, because he had been so quiet as he looked out of a window on the other side of Camay's bedroom.

"Go with y'all where, Prep?"

"Oxford Valley mall."

"Prep, Robbie wanna know if you'll drive to Philly with him to pick up his little sister?"

"Where he at?"

"Out in the hallway."

Tia kept her eyes on Camay as she walked past Prep and came back into her bedroom. She looked ten pounds thinner. The depth of her stress was visible in her eyes.

"I scheduled an appointment to get the abortion next Thursday."

"Cam, I'm so sorry you gotta go through-"

"Tia, this ain't nobody fault but mine, "Camay said, shrugging her shoulders. She looked at Tia and smiled sadly. "I got myself into this. Two wrongs don't make a right, and that night, me being mad at Robbie was really why I even considered havin' that threesome with you and Splash, Tia. I was drunk, but I wasn't that fuckin' drunk. This is what bein' spiteful got me. It got me pregnant by my best friend's husband, who like a brother to me at that."

Prep slowly stepped away from Camay's bedroom doorway with light steps. His ears were burning as he walked down Camay's hallway to her guest bedroom, where his seven hundred and eighty thousand dollars was hiding in a bag under the bed.

"What chu wanna show me?"

After Robbie stepped aside, Prep walked into Camay's guest bedroom and sat down on the bed.

"So, what's up?"

"How much you owe them Dominicans?"

"Somethin' small."

Prep had always looked up to Robbie, because he knew how to win in the streets. He was the guy to call for drugs when other so-called suppliers complained about a drought. His only problem was his mouth. He talked too much.

"Ay, Robbie I'ma show you somethin', but chu can't tell Cam shit, man."

"Alright."

"Dog, I'm fuckin' serious."

"Nigga, just show me what the fuck you talkin' 'bout."

Prep narrowed his eyes.

"Yo, I'm out."

"Robbie, that was me and my man that hit that armored truck down South Philly," Prep confessed, while he reached beneath the bed and grabbed the new love of his life. "That's why I came out here, 'cause I'm tryna stay under the radar, 'til I figure out my next move. You feel me? I got away with this, though."

"Oh, shit."

"Robbie, I'ma give you what chu need to pay ya connect back, but chu gotta do me a favor first."

"Damn."

Prep grinned and stood up, so Robbie could get a full view of all the thick stacks of money that were inside of his big, black, duffel bag. Each stack of money contained twenty thousand dollars. It was a total of thirty-nine stacks in the bag.

"What chu want me to drive you outta state?"

"Naw, not yet."

"What chu tryna do, then?"

"I want chu to help me fuck Tia."

"What?"

"And I wanna tape that shit, so I can send a copy of that shit to her fuckin' husband."

Chapter Fourteen

"They ran up in Gran' mom house yesterday, and Aunt Steph said they came back to her house this mornin'."

"What the fuck do the U.S. Marshalls got to do-"

"Craig, calm down and let Splash-"

"All them fuckin' pigs need to be slaughtered!"

Splash and his grandfather looked at each other with raised eyebrows. Neither of them wanted to get Splash's father any more worked up than he already was, so the two of them just kept quiet for a moment and watched him as he paced back and forth in front of them. Mentioning the cops around Splash's father was like a person saying Hitler's name in a room full of Jews.

Splash and his predecessors were inside of an old factory that was the size of a small playground. It was one huge room with a very high ceiling that had large, steel beams running parallel from one far wall to the other. There were no windows in the entire place. There were red light bulbs dangling from the ceiling all over the place, giving the factory's dusty, concrete floor an intense, reddish-glow.

It was here, where Splash's first dream with his father had taken place. It was here, where Splash and his father had hugged and cried without speaking one word to each other when their eyes had met under all of the glowing, red dots for the very first time.

"His only options is Canada or Mexico, 'cause him gettin' on a plane is out of the question."

Splash looked at his father and nodded his head in agreement. His grandfather did so as well.

"Gran' mom want Sabia to turn himself in, though."

Splash's father threw his hands in the air.

"Aunt Steph do, too."

"Barnes men don't surrender to nobody, Splash."

"Dad, I know that, but-"

"What do Sabia want to do?"

"Gran' pop, I still ain't talk to him, but I know he ain't with turnin' himself in."

"So, how you holdin' up?"

"Stressin'," Splash admitted, after wiping his hand over his face to clear the tears from his eyes. His pain was prevalent even in his dream-state of mind. "I feel like God just keep testin' me, and testin' me. Like-Like, he wanna see how much pain I can take, or somethin'. It seem like he keep takin' everybody I love. Y'all. My mom . . . Teek, my son. Shateek casket so little, I can carry it by myself."

"Splash, goin' through these difficult times is goin' to build your character."

"Dad, these difficult times is about to have me on some real bizzare shit."

"Son, I realize that you-"

"I wanna see my mom."

A loud silence followed Splash's request.

Splash switched his attention to the three-booth shooting range that was fifteen feet away from the wooden benches, where his father and grandfather were sitting. With angry eyes, he rose from the plastic crate he had been sitting on.

"We been over this a thousand-"

"I'm not gettin' in ya car no more, watch."

"Splash, you can't blame your father for your mother not-"

"Gran' pop, You had to die for you to even believe this could happen!"

"Apologize to your damn grandfather!"

"For what?! For tellin' the truth?!"

Splash didn't budge when his father stepped in his face.

"Apologize!!"

Even in his spiritual life, Craig Barnes was menacing. His anger had caused his eyes to become the same color as the countless light bulbs that were dangling from the factory's ceiling. He balled his fists and stepped closer to his only child. His heart wasn't even softened by the teardrops that were rolling down the front of his son's face.

"Apologize to your grandfather!"

Splash stared defiantly into his father's emotionless eyes as he curled the fingers on both of his hands into tight fists. If his father swung at him, he was going to swing back.

"Splash?"

Splash ignored his grandfather.

"Craig?"

"Dad, he gon' apologize to you, or-"

"Don't put ya hands on me, Dad."

"What?!"

"Don't put-"

"Smack!!!"

Splash snatched his eyes open and grabbed his face. His right cheek felt like he had gotten stung by a bee. His father had smacked him so hard that it woke him up.

The second Splash raised his fists to pound the dashboard of his father's vintage jeep, his cell phone started to ring in his pocket.

"What's up, Tuna?"

"I gotta situation here."

Splash frowned and rubbed the palm of his hand softly over his cheek.

"Splash?"

"I'm listenin'."

"It's a detective here."

"What the fuck he want?"

"You."

"Me?"

"That ain't the situation, though."

"What chu mean?"

"Sabia here."

"What?"

"I let him in through the back entrance."

Splash stepped out of his father's jeep and slammed the door with so much force that it shook the black, Nissan Pathfinder down to its four tires.

"Splash this mother fucker keep askin' me to give him a tour around the club."

"Where Sabia at?"

"Ya office."

"Here I come."

"Something ain't right about this detective, Splash."

"Tuna, don't let that mu'fucker in my office."

"Just hurry up and get here, 'cause I'm runnin' outta ex-"

"Tell him I'm on my way."

"Say no more."

It took Splash a little over an hour to make it to his club. Had it not been for the after work traffic on I-76, he would have gotten there a lot sooner. There were moments during his drive there, where he wondered to himself if the unknown detective would have to be killed, and if so, could he trust Tuna after the murder had taken place. Both of these thoughts walked around in his mind as he slipped his gun into his back pocket, and closed the heavy, metal door that he and Tuna sometimes used as a private entrance when they didn't feel like being bothered with going through the club's front doors.

To be sure that his cousin Sabia understood the gravity of the situation, Splash stopped at his office first to let him know what was going on.

"Yo, Bia, it's a fuckin' cop here."

"Come look at what this mu'fucker doin' to Tuna."

After Splash locked his office door, he walked around his office desk and joined his cousin at the split-screen, surveillance monitor that hung on the wall beside a large, framed-picture of him and Tia standing on a beach in St. Tropez.

The small screen in the bottom, left corner of Splash's surveillance monitor was showing a bizarre act taking place. Splash's manager was down on one knee, and he was letting a man not even half his size slap him in the face over and over again. When the detective started to unzip his pants, Splash pulled his gun out of his back pocket and told his cousin to lock the door as he stormed out of his office.

"I said put it in your fuckin' mouth!!"

The loud, freakish-command echoed off of every wall in Splash's nightclub.

"Do it!!"

Splash's nightclub was located on 3rd Street, in between the intersections of Market Street and Chestnut Street. It was a tall, handsome building that had three floors. On its left was a valet parking lot, and to its right stood a vintage jazz record store. On the first floor of the club, after passing a lounge area, and a unisex restroom, two giant champagne glasses commanded attention at the beginning of a long, twisting hallway, which led to Splash's office. Before reaching Splash's office, a set of stairs climbed up to the second floor, where the spacious dance floor, bar, and small stage were. There was another unisex restroom on the third floor, which was flanked by Splash's manager's office, a locker room that was used by the bouncers and other staff, and there was another room at the end of the hallway that wasn't used for anything, so its door was simply kept locked.

The idea to open up the nightclub had been a spontaneous move for Splash. It appeared to be a smart investment decision in the beginning, but after two months, he was noticing that he was in way over his head.

"Put it in your mother fuckin' mouth!!"

"Man, who the fuck is this freak ass fuckin' cop," Splash wondered, as he ran up the stairwell that led to the second floor of his club. He was taking the steps three at a time. "Why Tuna ain't tryna break this nigga in half? Fuck that. This faggot got the game fucked up if he-"

"I said-"

"Yo?!!"

With a calmness that impressed Splash, the little detective harassing Tuna spun around to face him with his dick in his hand, and a grin on his ugly face that would put fear inside of a ghost's spirit.

"Well, well, well."

"Ay, yo, Tuna, get the fuck up and come over here."

"So, the man of the hour has finally arrived, huh?"

There were tears in Tuna's eyes as he rose to his feet.

"Looks like you got saved by the bell, big fella."

The detective in Splash's nightclub was a deeply, disturbed individual. His name was Baron Konn. He was half Scandinavian and half black, and he was an opportunist that used his badge in every inappropriate way imaginable. His personality was as ugly as his features, and even his fellow officers despised him, because many of them suspected that he had set up his partner of ten years to be killed in an undercover drug buy gone wrong.

Tuna walked over to Splash and paused at his side. He opened his mouth to speak, but he couldn't put into words what he was feeling.

"Go to my office and lock the door, Tuna."

Once Tuna was gone, Splash returned his gun to his back pocket and looked around the second floor of his nightclub. His mind was playing a silent game of chess. He was fully aware that he had a dirty cop in his presence, and although the crooked police officer's motives weren't yet known to him, he wanted to be absolutely sure that his surveillance cameras recorded everything that was about to occur. He wanted to add what happened next, to what had already happened to his manager.

"You want a drink?"

"I'll take Cutty Sark, if you have it."

"Ice?"

"Straight."

As Splash walked behind his bar, he rubbed his hand over his cheek. Out of his peripheral vision, he saw that the detective was putting his dick back inside of the tight jeans that he was wearing. This gave him some relief, because had the detective made one sexual advance at him, he would have put a dozen bullets in his ugly face, and thought nothing of it. However, he was interested in knowing why the detective was there, so this made him anxious to hear what had to be said.

"I'm Detective Konn."

"Just get to the part where you tell me why you here."

"I knew your father."

Splash handed the detective his drink, but as he did, he gave him a suspicious look.

"I introduced myself to him just as he started to choke on his own blood, "Detective Konn said, before, throwing back his shot. "Looked him right in the eyes. Do you know what that sick bastard-Shit .Ain't nothin' like Cutty Sark, I tell ya. Make the next one a double, and leave the bottle here, so I can pour the rest myself. There you go. Yup. That'll do me just-"

"You one of the cops that killed my dad?"

"Does it matter?"

"Man, what the fuck you want?"

"Two hundred thousand by the end of the month."

"What?"

"It's either that, or get framed for a couple of homicides."

Splash's sudden lost for words earned him a smile from Detective Konn.

"Consider it a payoff for the work you and your wife do for Trixie Masino."

"Who the fuck is that?"

"She's your wife's fuckin' aunt, and the lady that pays the both of you to commit murders, Rasool Barnes."

Splash understood that Detective Konn's purpose of using his real name was to only show him how well he had been doing his homework.

"Your father spit blood in my face and smiled, before he died that day."

Detective Konn reminded Splash of the unsightly creature from the movie 'Lord of the Ring'. He looked like Smeegor. All of the features on his face belonged to a person with a bigger head, and his albino complexion was highlighted by his salt and pepper hair that was running away from his forehead. His face was clean, except for a few strands of gray hair that was under his thin, lower lip. He grew uglier when he smiled. His physical appearance would make a person think God was angry when he fashioned his mold.

"Who told you about me?"

"Who my sources are don't concern you."

"Alright, well, what makes you think I got two hundred thousand fuckin' dollars, then?"

Detective Konn swallowed his fifth shot of whiskey and sat the shot glass beside the tall bottle of Cutty Sark. Without removing his big eyes from Splash's face, he unholstered his gun and put it on the counter of the bar with the barrel pointed at Splash's chest.

Unimpressed, Splash pulled out his own gun and shrugged his shoulders.

"Is that registered?"

"It's good to go just like yours is."

"Don't let my size, or this gray hair fool you."

"Shit like that don't cloud my judgement," Splash clarified, as he flexed the fingers on his right hand around the handle of his gun. He always wanted to kill a cop. "See one thing about me... I know that killers can come in all shapes and sizes. A bee can kill a mu'fucker, if he allergic to it. Now, for you to pull that nut ass .357 out on me, though, that just tell me that you underestimate me, or you think my chest ain't got no heart in it. I-Yo, then, you talkin' 'bout my fuckin' dad like just on the strength of that alone-"

"Relax, and put that gun away."

"Man, who fuckin' told you about me?"

"Would you believe that I had so much respect for the man your father was, that I let your grandfather get away with robbing and murdering those Cuban guys your father used to do hits for?"

Splash narrowed his eyes.

Detective Konn poured himself another drink with a smile on his face.

Splash's cell phone started to ring.

"I'll be here on August 1st for my two hundred grand. and throw in a case of Cutty Sark, too."

"And what if I don't have it?"

"Well, consider yourself at war with God, then."

"I ain't got no problem bein' the devil."

"Nice comeback."

"See you on the 1st."

After Detective Konn poured himself another shot ,and downed it, he re-holstered his gun and climbed off of the tall aluminum stool he had been perched on. He had to back away from the counter of the bar to look Splash in his eyes.

"Tell that manager of yours that I'll take a rain check on that blowjob when you see him."

Splash's cell phone started to ring again.

"Oh, and by the way. This nut ass .357 was the gun that put your father on his back."

"I bet it won't be the one that put me on mine."

"We shall soon see."

Twelve minutes later, Splash stood at the double-doors of his nightclub with his cell phone pressed to his ear. His instincts were telling him to call his lawyer, but he wanted to return his grandmother's two, missed calls first. When she didn't answer, he put his cell phone back in his pocket and watched Detective Konn as he pulled away from the curb in a clean, white, Grand Marquis.

"Ay, that cop on some bullshit, ain't he?"

Splash turned around and looked at Tuna. It was impossible for him not to look at Tia's uncle in a different light.

"You was gon' suck that nigga dick, wasn't chu, Tuna?"

"Fuck no."

"Even rubber bands got limits, before they fuckin' snap, Tuna."

"Splash, I-"

"Sabia still in my office?"

"He left."

"Man, why the fuck you let him-"

Splash snatched his cell phone out of his pocket when it began to ring. He gave the screen of his iPhone a quizzical look, because the caller was his grandmother's neighbor.

"What's up, Mrs. Perez?"

"Baby, you-You got to-Splash, some man just killed your grandmother, and now he got the people that just moved next door hostage in their-"

"What?!"

"Some white man just killed your grandmother."

Chapter Fifteen

No.

More.

Pain.

In the city of Philadelphia, tragedies were born every second of the hour. No summer ever ended without leaving new tombstones in the cemeteries, and old chalk-lines on the streets. It appeared as if the devil and his evil fleet of followers all had personal grudges against the city of brotherly love, and sisterly affection. Some children couldn't even enjoy their neighborhood playgrounds, because other children like them had lost their innocent lives to stray bullets at those very same places summers before.

Splash's grandmother lived on 6th and Cecil B. Moore Avenue. Her house was the prettiest one on the block. For years, Splash had begged her to let him move her to some place nicer, but she had always refused, because the house had been a wedding gift from her parents.

"Tuna, make a fuckin' path for me!!"

The scene on Splash's grandmother's block was like something out of a movie. On 6th Street, from Montgomery Avenue, down to Cecil B. Moore Avenue, there were hundreds of people, a SWAT unit, police officers, and local news reporters. There were two news helicopters hovering up in the sky, and one police helicopter that was doing wide circles around the entire perimeter. The news of Splash's grandmother's death ,and the hostage situation that was happening next door at her neighbor's house had spread quickly.

It wasn't easy, but Splash and Tuna reached the line of police barricades that were set up to keep the crowd and the news reporters back.

"Aunt Steph?!!" Splash hollered, shoving pass a cop that made an attempt to grab him by his arm. This brung several other officers to his face."Yo, that's my fuckin' gran' mom house! Get the fuck off me! Aunt Stsph?! Ay, Aunt Steph?!! That's my-"

When the coroners stepped out of Splash's grandmother's house carrying her inside of a body-bag, Splash went bezerk. At that same moment, his grandmother's murderer was surrendering himself and releasing his hostages two houses away.

Seeing a smile on the killer's face turned the huge crowd into an angry mob. When someone hollered out 'Get that pussy', all hell broke loose. People began to hurl rocks, bottles, and anything else they could get their hands on. Some people even threw their cell phones. Others rushed the police barricades swinging their fists at the cops.

A second before the prongs of a police officer's tazer-gun grabbed Splash's chest, he was able to get a brief glimpse of his aunt clawing at his grandmother's killer's face. As his body began to spasm and fell to the street, he released a gut-wrenching howl that had nothing to do with the volts that were coursing through his body. His grandmother's killer was Angelo.

Angelo.

Tia's brother.

Angelo had killed his grandmother, and he was smiling at him.

Two hours later, Splash was inside of a holding cell at the police station on Richmond and Girard Avenue. He was sitting on a cold metal bench with his face in his hands, and his elbows on his knees. As hard as he tried, he couldn't stop himself from crying. His loud sobs were echoing around the entire police station. His pain was felt by everyone that heard him. The horrible news of how his grandmother had been brutally raped and bludgeoned to death had hit home with some of the cops, as well as the rioters that had gotten arrested, who were being held in the police station's other holding cells.

Another hour had passed, and Splash was still crying his heart out in the holding cell at the police station. He was down on the dirty, piss-stained floor, and he had no idea that Detective Konn was watching him from the other side of the paint-chipped bars.

"Rasool?"

Splash opened his eyes and stared at a pair of black, Puma sneakers that he thought looked oddly familiar. The silver laces on the old sneakers were tied extra tight, and they were flipping up in the front.

"Hey, Rasool?"

Splash wiped his watery eyes and looked up at one of the ugliest faces he had ever seen.

"You ready to get out of there?"

"No."

"Why not?"

"'Cause I'ma kill everything I see, as soon as they give me my fuckin' gun back."

"You wouldn't do that, Rasool."

"You don't fuckin' know me."

"What if the first person you saw was an old lady?"

This question made Splash rise to his feet.

"That's what I thought."

After pacing back and forth a few times, Splash took a seat on the metal bench and exhaled a long sigh, which transformed itself into a series of muffled sobs. His brain knew that his grandmother was no longer alive, but his heart wasn't ready to accept that reality.

"Know this guy?"

Splash looked at the black and white mug shot of Angelo in Detective Konn's right hand and shook his head.

"Sure?"

Splash nodded his head.

"Rasool, I've been a detective for a long time, "Detective Konn boasted, returning the picture of Angelo to the folder in his left hand. He lowered his voice to a whisper and took a step closer to the bars. "I know about scandals that can sink our last three mayors. Rasool, if I wanted that spot William Penn got on City Hall I can make them change it. You know why? 'Cause for twenty-two years, I been collectin' dirt on every badge in this city, and they all know it. It ain't my looks that make 'em cringe when they see me comin,' Rasool. It's what I know. It's what I know that allows me to walk around our lovely city like I'm a fuckin' handsome giant. Because of me, you're not going down 8th and Race and getting booked for a long list of charges. That riot sent eleven cops and three news reporters to the hospital, Rasool."

"Mother fucker, that riot started 'cause that pussy sent my fuckin' gran' mom to the morgue!!"

"And I'm sorry for your loss, and I know that this must be a really difficult time for you right now."

"I gotta bury my little cousin tomorrow, man."

"Yo, Splash?"

The loud conversations in the other holding cells paused.

"Who that?"

"It's Silk."

"What's up, Silk?"

Silk was one of the many rioters that had gotten arrested. He lived around the corner from Splash's grandmother.

"You cool?"

"Yea, I'm good, Silk."

"Ay, yo, you know I knocked out that nut ass cop that tazed you wit' that tazer-gun, right?"

"Yea?"

"Ay, no question."

Splash eyed Detective Konn's pale, ugly face. He was having a premonition that he would one day get the chance to get revenge on the cop for his part in his father's death.

"Yo, Splash?"

"Yo?"

"Me, Marty, and Radio, treated that nigga."

"As y'all should've."

"I'm sorry about ya gran' mom, dog."

"Silk, they about to let me go, but I'ma send the manager from my club to pay y'all bail, once y'all get down 8th and Race, al-"

"Yo, Splash what about us?"

"Who that?"

"Ben."

"From Marshall Street?"

"Yea."

"Who else got locked up wit' chu?"

"Oh, um, Alf, Steven, Cook, Aubu and them mu' fuckers got my sister, Carmen and, uh, Girty on the other side, where they keep all the chicks at."

"I'ma have my lawyer and my manager down there for all of y'all, alright?"

For five minutes straight, the young, rioters whooped and hollered. They all calmed down when a young, black, police officer made a threat to put a dope fiend that had shitted on himself in one of their holding cells, once the dope fiend was done with getting processed.

"Wanna know why I had so much respect for your father?"

"I wanna know who put chu on me?"

"I put myself on you, Rasool," Detective Konn revealed, raising his bushy right eyebrow. He waved the folder in his hand behind his butt, after he let go a long,wet-fart. " 'Scuse me. See, I had this fascination with knowing how your life turned out, after you lost both of your parents that day. It was my first day on the job. So, when I heard how your father was a legend, and how those Cubans had sold your mother that dope, and how it was your birthday, I felt compelled to follow your story, Rasool. I wanted you to make something better of yourself, and you didn't. You threw away a scholarship to play basketball to kill people for money. Maybe you tryna be like your father. Who knows. I just want you to know that your run is done, if you don't have what I asked for. Your nothing like your father. What happened today would've never happened on his watch. I came here from headquarters to tell you Angelo Masino got the DEA,FBI, and ATF, in line to talk to him, and he ain't keeping no secrets. He told me what happened out at your house, Rasool. I know everything. I even know about Mikey. I know about them safes you have, too."

"Who gave him my gran' mom address?"

"Your boss gave it to him that night him and his cousin went to your house."

Splash stepped back when Detective Konn farted again.

"He's willing to testify against your wife for killing his cousin, too."

"My wife ain't kill his cousin."

"I'm not the person who has to believe you."

"So, you still gon' get them to let me go?"

"Will that gesture change how our conversation ended this afternoon?"

Splash nodded his head.

"Shake on it."

Splash felt like he was making a deal with the devil when he stuck his forearm through the bars and shook Detective Konn's sweaty, little hand.

"Don't even try to fuck me over, 'cause I'll unleash a world of hurt on you that you'll never find help for."

When Detective Konn made that statement and walked off, Splash backed away from the bars of his holding cell and sat back down on the metal bench. He was feeling overwhelmed. He had thoughts hopping in and out of his head. He had the agony and pain of his grandmother's death digging holes inside of his heart, and in less than twenty-four hours, he was going to be speaking from a podium at Shateek's funeral.

"Let's go."

The same cop that had put Splash inside of the holding cell, turned out to be the same one who had come to let him out of it. He was young, white, and he had a nice attitude.

Seconds later, Splash was having all of his personal belongings returned to him at a very tall desk that faced the police station's entrance. He was given his gun, his gun permit, and his license to carry last.

It was just beginning to turn dark when Splash stepped out of the police station. He had expected to see Detective Konn waiting for him outside, but he was nowhere in sight. Splash let out a long sigh and looked up and down Girard Avenue, as he powered his cell phone back on. His car was parked on his grandmother's block, which was over twenty blocks away from where he was standing, so he took a deep breath and started to walk west on Girard Avenue.

Tuna pulled up beside Splash at Frankford Avenue and honked his horn twice. He had his girlfriend Victoria with him.

Splash slid into the backseat of Tuna's 2011 black, Chrysler 200, and pulled the door shut behind him. He placed his cell phone back to his ear and went back to waiting for Tia to answer her cell phone as Tuna pulled back into traffic.

"Hello?"

Splash's neck recoiled at the sound of another man's voice on the other end of Tia's cell phone. He looked at the screen of his own phone to make sure that he had the right number, then he placed it back to his ear.

"Yo, who the fuck is this?"

"What?"

"What chu just found this cell phone somewhere, or somethin?"

"Nigga, the person that own this fuckin' phone right in front of me."

Splash and Tuna shared a brief stare in Tuna's rearview mirror.

"Who the fuck is this?"

"Prep."

"Yo, man, give-"

"I just spent ten stacks on ya wife. Help her pop the tags when she get home, lame."

Up until that moment, Splash never had a reason to question Tia's loyalty. In his eyes, he had the perfect wife. However, as he stared out of Tuna's rear window at the passing streets and traffic, he saw a new flaw in his marriage that could possibly be a deal breaker for him.

"You ain't got no rap, now, huh?"

Instead of answering the guy with Tia's phone question, Splash just ended their call and stuffed his cell phone into his pocket.

"You okay?"

Splash met Tuna's eyes in Tuna's rearview mirror.

"I need you to call Tobi and tell her to meet you down 8th and Race, so y'all can bailout everybody that got locked up on my gran' mom block earlier."

"I'm on it."

"Why you ain't turn up 5th Street?"

"Sabia and Trixie wanted me to bring you to them first."

"I'm sorry about your grandmother, Splash."

"Thanks," Splash replied, cutting his eyes at Tuna's girlfriend Victoria. Her perfume was making him feel lightheaded. "Ay, Tuna, I want chu to start runnin' the club by yourself, alright? I'ma still be comin' through, but I-"

"That's them in that Lacrosse."

Splash stared out at the gold, Buick Lacrosse that was parked in the gas station on 6th and Girard. The windows were tinted. The car looked brand new.

"You heard me, Tuna?"

"Anything you need me to do, I'ma take care of."

"When the last time you talked to Tia?"

"I kept tryna call her earlier, so she could come down to the police station, but she never picked up."

"Naw?"

Tuna pulled his car to a stop beside the vacuum machines in the gas station, then he looked in his rearview mirror at Splash.

"Try her again for me, and let me know what happened."

"Alright, be safe."

Splash climbed out of Tuna's car and closed the door. It was sticky and humid outside. As he walked over to the car that his cousin and Trixie were in, he noticed how empty he felt inside. He felt like his heart and soul had been stolen from him. Losing his grandmother made him care about nothing else. In just a matter of hours, all of his concern for others had been stripped out of his being. His ability to love had died with his grandmother. The only emotion remaining in his body was hate. He was crying again, and he was so numb that he didn't even feel his own tears, as they ran from his eyes down the front of his face.

The strong smell of weed gave Splash a fit of coughs when he got into the car with his cousin and Trixie.

"My mom just left the medical examiner's office from seein' gran' mom body."

"Hey, Splash."

Splash ignored Trixie and looked at the back of his cousin's head. Him and his cousin were only four years apart in age. They had a bond that brothers shared.

"Y'all want me to get out to give y'all some privacy?"

Splash met Trixie's gray eyes in the rearview mirror. She was sitting in the driver's seat with a Dutch in her hand. Her long hair was pulled back into a ponytail, and all of the bruises on her face had cleared up. Even with her beauty returned to her, the look in her eyes reflected a deep sense of turmoil that she could never hide from anyone. She was still using weed to cushion her fall from shame and guilt.

"Splash, can I say somethin' to you?"

"Take me to my car."

Trixie handed Sabia the burning Dutch and pulled out of the gas station. She turned down Marshall Street and drove in silence, until she reached the corner of Thompson Street.

"Can I talk, while I drive?"

With a sigh, Splash slouched further down in the backseat. He was getting a contact from the weed Trixie and Sabia was smoking.

"Yo, ya phone ringin'."

Splash gave his cousin a strange look, then followed Trixie's right hand to the knob of the radio. The lower the music got in the car, the louder his cell phone rang in the pocket of his red, D&G shorts. He pulled out his iPhone and immediately felt a rush of hatred when he saw that it was Tia, who was calling him.

"What the fuck you want?"

"Bay, where you at?!"

The urgency in Tia's voice let Splash know that Tuna had gotten through to her, and that he had told her about his grandmother and everything else that had happened.

"Bay?!"

"What?"

"Where you-"

Splash powered his cell phone off and stuffed it back in his pocket. When him and Tia talked, he wanted them to be face to face. He wanted to look in her eyes as she tried to explain herself out of the trouble she was in.

"I'm comin' to Shateek funeral tomorrow."

"And ya dumb ass gon' get locked the fuck up, too."

"Trixie gotta disguise for me."

"Pull over right here, Trixie."

"Ain't nobody gon' know it's-"

Splash hopped out of Trixie's rental car when she pulled over at the top of his grandmother's block on 6th and Montgomery. He slammed the door and stormed off. He only stopped, because he heard another car door slam behind him.

"Splash?"

"Bia, this shit ain't no fuckin' game," Splash warned his cousin, as he stared past him down their grandmother's block. He was touched by the small crowd of people that was holding a candlelight vigil in front of his grandmother's house. "You talkin' about disguises 'n shit, like, ain't nobody gon' recognize you, or something.' Nigga, you hot as shit. You fish grease, Bia. Then, you wit' that bitch of all people? Gran' mom dead because she told her fuckin' nephew this where her house was, Bia. That bitch poisonous, man. Look how she did me and Tia, and we been fuckin' wit' her for- She the one that told you about Jen, ain't she?"

"She puttin' me on a sting for a million dollars."

"What?"

"Some niggaz robbed this armored truck last week, and one of 'em got away."

"Bia, I'll give you a fuckin' million dollars."

"I know, but-"

"Here come ya mom."

As him and his cousin watched the steady flow of traffic come down 6th Street, Splash was reminded of their younger years when life was much more simple. A flash of priceless memories came and went in Splash's mind, influencing him to put an arm around his cousin's shoulder. He stood there wishing that there was a way for them to escape to the past, and rewrite their destinies.

"I love you, Bia."

"I love you, too."

"Don't-"

"There go Tia."

Splash took his eyes off of his aunt's car, which had pulled to a stop at the curb in front of him and his cousin, and looked at Tia's Cadillac wagon, that was parking behind the gold Buick that her aunt Trixie was sitting in. His aunt and Tia exited their cars at the same time. Trixie stepped out of her car three seconds later.

"Sabia, I think we should go."

"He shouldn't 've been here in the first place!"

It was obvious that Splash's aunt didn't approve of her son dealing with Trixie. She went into a tearful tirade of how Trixie had been like a bad omen in his life, since the two of them began dealing with each other, and how in just two weeks, they had lost two important people in their lives that mattered most to them. She then began to scream that he should turn himself in, because the cops had told her that they were going to kill him if he continued to evade authorities.

"I'm not turnin' myself in!"

Those were Splash's cousin's last words, before he got back into the car with Trixie. His mother hopped in her car and followed them when Trixie pulled away from the curb with screeching tires.

"What happened, Bay?"

Splash raised his eyes up to the full moon up in the dark sky and shook his head. The feeling of Tia's hand rubbing circles on his back provided him with some comfort, but his sadness for his family was rising like tidal waves in his chest, and the sound of someone singing down the street at the vigil in front of his grandmother's house was sending tremors through his body. He felt like a fish out of water.

"Bay?"

"Who was you with today, Tee?"

"Huh?"

"You heard what the fuck I just-"

"I was with Camay at the mall."

Splash looked Tia in her eyes and searched them for deceit. He only found tears and loyalty, but his own heart had already convicted his wife of being unfaithful to him.

"Why didn't chu call me, Bay?"

"Who was you with, Tee?"

"Why you keep-"

Splash walked over to Tia's car and pulled the back door open. His face frowned at the sight of all the shopping bags piled up on her back seat. When he began to toss the bags out onto the sidewalk, Tia ran up behind him and grabbed him by the arm.

Sadly, Splash's suspicions were wrong, but because he thought he was right, he grabbed Tia by her neck and shoved her down to the ground. It was his first time ever putting his hands on Tia in that type of way.

The commotion between Splash and Tia got the attention of the people attending the candlelight vigil down the street.

"Splash, what's wrong with you?!"

"What the fuck you think I'm stupid?!"

On any other day, Tia would have jumped to her feet and fought Splash back. Today was different. As her husband stood over her, she looked up at him shocked and confused. She had no idea of what was going on. A half an hour earlier, while she was at Camay's house, she had gotten a call from her uncle, and he had told her that Splash's grandmother had been killed, and that Splash had gotten tazered and arrested by the cops. That phone call had made her heart skip two beats. When she called Splash, their call had dropped, and when she tried calling him back, his cell phone kept going to his voice mail, so she called her uncle back and found out where he was.

"Some nigga answered ya phone when I called you."

"Bay, besides Camay, the only other person I was around was her cousin Prep."

"What the fuck was he doin' with ya fuckin' phone?"

"He must've-Bay, he must've answered my phone when I was in the bathroom."

Splash stepped back as Tia stood up.

"What he say?"

"So, Cam cousin just, spent ten stacks on you for nothin'?"

"Bay, he was buyin' stuff for Cam, too."

"Do you know what the fuck I been through today?"

"Bay, I-"

Splash pushed Tia away when she tried to hug him. His rejection brung her to tears.

"Ya fuckin' brother killed my gran' mom."

"Wh-What?"

"You was out fuckin' shoppin' when I needed you most," Splash argued, staring into Tia's watery eyes. Deep down, he knew that she wasn't the blame for all that he had went through, yet he found himself blaming her for his pain still. "Trixie gave Angelo my gran' mom address that night they came out to the house. He raped her, Tee. That pussy killed-He killed my gran' mom, and now he down 8th and Race rattin' about how you rocked his cousin, the fuckin' safes, and all types of fuckin' shit. Then, I got this freak ass cop tryna blackmail me for two hundred thousand. Now,you wanna pull up like you give a fuck about somebody? It's too late for that shit-"

"I loved your gran' mother just as much as-"

"Bitch, go suck Cam cousin dick, and when you see me at Teek funeral tomorrow, you better not say shit to me, or I'ma spit in ya fuckin' face."

Splash had no clue that Camay's cousin was the same person that his cousin Sabia was searching for.

"I'm filin' for divorce, too."

Chapter Sixteen

"So, the nigga Hasaan don't even know his right hand man about to set him up, huh?"

"He think he comin' to cop two bricks."

"That's crazy."

"All we doin' is playin' decoys, so my cousin can air him out, and we-"

"And his man just gon' stand there and let him get rocked, and he ain't gon' do shit?"

"His man the one that's gon' help my cousin take over they dope strip."

"Niggaz can't be trusted for shit."

"Without trust, there's no betrayal, Prep."

"What the fuck that mean?"

"A mu'fucker can never betray you, if you don't give them ya trust."

It was 9:36 a.m., and Prep and Robbie were up to no good. The two of them were sitting inside of Camay's Lexus jeep on Frankford Avenue. They were both eating their breakfast from the Styrofoam trays that they had ordered at the breakfast store up the block on Orthodox Street. Across the street from them, Robbie's cousin was parked in his white, Ford F-250. The three of them were about to orchestrate the murder of a man that had more respect in North Philly, than the mayor of Philadelphia himself.

"Ay, you know shorty Tia little cousin, right?"

"Who?"

"Shorty hidin' in the back of my cousin truck."

Prep took a sip of his orange juice and looked across the street at Robbie's cousin's pick-up truck. There was a brown refrigerator standing up in the back of it.

"What the fuck she hidin' in the 'frigerator?"

"Naw, she layin' down."

Prep took another sip of his orange juice.

"They call her Rock 'n Roll Rhonda."

"I ain't never heard of her."

"You will this summer."

Prep and Robbie had been spending a lot of time with each other. Prep's money had made them the best of friends, and to the naked eye, it did appear like the two of them were getting along extremely well.

"You tryna hit that club Gossip Alley tonight?"

"That's Tia husband joint."

"So."

"Prep, dude ain't to be fucked wit'."

"I don't give a fuck about that nigga, Robbie."

"I'm serious, Prep."

"Oh, so now that chu paid ya connect off, you tryna get on some nut shit?"

"Man, I'm just tryna put chu up on game."

"Fuck that nigga."

"Prep, I'm tellin' you-"

"That nigga fucked Cam, Robbie," Prep confessed, after he cracked the passenger door and threw out his breakfast platter. He sat his orange juice between his thighs and pulled the door back shut with a sigh. "She pregnant by that nigga, dog. I heard her and Tia talkin' 'bout that shit the other day. Cam had a threesome with- Who this?"

"Oh, shit, Prep!"

Robbie had gotten so caught up in what Prep had been telling him, it slipped his mind that he was supposed to signal his cousin by pressing down on his horn twice when the black, GMC Yukon pulled up.

In open-mouthed fascination, Prep sat beside Robbie and watched as the movie-like scenario played out in front of their wide eyes. He knew that what he was witnessing would never be forgotten by him, because he was being provided with a front row seat to see for himself just how crafty the game of death was.

Overhead, a passing el-train was going northbound. As it moved loudly on the steel bridge, it drowned out the sound of Robbie mashing down on the horn in Camay's Lexus jeep.

The occupants of the GMC Yukon stepped out of the SUV smiling and talking. Both of them were wearing white kufis on their heads. They were childhood friends, and shared the same religion, but they had division amidst their team, because their dreams for their territory kept colliding with each other. The passenger was married to the driver's sister. Their family ties went so far back that their great-grandmothers used to be best friends.

Hasaan was the driver.

The tall, muscular man with the hazel eyes and thick beard, who was walking beside Hasaan was a snake in a human's body. His name was Drees, which was short for Idris, and he was as shady as they come. Because he wanted his brother-in-law's position, and all of the esteem that would come with having his powerful spot, he had hand-delivered him to Robbie's cousin, who just happened to be Hasaan's worst enemy.

Prep would never admit it to anyone, but he felt sorry for the way Hasaan had to meet his demise.

"Prep, hurry up and get in the back, so Drees can get in the-"

At that very moment, two bike-cops turned the corner of Frankford Avenue. Just as they were steering their bikes out into the street, Robbie's cousin was pulling his pick-up truck out of the space where he had been parked. The big tires on the Ford F-250 screamed as they bit into the street, immediately grabbing the attention of both police officers, who were only ten feet away. It was the sight of Rock 'n Roll Rhonda standing up in the rear of the pick-up truck cradling an AR-15 that drained all of the blood out of their white faces.

"Blat... Blat... Blat... Blat... Blat... Blat... Blat... Blat..."

From the backseat of his cousin's jeep, Prep watched as Tia's cousin released hell from the machine gun in her hands. Her upper body was vibrating as she lit Hasaan's chest up with a hail of bullets. After he fell to the pavement beside Drees' feet, she twisted her waist, and with a smile on her pretty face, she sent another hail of bullets at the two bike-cops when Robbie's cousin pulled up beside them and hit the brakes.

The sound of another el-train passing by overhead made the noise of the gunshots weaker.

"Pull off!!"

Robbie made a wild U-turn and slammed his foot on the gas pedal when Drees hopped in Camay's Lexus SUV with him and Prep. Once he made it to the corner of Frankford and Orthodox, he made a hard left, and then slowed down to avoid bringing any unwanted attention to himself. He had fulfilled his end of the bargain with his cousin, now all his cousin had to do was come out to his house and kill Camay and Prep, and take all of Prep's money, and that would make them both even with each other.

The West Philadelphia church on 43rd and Parkside was packed with mourners. Black was the color that everyone wore to the funeral. Sadness and a deep sense of sorrow were just some of the emotions that were resting in the hearts of the people sitting in the pews. Other feelings like anger, blame, and high levels of despair lived in the chests of some of the others as they stared at the tiny casket surrounded by flowers at the front of the church.

The coffin was three and a half feet in length, and three feet in width. It was made from the blackest pearls that the ocean had to offer. Inside of it, an innocent, five-year-old boy's body laid soulless. His story was written with the liquid of teardrops. His untimely loss had erased the silver-lining in the sky for some of the mourners sitting in the church.

Shateek Barnes was loved by a lot of people, and by God's mercy, he died knowing so.

"I, um, chose to speak first, because I wanted to give my husband and his aunt a chance to gather their thoughts, "Tia announced, staring from the church's stage at all of the sad faces looking back at her. She held onto the podium in front of her for support, because her legs felt weak. "Maybe I was wrong for doing that, because I've never been good at expressin' myself, but-But-"

Tia got choked up, and as she began to cry, she glanced at the front, left pew, where Splash was sitting beside his aunt, but even in her moment of being overcome with emotions, he still refused to acknowledge her. He had stayed at a hotel the night before, and he still wasn't speaking to her.

"I'm-I'm sorry," Tia apologized, wiping her falling tears. She felt embarrassed, but her embarrassment was quickly overshadowed by gloom when she placed her eyes on Shateek's small casket. "I remember the first time I saw Shateek. I thought that he was the prettiest baby that I ever seen. I'm the one who cut his umbilical cord. I got to hold him before Jen did. I loved him like he was mine. So, I-I, um, I just been lyin' to myself by sayin' that all of this is just a nightmare, and that- And that I'm gon' wake up from it, but it's not a bad dream. This is real, and it-It hurt so, so much. I loved that little boy with everything I got in my heart. He was my heart. He was my godson, and I'm gon' miss him so-I'm gon' miss him-so-"

No one had seen, or heard from Jen, since Splash's birthday party, so when she came walking down the center aisle of the church with a black rose in her left hand, her presence not only made Tia's voice disappear, but it caused a lot of whispering up and down the pews.

The murmurs stopped when Jen reached her son's casket and removed her sunglasses. Her pain was understood by many, but not by all. None of her family members had attended the funeral. She had even thought twice about coming herself. Her spiritual attachment to her son had influenced her to see him buried that morning. She had a long list of regrets, and she didn't want to add not being at her only child's funeral as one of them.

"I'm so sorry."

Invisible wings carried Jen's apology to her son around the entire church. She had only meant for it to be a soft whisper, but her grief-stricken soul wanted her baby to awaken from the dead and hear what she had to say, so her sincere sentiments left her trembling lips with enough volume to get God's attention.

Teardrops left the eyes of everyone, except Sabia's. No one knew he was at the funeral. He was sitting in one of the last pews with his disguise on. One of his mother's friends was to his left, and she didn't even know it was him.

After some prodding from a few of the older mourners in the first pews, Jen walked up on the church's stage and joined Tia at the podium. She had been asked to give her testimony, so when Tia left her there standing alone, she searched her soul for something to say.

"This week I found out how much I don't love myself," Jen revealed, after placing her sunglasses next to the Bible laying on the podium. A chill ran through her body when she ran her fingers over the gold-lettering on the front of the black Bible, because she had never touched one before, much less opened one. "I've come to terms with accepting that I hate everything about me. My chinky eyes. Just everything about me. I hated that I was Cambodian when I was growing up. I wanted to be black more than anything. Instead of me being happy with who I was, I hated myself for who I wasn't. I swear to God in front of all of y'all that I didn't mean for my bad ways to come back on my son. I didn't. It wasn't until I looked at him when he was born that-That I realized that I was pretty. He looked just like me, so when I heard Tia, and Camay, and all of the doctors and nurses sayin' how pretty he was, for the first time, I felt like I was, too. I'm not-I'm not standin' here tryna make this about me, 'cause it's not, but I, um, I-I-I just want y'all to understand me, and know that no matter how much some of y'all hate me, I already hate myself more than any of y'all ever can."

Jen opened her mouth to say more, but nothing, except for a sob came out of her mouth. She raised her hand to offer her apology, then placed that same hand over her mouth when a series of loud sobs forced their way through her trembling lips.

Splash walked up on the stage and stood beside Jen at the podium. His presence seemed to give her the strength she needed to continue speaking.

As Tia listened to Jen pour out her heart and soul, she sat there quietly realizing that there were a lot of things about her best friend that she did not know. It was difficult for her to see Jen as a grieving mother, because when Shateek was alive, Jen dealt with him like he was an accessory. On Easter, she treated him like a doll. For Christmas, she always left him with Sabia's mother. She loved the idea of being a mother more than she liked the responsibilities that came with actually being one.

Sabia rose from his seat when Jen exited the stage and walked down a hallway that led to the church's restrooms.

Tia got up and followed the Muslim lady in all black that was walking behind Jen.

At the very moment that Splash was about to speak, a loud scream escaped from the ladies' restroom. This brought everyone in the church to their feet. The pastor was the first person to make it to the bathroom, but unfortunately for him, as everybody looked on in open-mouthed shock and sheer disbelief, he came stumbling backwards out of the bathroom's door with a Muslim lady all over him. Her hands were moving like the wind as she landed a combination of punches to the pastor's face, head, and thin body. Before he crumpled to the floor, the pastor got the opportunity to snatch off the Muslim lady's face-veil.

"That's a damn man!!"

"Sabia?!"

"Oh, my God!"

Nobody tried to stop Sabia when he bolted for the church's exit. The shiny gun that he had pulled from under his long, black, over garment had convinced people to leave him alone.

Splash was frozen where he stood. He was still up on the stage standing behind the podium. His eyes were glued to the black rose that Jen placed on the top of her son's coffin. In his heart, he wanted to go check on Tia and Jen. His mind was telling him to go after his cousin. His soul was begging him to open Shateek's casket. A teardrop slid down his right cheek. Another one crept down his left. Two more left both of his eyes at the same time.

Tia and Jen came out of the bathroom at the same time. Jen had her right hand over her right eye. Her nose was bleeding and her lower lip was swollen.

With the help of others, the pastor was back on his feet. His legs were unsteady, so he was helped to a nearby chair. As soon as he sat down, Sabia's mother ran past him and the people aiding him and attacked Jen with one of her shoes.

The house of worship had become the house of blame and sin.

God was upset.

The angels were appalled.

The devil had a grin on his face.

Chapter Seventeen

Two days later . . .

"Bleach wanted me to tell you that he appreciate you gettin' him out on bail."

Trixie looked up from her iPad at Sabia and smiled at him. Her smile vanished when he sat down on her waterbed beside her, because his eyes were dark and stormy. She wasn't sure if his eyes were red from crying, or if they had gotten that way from the weed he was smoking with his friends out in her living room.

"Trixie, can I ask you somethin'?"

"You can ask me anything."

"What made you tell me that Shateek wasn't my son?"

Trixie lowered her eyes down to the blue, little man and horse on Sabia's white, Polo shirt.

"I know you probably thinkin' 'bout what chu gon' say, but I want chu to look me in my eyes when you talk to me, Trixie."

"Sabia, my intentions were in the right place when I told you what I-"

"You not lookin' at me."

Trixie raised her gray eyes and met Sabia's stare.

"Now, go 'head."

"I felt indebted to you, "Trixie admitted, staring into Sabia's eyes, so that he could investigate the windows to her soul. It was important to her that he knew how deeply she felt about him. "My life was literally on the line at Tia and Splash's house, and you stood up for me. Sabia, you took me to the hospital that night. When I was at my weakest, you-Sabia, I been beatin' myself up all week, 'cause now I regret tellin' you about Jen and Camay's boyfriend. I-I just wanted you to know. I just wanted you to know the truth. Sabia, I thought that you deserved to know. It was more about you, than it was about me payin' Jen back for givin' my nephews my address. To be clear, it was only about you, Sabia. I didn't think it would get this bad, and I swear, I never wanted anything to happen to your-Well, to Jen's son. Sabia, I don't even remember tellin' Angelo where you and Splash's grandmother lived. Him and-They was doin' so much stuff to me in here. Rapin' me, beatin' me up, askin' me shit, torturin' me. You have every right in the world to sit there and question my motives, but I can look you in your eyes and honestly tell you that I'm simply doin' for you what you did for me, Sabia. My issues with Jen don't have anything to do with what we creatin'. Do you see what you lookin' for in my eyes? Do you see my honesty? If it was possible, I would let you dig in my chest with your hands, so you could pull out my heart and see what it say with your own eyes, Sabia."

"I believe you."

"Sabia, I really didn't mean for shit to get this bad."

"I know."

The sadness in Sabia's eyes made Trixie sigh. She grabbed his hand when he moved to rise to his feet.

"We in this together, okay?"

"What about when I get caught?"

"You can't think like that, Sabia."

"Trixie, the longer I stay in Philly, the higher my chances-"

Sabia's friend, Bleach, rushed into Trixie's bedroom with his gun in his hand. Moo, Sabia's other friend, was right behind him.

"Yo, somebody at the door."

"He look like a fuckin' cop, too."

The smell of weed was strong throughout Trixie's entire condo. Before she went to see who her uninvited guest was, she opened her all-glass, balcony doors, then looked around her living room. Besides the aroma of weed in the air, everything else looked presentable as it always did.

It was 10:47 at night, and Trixie wasn't expecting any visitors. After looking through the peephole in her door, and quickly taking note that she didn't know who the small, ugly man on the opposite side of her door was, she pulled her door partially open and frowned at the pint-sized stranger.

"Trixie Masino?"

"And you are?"

"Detective Konn."

"And?"

"I'm here unofficially to make a bargain with you."

"About?"

"Well, for starters, can I come in, or would you like to hold this discussion like this?"

Trixie wrinkled her nose when the smell of liquor and cigarettes bit at her nostrils. She recoiled her neck when Detective Konn opened his mouth to speak again.

"I have some information that will serve you and your brother Salvatore very well."

"Let me see your badge."

Trixie stole a quick glance over her shoulder and looked into her condo when Detective Konn dug in his pocket for his badge. Sabia and his friends were hiding in her bedroom. Sabia's friend, Bleach, was okay, because she had just paid his bail earlier that morning, but the same couldn't be said for Sabia, or for his friend, Moo. Sabia was a fugitive, and Moo was on the run for shooting at the cops on 60th and Market out West Philly.

"There you go."

Trixie took Detective Konn's badge from him and scrutinized it for a few seconds. Sighing, she handed back the badge, and with a sense of nervousness that was causing sweat to trickle down her sides from her armpits, she reluctantly stepped aside and let the ugly, foul-breath smelling cop into her condo.

"Nice place."

"Thank you."

"Nice smell, too."

"I had company earlier."

"That's funny, because before I knocked on your door it sounded to me like you still did."

To appear like she was calm, Trixie sat on her leather couch and crossed her legs. Her armpits were crying sweat.

"Do you mind if I park my ass somewhere, too?"

"It all depends on where you park it."

"How about right there?"

Detective Konn pointed at a clear chair that was against the half-wall that separated her kitchen from her living room. It had a round, aluminum base, but everything else on the chair was clear. It looked inexpensive, but the see-through chair had cost Trixie two thousand dollars. She had another one in her bedroom.

"So, where would you like me to start?"

"Start with why you're here."

"Okay," Detective Konn chuckled, adjusting himself in Trixie's expensive chair. His old Pumas left the floor when he sat back. "I stopped down South Philly first, but I was told that your brother Salvatore wasn't in the city at the moment. So, I figured I'd come by here and-Hey, do you mind if I smoke?"

"No."

Trixie didn't like Detective Konn. His unsightly looks had nothing to do with her distaste for him. It was the way that he was pretending to have manners that made her dislike him. He was a fraud ,and it showed all in the way he carried himself. Another thing that kept irking Trixie was his smile. Not only didn't it reach his eyes, but it was creepy as hell.

"Your nephew Angelo was down 8th and Race the other day, and he threw you and your brother Salvatore under the bus."

"I already know that."

"Really?"

"You can't honestly believe that you're the only crooked cop in Philly?"

Detective Konn smiled and blew a cloud of cigarette smoke at Trixie's living room ceiling.

Trixie stood up and walked over to her door and opened it. Detective Konn followed her with a smug look on his face.

"It was nice meeting you, Trixie."

"I'm sorry that I can't say the same thing."

"Ouch."

"Let this be the last time that you come to my house."

"Duly noted."

Trixie closed her door behind Detective Konn and let out an exasperated sigh. After she locked it, she placed her left eye to the peephole in the middle of her door and watched Detective Konn as he walked down the hallway to her condo's elevators.

Thirteen minutes later, everything was back to normal inside of Trixie's condo; well almost. Sabia and his two friends were out in Trixie's living room smoking weed again, and Trixie was standing out on her balcony talking on her cell phone to Kenyatta Bey.

"How's your mother doin'?"

"Better than you."

Trixie's balcony overlooked the I-95 expressway. She could see as far north as the Girard Avenue exit, and as far south as the Callowhill Street exit, and there were tall, industrial factories, the nightclubs on Delaware Avenue, and the sight of residential houses, all in between.

"How'd you get my number?"

"I know somebody that know somebody."

"So, is this a social call?"

"Shit pass bein' social, Trixie."

"Well, let your mother know that I'm pass the bullshit," Trixie snapped into her cell phone, walking over to the patio set on her balcony. After sitting down, she crossed her legs and stared at her bare feet. "Kenyatta, all of this started over a misunderstanding. I know it. Ya fuckin' mother know it, and you know it, too. How was I supposed to know who one of her employees was married to? We like family, Kenyatta. I changed your pampers be-"

"You still live in them condos down Delaware Avenue, Trixie?"

"No, I moved last month."

"So, the white bitch sittin' on ya balcony with the cell phone to her ear is ya fuckin' clone, huh?"

Trixie jumped to her feet.

"You can sit back down."

Trixie stayed standing with her cell phone pressed to her right ear. She could feel the approach of fear as it crept up the veins in her legs, and made its way to her chest, where her heart was beating out of control. Swallowing nervously, she stepped to the waist-high, aluminum gate that surrounded her balcony and looked out at all of the places she thought Kenyatta could possibly be.

"Trixie?"

"I'm here."

"You look like you just saw a ghost."

Trixie's eyes found Kenyatta. He was on the northbound lane on I-95, standing beside a four wheeler. He had a pair of binoculars up to his eyes.

"On the strength of Salvatore, my gran' pop told my mom to ease up on you and to call off the war, but between me and you, I'm just gettin' the fuck started."

"Kenyatta, this shit is uncalled for."

"Tell all them niggaz in ya spot to get out they fuckin' war paint, bitch."

"Why are you-"

Before Trixie could get out the rest of her sentence, Kenyatta hung up on her. He had blocked his number when he called her, so she couldn't call him back like she so desperately wanted to as she watched him pull off on his four wheeler.

"Yo, why you lookin' like that?"

Trixie sat her cell phone down on her patio table and turned around to face Sabia.

"What chu out here stressin' about that cop dude that came through earlier?"

"No, but speakin' of him," Trixie said, stepping into Sabia's embrace. Her collarbone wasn't fully healed, and because Sabia was aware of this, he was extra careful as he pressed his body against hers. "Do you really think that he was the same one that was at Splash club?"

"From the way you described-"

"Did Splash say what he wanted?"

"I left remember?"

Trixie sighed and nodded her head against Sabia's chest. She felt safe in his arms. He made her feel protected.

"Bleach girl on her way."

"Why your friend Moo never smile?"

"He smile."

"He ain't smile since he been here."

"He mad at me for dressin' like a Muslim lady the other day."

"Why?"

"It's a long story, Trixie."

"Tell me the short version, then."

"Alright," Sabia agreed, releasing Trixie from his hug. "My man Moo been Muslim all his life. He pray five times a day . . . fast. He do all that shit, Trixie. He caught his case, 'cause the cops he shot at had dragged his wife out of her car, 'cause they was looking for some nigga that robbed this store dressed like a-"

"Muslim lady."

Sabia nodded his head.

"And Moo was with her?"

"He was in the barbershop waitin' for her to pick him up, and somebody told him the cops was outside snatchin' his wife stuff off her head and face."

"Oh, my God."

"Yea, so, like, he-"

"Sabia, I only picked that stuff out, because your face would be covered and I didn't-"

"I know, but that shit wasn't cool, though."

"I feel so bad, now."

"Come on inside."

After getting her cell phone, Trixie took Sabia's outstretched hand and followed him back into her condo. The change from the warm air outside, to the cool air in her condo made her nipples harden beneath her red, Whiting+Davis tunic. It didn't help that her physical attraction for Sabia was through the roof. Her skin caught fire every time he touched her, and although she was twice his age, and more mature than him in certain areas, he was still more man than any of the men she had ever dealt with. He had potential, and because he did, she was going to use all of her resources to mold him into a powerful man in the city of Philadelphia, then she was going to marry him afterwards.

"I ain't know the pizza was here."

"Oh."

The aromas of pizza, honey-barbeque wings, and weed, filled the cold air in Trixie's condo.

Trixie's Bose sound system was playing Jill Scott's latest CD. The soul singer's voice was influencing a peaceful aura, and it could be seen in the way that Sabia's friends were eating and talking. They weren't even paying any attention to the UFC fight that was showing on Trixie's wide, flat-screen T.V.

"How would y'all feel, if we go to my brother's house at the shore in Cape May?"

"That's in Wildwood, right?"

Trixie looked across her living room at Sabia's friend, Moo, and nodded her head. His smile made her smile.

"You can bring your wife, and Bleach, your girlfriend can come, too."

"Yo, Trixie, let me holla at chu in ya room real quick."

With confusion written on her face, and questions shining in her eyes, Trixie sat her half-eaten slice of pizza on her paper plate that was on her coffee table and stood up. Without saying anything, she followed Sabia down her mirrored-hallway to her bedroom.

"What's all that about?"

"What?"

"Yo, Trixie, me and my niggaz tryna get at that fuckin' paper, and you talkin' 'bout goin' to some fuckin'-"

"Do you trust me, Sabia?"

"Man, listen, I'm-"

"I asked you a question, Sabia."

When Sabia blew out a long sigh and turned his back, Trixie sighed herself and walked over and shut her bedroom door.

"Sabia, let me just at least say this to you," Trixie reasoned, after closing her door. With both hands, she finger-combed her long hair and plopped down on the edge of her round waterbed. "This not gon' work between us, if you don't start trustin' me. Wasn't I out there in front of that church waitin' for you the other day, just like I said I would? Did I not drop everything I was doin', and got down to Splash club as fast as I fuckin' could when you called me and told me that it was a cop there, Sabia? I would think that by now, we would be on the same page, but you got me thinkin', we not even in the same book, from the way you turned your back on me a second ago."

"We was on the same page, but chu just changed lanes on me."

"Sabia, changed lanes on you how?"

"Man, fuck it."

Trixie stood up and blocked Sabia's path when he made a move to walk out of her bedroom.

"How did I change lanes on you?"

"It ain't about nothin'."

"Well, evidently it is, "Trixie replied, rolling her eyes at the large, expensive, framed-painting that hung on the wall over her oval-shaped waterbed. "Am I missin' somethin' here, Sabia? Please do me a favor and fill in the blanks, 'cause I'm standin' here lost. I really am. Up to this point, I've done everything you asked me to do, Sabia. Everything. I went and paid Bleach bail, drove all the way to New York and picked up Moo from Brooklyn, and now I'm tryna-"

"And now you tryna take these niggaz on a fuckin' vacation, after I told them we was gon' get on top of that nigga that got that fuckin' money."

"Sabia, did you hear me say anything about a vacation?"

"What chu call it, then?"

Trixie backed away from Sabia and sat back down on her waterbed. She didn't want to spend another minute talking about something that seemed senseless to her.

"So, you tryna tell me goin' to ya peoples house in Jersey ain't a vacation?"

"Yes. That's what I'm tellin' you."

For seven seconds, Trixie and Sabia didn't say anything else to each other. The silence wasn't uncomfortable between the two of them, because while they weren't speaking, the solitude of their private thoughts were actually navigating back to the same path.

"Trixie, I trust you."

"Well, why didn't you show that you trusted me when I suggested that all of us go-"

A knock at her bedroom door stopped Trixie from talking.

"Who that?"

"Ay, Bia, it's me."

"What's up, Bleach?"

"Ay, yo, tell Trixie Ashley down in the lobby, and that dude at the desk won't let her up."

"Alright."

Trixie stared at her bedroom door and sighed. She was anxious to meet Bleach's girlfriend, because she was the key to finding the guy that had gotten away with robbing the armored truck down South Philly. Shortly after the heist had taken place, she had received a call from an old friend. This old friend told her how he and his brother had followed this guy that had a large bag of money, and that after a brief battle of words, the guy gave them twenty thousand dollars to leave him alone. Initially, Trixie had no interest in anything about the situation, but the next day, Sabia had received a call from jail, and it was his friend, Bleach, telling him that his cousin got killed by the cops trying to rob an armored truck. She became more intrigued when she learned that Sabia's friend, Bleach, was engaged to the armored truck robber's son's mother.

"So, are we okay, or what?" Trixie asked, from deep inside of her large, walk-in closet. After slipping her bare feet into her Enzo Angiolini sandals, she walked back out into her bedroom, where Sabia was waiting for her. "And just so you'll know, I only suggested that we all go to Cape May, because way too much is going on right now, Sabia. With the shit my nephew know about me, I could be under indictment at this fuckin' very second. I got crooked cops comin' by here unannounced, and need I mention that you're number one on the Philly's Most Wanted List? A change of scenery will do us all some good, Sabia. We can clear our heads, Moo can spend some time with his wife, Bleach and his girlfriend can relax a little, and we can come right back as soon as we find this guy that we're-"

Another knock came at Trixie's bedroom door.

"Here we come right now, Bleach."

"This Moo . . . Bleach downstairs with Ash-"

When Sabia pulled Trixie's bedroom door open, his friend, Moo, handed him a cell phone.

"Some mu'fucker on there talkin' 'bout he heard everything me and Bleach was-"

Sabia put his index finger up to his lips. When his friend got silent, he placed the cell phone he was given up to his right ear.

"Who the fuck is this?"

"Detective Konn."

"What? Man, how the-"

"If you don't pass that fuckin' phone to Trixie Masino, I'ma have every cop that work in that district comin' there in . . ."

Trixie placed the cell phone to her ear when Sabia handed it to her.

". . . three minutes."

"H-Hello?"

"I want in."

"In on what?" Trixie asked, flicking her eyes from Sabia to his friend, Moo. As she listened to Detective Konn chuckle at her question, she felt her heartbeat pick up speed in her chest. "What are you talkin' about?"

"Trixie, I can make your life go from sugar to shit, before the sun show his hot ass tomorrow."

"Well, I'm all for that not happenin'."

"I left behind that cell phone when I left your place."

Trixie placed her hand over Detective Konn's cell phone and whispered for Sabia and Moo to get their things quickly, and to go and wait for her down in the lobby.

"I left it in that pretty chair of yours."

"Okay."

"And so lucky me, from my other phone, I got to listen to a lot of shit that had me sitting here in my car feeling like I hit the jackpot."

"I don't see how you could have overheard anything here that would possibly make you feel like that."

While Trixie was talking to Detective Konn, she was packing a small suitcase. The sound of her front door closing made her move faster.

"I heard your company talking about the guy that robbed that armored truck two weeks back, and I want in on it when y'all find him."

"Why didn't you just say so?"

"I heard you talking about me to your friends when I left."

Trixie stopped in her living room and sat her goat skin, Eddie Bauer suitcase by her door, then walked back across her living room and went out onto her balcony.

"Did I hurt your feelings, Detective Konn?"

Trixie covered her mouth to stop her giggles from being heard through the cell phone.

"I've heard worse things said about me, so actually-So, one of the guys at your condo is related to Rasool, huh?"

"Rasool?"

"Splash."

"Oh, um, not that I know of."

"Trixie, I heard him telling all of y'all that he seen me at-"

"Detective Konn?"

"Yeah?"

"Can you hold on for a second?"

"Make it quick."

"Okay."

Trixie took a step back, and she threw Detective Konn's cell phone as far into the night air as she possibly could. There was a time when she would have gladly used the cop's crookedness as an opportunity to gain an ally on the police force, but now things in Trixie's life were much different, considering that her nephew Angelo was cooperating with the likes of every police agency known to man, there was no way that she could be impetuous with the way that she made her decisions from here on out.

It.

Was.

On.

Chapter Eighteen

"Stop tryna tease me, and put all of it in ya mouth."

Prep gave the order ,and Tia quietly did what he had asked.

"Yo, look at me, so I can see them pretty eyes, while you suck it."

After giving Prep's dick one last long, and sloppy lick, Tia locked eyes with Prep, and slowly took the length of his hard dick into her mouth with a humming sound that lasted until her lips reached his balls.

"Damn, Tia."

Prep was finally living out one of his biggest dreams. He felt like a king. Having sex with Tia was a fantasy of his, since he was fifteen-years-old, and it was exactly like everything that he had expected, and more. Tia was proving herself to be a real freak, and he was grateful that his body was the recipient of her freakish ways, because what she was doing to him was psychedelic. She had pop rock candy in her mouth, while she was sucking his dick. Sensations of the candy making small explosions all around his dick was a feeling that he couldn't put into words, even if he had to describe the experience to keep all of the money he had beneath the bed he was stretched out on.

For Prep, getting Tia to the point where he had her at hadn't come easy. Fate had done a favor for him, and being the opportunist that he was, he basically had taken advantage of Tia in her moment of being stressed out, weak, and vulnerable. Her endless tears had created the opening for him to offer her a hug. His comforting words had caused her to cry harder, but those same kind words had given their hug a longer life. The two of them were all alone in Camay's big house. Camay was at work. Robbie and his little sister weren't there. It was just him and Tia. His first kiss had landed awkwardly on the corner of her mouth. It had been inspired by a silent dare in his head. That kiss made Tia search his eyes with her own. In the moment of those prominent seconds, he dug deep in his soul and forced his bad spirit to give both of his eyes a river of tears, and everything from that moment on just paved the way to the erotic position he was in now with Tia between his legs in his cousin Camay's guest bedroom.

"You know that nigga don't deserve you right?"

Tia nodded her head as she sucked Prep's dick with no hands.

"Yo, that shit-Damn."

"You can take better care of me than my husband?"

Tia's question made Prep open his eyes and prop himself up on his elbows. He watched Tia as she wiped her chin, cheek, and lips, clean of all the wetness that came from sucking his dick. Her left hand was doing a better masturbating-job with his dick than he ever could. Her hand felt like a mouth, and her mouth felt better than every piece of pussy he ever stuck his dick into, since he lost his virginity. He was whipped without even fucking her yet.

"Tia, I can-"

A knock on the door ended Prep's sentence, and sent Tia jumping off the side of the bed with wide eyes. Her panic made Prep angry. He looked around the darkness of the bedroom for something of his to put on. When the knocking got louder, he snapped.

"Who the fuck is it?!"

"It's Tia!"

Prep snatched his eyes open and sat up in his bed. Moving too fast had given him a dizzy-spell, so he laid back down. The feeling of confusion slowly left his mind as he realized that he had been having a crazy dream. His dizziness subsided, so he sat back up.

"Prep?!"

"Who that?!"

"It's Tia!"

"Alright, hold up."

Prep slid out of bed feeling confused again. His head was full of cobwebs that was making it difficult for him to separate what happened in his dream, from what was actually taking place at the present moment. There were countless shopping bags all over, so he had to do small hurdles, and hop-scotch his way to the door.

"Open the door, Prep!"

Unlike the dream that he had just awakened from, Tia didn't show any signs of weakness, or vulnerability, when Prep pulled Camay's guest bedroom door open and looked into her eyes.

"Prep, what the fuck did you tell my husband when you answered my fuckin' cell phone the other day?!"

Prep didn't know what Tia was made of. Her wiring couldn't be explained by the best psychologist that the world has ever seen. Her thought process alone set her apart from other women. Her mean streak didn't have any gray-areas. Her wrath was like a hundred women scorned with your name, number, and address. Herself, her husband, and her marriage, were all that mattered to her at the end of the day, and Prep had showed ignorance to what she cared most about, and that was a very bad mistake for anyone to make.

"Man, I ain't tell ya husband shit, and get ya finger outta my fuckin' face."

"You a fuckin' lie, 'cause Cam told me you was messin' with my phone when I was in the damn bathroom, after we got back from the fuckin' mall."

"Yo, man, I ain't tryna hear-"

Prep closed his mouth and poked his head out into the hallway. There were several shopping bags lined up against the wall beside the door of the guest bathroom across the hall. They were all of the things that he had bought for Tia when him, her, and his cousin Camay, were at the mall a few days earlier.

Tia was two seconds away from pulling her registered, Glock 40 out of her oversized, stop-light green, Vivienne Tarn pocketbook, and one second from putting it to Prep's face and squeezing the trigger.

"I 'on't want that shit back."

"Prep, I really could fuckin' care less!"

"Ay, Tia, man, I told you to stop pointin' ya fuckin' finger in my-"

When Tia introduced her gun to Prep's forehead, a quick and profound silence was born.

"Tia, this shit not even that deep, man."

"What the fuck did you say to my husband when you answered my fuckin' cell phone, Prep?"

Tia's voice was even and steady, just like the gun in her left hand.

"I, um, I just told him to, uh, I told him to unpack ya bags when ya got home, that's all."

"And what else?"

"That's all I said."

"That ain't the fuck all you said to-"

"Ay, yo, Prep?!"

Robbie's voice came from downstairs in Camay's foyer. The soft sound of him shutting Camay's front door, then his footsteps coming up the stairs were next.

"Yo, what the-Oh,shit."

After those few words left Robbie's lips, he slowly raised his palms to the ceiling and stood still like a wax statue.

Robbie knew that Tia was a killer.

Prep didn't.

"Do I need to pull my other gun outta my pocketbook, Robbie?"

"Naw."

"Was it a good idea for Prep to answer my fuckin' cell phone, and tell my husband some bullshit that wasn't true?"

"Fuck no."

Prep cut his eyes down the hall at Robbie.

"I spent ten thousand dollars on keepin' my swimmin' pool and yard clean last summer, "Tia whispered, as she dug her right hand into her pocketbook for her cell phone. Her chest felt like a jungle full of wild emotions. "My fuckin' dog wear a black, diamond collar that cost half of that, Prep. My damn gas card probably got that much money on it. And don't think 'cause you spent a little money on me that you did some boss shit. Prep, that shit you did at the mall wasn't new to me and Camay. Obviously, it's new to you, though. In any one of them fuckin' stores, I could've whipped out one of my credit cards, and paid for my shit, what Camay had, and got you whatever the fuck you wanted to. That little money really went to ya fuckin' head, but chu wanna know what chu gon' do? You about to tell my husband that chu was fuckin' high, drunk, delirious, or whatever you wanna claim ya fuckin' excuse was, but you gon' put this fuckin' cell phone to ya damn ear, and you gon' tell him what the fuck happened, 'cause I refuse to fuckin' believe he as mad as he is at me, 'cause you just told him to help me unpack my fuckin' bags when I got home, dickhead."

Prep took Tia's cell phone and placed it to his ear. She still had her gun kissing his forehead. The way that she was holding it let him know that she was comfortable with the charcoal-black weapon. It was this recognition that stopped him from making an attempt to wrestle her down, and wrench it from her hand. As he listened to her husband's end of the cell phone ring in his ear, he looked into Tia's gray eyes, and thought of the things that she had said to him. Her words had done a job on his pride the way a demolition crew tore down a building.

"It went to his voice mail."

"Leave him a message, then."

When Prep lowered Tia's cell phone down to his side, Tia's eyes became slits. Clinching her jaws, she brought her right hand up, and joined it with her left hand around the handle of her gun.

"T-Tia, I'm-Yo, I was on some-"

"Say that shit to the fuckin' phone!!"

After a long sigh, Prep raised Tia's cell phone back up to his ear and left her husband a message that helped remove the gun out of his face.

"Prep, God not gon' be able to fuckin' help you, if my marriage fall apart, because of-"

Tia's cell phone started to chime in Prep's hand.

"Gimme."

Tia snatched her cell phone from Prep, thinking that Splash was calling her back. She rolled her eyes at the screen of her iPhone when she saw that it was her cousin Rhonda, and after rolling her eyes at Prep, she accepted her cousin's call, put her cell phone to her ear, and began to walk in the direction, where Robbie was standing at the top of the steps.

"Rhonda, what do you-Hold on."

Tia stopped beside Robbie and pulled her pocketbook off of her shoulder. Sucking her teeth, she dropped her gun inside of it, and grabbed the two stacks of money that she had forgot to give to Prep.

"Give this to him, and tell him he need to be spendin' some money on his fuckin' son, 'cause he sure didn't buy him shit when he was spendin' all that money on me and Cam."

"Alright."

"Did you find a place, yet?"

"Naw."

"Well, hurry up and find one, then."

"Can you holla at ya cousin Zainab for me?"

"For what?"

"I need some pay stubs."

"Alright."

Chapter Nineteen

"Say it wit' cha chest!"

"Gunna, be quiet!"

Tia huffed out an annoyed sigh, and switched her cell phone to her other ear. She was in her home theater in the dark, talking to her cousin, Zainab, who, at the moment, was laughing hysterically on the other end of her cell phone, because she had overheard Gunna mimicking the comedian, Kevin Hart.

"Girl, go 'head. I'm so sorry, but can you go somewhere else, cause ya bird gon' keep makin' me laugh, if-"

"So, you really think I should go to the hotel, where Splash been stayin'?"

"The Tia I know would've already been there and done that."

"Zainab, I know, but the way he been actin', I think it might-"

"Say it wit' cha chest!"

"Shut up, Gunna!!"

"One man! One pillow! In the yard!"

"Gunna?!"

"By myself!"

"Shut the fuck up!!"

"The cabs are here!"

Tia stood up and hurled her half-eaten carrot stick over at Gunna's birdcage. His silence prompted her to continue the conversation that she was having with her cousin on her cell phone.

"Like I was sayin', I-"

"Nomyo . . . rang . . . yekyo."

"Oh, my fuckin' God!" Tia snapped, switching her cell phone to her other ear. Accepting that Gunna was never going to stay quiet, she decided that she should go up to her bedroom to finish talking to her cousin. "I just don't want it to turn into some real big fight, Zainab. I just want him to come home. I-His gran 'mother was like a gran 'mother to me, too."

There was once a time in Tia's life, when her own existence didn't have any value to her. Days after her mother's death, she had found herself in a very dark place, and it was there, in the confinement of this dark place, where Tio's mind, body, and soul, was repeatedly, and unmercifully, attacked by depression and anguish. She hid herself from everyone that she knew, and had missed three straight weeks of school. Besides Splash, her only other company was misery in her house.

It could be said that Tia lost herself when her mother died, because she had actually lost her own sense of self. For those three weeks, she cried, slept, and only dragged herself out of bed when she had to use the bathroom. Not having the closure of giving her mother the respectable burial service that she felt her mother deserved had been a very painful ordeal for Tia to deal with. At the young age of seventeen, life had forced her to become a grown woman, at a time in her life when she was reveling in the joys of being a spoiled teenager, who got whatever she wanted from her mother.

Splash's grandmother was the only person able to get through the otherwise impenetrable wall that was built around Tia's heart back then. She was also the crutch for Tia when she had her miscarriage a month and a half earlier. During each of these rough periods in Tia's life, Splash's grandmother was there with the wisest of words, love and her listening ear.

As Tia left her home theater and walked out into her foyer, she thought of Splash's grandmother. Her soul didn't want to absorb the impactful loss. She was still struggling with coming to grips with the fact that Splash's grandmother was actually no longer alive, and that it had been her estranged brother, who had been behind her untimely death. Being so closely connected to Splash's grandmother's murderer, and along with the guilt that came with knowing who this individual was, put Tia in the mindset of thinking that Splash's anger towards her was because she was Angelo's sister, and that it had nothing to do with him believing that she had been unfaithful to him.

"Zainab, can I ask you somethin'?"

"Go 'head."

"What do Muslims believe happen when people die?" Tia asked, as she climbed onto her huge bed and reached over to Splash's side of their bed for his pillow. Closing her crying eyes, she hugged the big, fluffy pillow, and inhaled Splash's scent, that was still lingering on the white, cotton, Martha Stewart pillow case. "Do all of y'all think y'all goin' to paradise, or whatever? I remember Jamillah told me a long time ago that people still be alive when they be in their graves. You know what I'm talkin' about? I'm probably sayin' it all wrong."

"Tia, the last time we talked about religion, you hung up on me and ain't speak to-"

"Zainab, I just wanna know if Shateek and Mrs. Barbara gonna make it to heaven, or not?"

"Only Allah know the answer to that, Tia."

"So, what Jamillah was-"

"Let me finish."

Tia sat up in her bed and switched her cell phone to her left ear, then wiped her face clean of her tears.

"The pen is lifted from babies, until they reach the age of puberty."

"What that mean?"

"Well, um, okay, let me just back up."

"Zainab, you know you gon' have to dumb down for me, 'cause I don't know nothin' about what chu talkin' about."

Tia and her cousin shared a brief laugh that lightened the moment.

"Okay, so, all of us have two angels that be recordin' all of the deeds that we do everyday."

"All of us?"

"Yup. It's one that record all of our good deeds, and the other one record the bad ones that we do."

"And how you supposed to believe in somethin' like that, if you never can see them, Zainab?"

"Do you believe in oxygen, Tia?"

"Girl, what type of question is that?"

"Do you?"

"Of course I do, I'm breathin' it right-"

"Can you see it?"

"No."

"I rest my case."

The thought of unseen angels being in her presence made Tia suddenly conscious of her naked body. She grabbed a handful of her top bed sheet and pulled it all the way up to her neck.

"Tia?"

"I'm still lis-"

When her bedroom light was cut on unexpectedly, Tia's eyes were momentarily blinded by the sudden flood of bright lights, but even with her sense of sight gone, her hand coordination and sense of touch were still reliable.

Snookums' incessant barking filled her ears. The Walther PPk 9mm under her pillow filled the palm of her left hand. As her vision was adjusting to the lights, she aimed her gun at her bedroom doorway and squeezed off two shots, then rolled behind her bed for cover.

"Yo, man, you almost fuckin' shot me!!"

Snookums bared his little, pointy teeth, and charged at Splash. This earned him a soccer ball kick to his side, which sent him up in the air.

"Bay, what chu-I ain't know that was you!"

"Man, who the fuck else was gone be able to get in here?!"

"But I ain't know you was comin' home, and then you just cut the light on, and ain't even say-"

Snookums barked and charged at Splash again, but when Splash cocked his right leg back, he hit his brakes and scurried over to where Tia was standing beside her and Splash's bed.

"Who the fuck was you talkin' to?!"

"What chu talkin' about?"

Tia's nerves were still a little rattled, so she didn't understand what Splash was talking about, until she climbed on their bed and heard a light scream coming from the small speaker on her cell phone.

"Zainab?"

"Was that gunshots I heard?!"

With her eyes on Splash, Tia explained what had happened to her cousin, then ended their phone call with a promise that they would finish their conversation the next day.

"You alright?"

"Ya brother killed my gran 'mom."

"Bay, me and you met that mother fucker the same time, so-Don't do me like-"

"Ya blood killed my blood, "Splash slurred, shuffling his feet to keep himself from falling to the floor. He had enough Nuvo in his system to make two people drunk, and another one tipsy. "That nigga-Tee, that bitch ass nigga-Yo, he raped my gran 'mom, man. He did all that shit to her, 'cause he wanted to hurt me, Tee. I got somethin' for his ass, though, watch. Don't have no mu'fuckers leavin' no more fuckin' messages on my phone, either. It's-It's too late to clean that shit up now, Tee. You caught. It is, what it is. You was in the mu'fuckin cookie jar, crumbs all on ya lips 'n shit, and you just think I'm-I'm up on game, Tee. It's cool if you gave that nigga some yams. Fuck it. I'm tired of fuckin' you anyway. Fuckin' you be feelin' like I'm stickin' my dick in a bucket of water. I'm-I'm cool. You can have all this shit. I'm movin' back to my gran 'mom house any-"

As soon as Splash made contact with his bed, he passed out. The lower half of his body was hanging off, and the upper half of his body was sprawled across Tia's lap.

Tia looked down at Splash through her tears and sighed. His drunken honesty had pierced the armor around her heart. She ignored her cell phone when it began to ring, and only when it got quiet, after rolling Splash off of her legs, did she finally acknowledge it by picking it up to see who the caller had been. For a few seconds, she just stared blankly at the unfamiliar number on the screen of her iPhone. The things that Splash had said still had her spinning in circles. Without thinking, she thumbed the screen of her cell phone to return the unfamiliar number's call, and placed her cell phone up to her ear as she crawled slowly over Splash and got out of bed.

"Yo?"

"Who this?"

"Who this?"

"Somebody just called my phone from this number."

"Oh. Ay, yo, Bia?!"

With Snookums close behind, Tia walked into her huge, walk-in closet, and followed the carpeted walkway that led to the oval window in the rear wall that overlooked her driveway. It was 2:24 in the morning, and she was far from being tired.

"Tia?"

"What's up, Sabia?"

"Yo, my cousin cool?"

The concern in Splash's cousin's voice, coupled with what Tia saw when she looked down at her driveway, made her heartbeat speed up. The entire passenger side of Splash's car was mangled.

"Sabia, what he do to his car?"

"He told me he banged out against a guardrail on the e-way."

"On his way here?"

"I think so."

"So, he did make it home, though?"

"Yeah, he here."

"Yo, that nigga just had me in here trippin', 'cause his fuckin' phone died while we was talkin' and I thought-Aww, man."

Tia left her walk-in closet and went back into her bedroom. Splash had moved from their bed. She followed the sound of him vomiting to the closed door of their master bathroom.

"Ay, Tia this my man number. When that nigga wake up tell him to call me, alright?"

"Okay."

"You cool?"

"Yeah, I'm okay."

"Ay, Tia?"

"Yeah."

"Yo, Gran 'mom told Splash one time that chu was the best thing that ever happened to him."

"Too bad ya cousin don't feel like that."

"Y'all gon' be cool."

Those were the nicest words that Splash's cousin had ever expressed to Tia. Their relationship had always been rocky.

"Thanks, Sabia."

"Take care of my cousin, alright?"

"Alright."

"I know I'm hot right now, but if you ever need me to show up, I'll come, Tia."

"I know."

"Don't forget to tell Splash what I said, alright?"

"I won't."

Tia ended her call with Splash's cousin and tried to open her bathroom door, but it was locked. When she raised her hand to knock on the door, it swung open.

"You okay?"

"Move, man."

Splash shoved pass Tia and walked back over to their bed and laid down. After kicking his blue, Ed Sherman sneakers off, he sighed and pulled his plaid, Ed Sherman shirt over his head without bothering with the buttons.

"You know you messed your car up, right?"

"At least I ain't mess up my fuckin' marriage."

"Bay, I can call Cam right now, and she'll-"

"I ain't got no fuckin' rap for none of y'all."

"So, you really movin' out?"

"The movin' truck gon' be here in the mornin'."

"You gon' leave me here by myself?"

"You was by ya fuckin' self when I got here."

"Bay, all this over somethin' that I didn't even do?"

"I'm goin' to sleep, man."

"So, you just gon' give up on us that easy, huh?"

"Yup."

The next morning, Splash woke up to the sound of Anita Baker singing about apologizing to her man. He didn't remember coming home, and he had no recollection of the accident that he had gotten into on the I-95 expressway the prior night. Everything about the day before was foggy to him. His memory stopped after he had visited the cemetery, where Jen's son, Shateek, had gotten buried. It was there, where he had finished a bottle of Nuvo all by himself, while watching another family off in the distance bury one of their own.

Splash sat up in bed just as Tia was coming into their bedroom. Snookums was right behind her. He followed Tia into her walk-in closet, and as if he was her security guard, he returned to the doorway of Tia's walk-in closet, and sat back on his hind legs and put his eyes on Splash.

Splash didn't remember kicking Snookums.

Snookums did.

"What time that truck supposed to get here?"

"What fuckin' truck?"

"Forget it, Splash."

Splash watched Tia as she carried an outfit and a pair of her sandals out of their bedroom with her. His worst animal-enemy was right on her heels.

Anita Baker was still singing her apologies through the many wall-speakers in Splash's and Tia's humongous, master bedroom.

Two hours later, Splash was standing out in his driveway totally stunned at the sight of his Chevy Camaro. It was totaled. How the car made it to his house was beyond his comprehension.

"Damn, man."

"That shit fucked up like that?"

"Bia, this shit look like I was playin' chicken wit' a fuckin' airplane, or somethin'."

Splash looked at his cell phone when it alerted him that he was getting a second call.

"Yo, Bia, hold on."

"Alright."

After accepting his second call, Splash put his cell phone back up to his ear and walked into his garage, because the sun had his shirtless back feeling like it was getting cooked.

"What's up, Jen?"

"Splash, I-I know I'm the last person that should be askin' you for a favor, but can I still keep my job?"

"Jen, you never lost it."

"I-Splash, you gon' let me keep my job?"

"Yea, man."

"Oh, 'cause I thought-"

"Brothers get mad at they sisters, but they don't turn they backs on them, Jen."

"I didn't try to hurt Sabia, or ya aunt intent-"

"I'ma see you at the club tonight, alright?"

"Thank you, Splash."

Splash sighed and switched back over to his cousin. As soon as he did, his cell phone alerted him that he had another call.

"Ay, Bia, hold on again real quick, alright?"

"Don't forget I'm on the phone, man."

"Naw, I'm right back at chu, cuz."

"I gotta holla at chu about somethin', too, man."

"Alright, hold up, 'cause I got some rap for you, too."

"Alright, hurry up, 'cause this battery about to die."

"Alright."

Although he really didn't want to, Splash still accepted the call that he knew was going to make him more upset than he already was. He took a seat on his motorcycle and gritted his teeth.

"Splash?"

"What's up?"

"This Trixie."

"I know who the fuck it is."

"Oh, I-I just thought you might've erased my number out of your phone."

"I am as soon as you tell me why the fuck you callin' me."

"Did your cousin tell you that the same cop that came to your club stopped by my house the other-"

Splash switched back over to his cousin.

"Bia?"

"Yo?"

"Ay, yo, that mu'fuckin' cop that was at the club came to-"

"You 'on't remember me tellin' you that shit last night?"

"Man, fuck no."

"So, how you just-"

" 'Cause Trixie just told me."

"Dog, last night, you had me thinkin' you smoked some fuckin' wet, or somethin'."

"Fuck you talkin' 'bout?"

"You was talkin' some crazy shit about how you be chillin' wit' cha dad, and Gran 'pop, in ya-"

"Yo, that cop ain't see you when he was over there, did he?"

"Naw, but he left this fuckin' cell phone in one of Trixie chairs, and that nigga was ear hustling everything that we was fuckin' talkin' about."

Splash stood up and walked back out into the sunlight. He was worried about his cousin's safety, because after meeting Detective Konn, he was certain that the ugly, little cop was an enigma, and he didn't want his cousin anywhere around him; especially while his cousin's predicament was so questionable.

"What made that nigga come there, Bia?"

"Man, that freak tryna bribe Trixie and her brother, 'cause they nephew rattin'. So, he on some shit, like, he can dead the whole situation for a couple dollars."

"Bia, wherever the fuck y'all at, stay there."

"We over-"

"Chill."

Splash squinted up at the sun as he wiped his hand over his head. He stepped back out into his driveway, but one look at his car sent him reversing back into the shade of his garage.

"Alright, listen," Splash spoke, after switching his cell phone to his left ear. He looked out of his garage at Tia, as her and Snookums crossed their lawn and went for a walk. "Nix that situation that Trixie tryna put chu on. I got chu, Bia. What I told you I had for you when we was out on Gran 'mom block, I'ma bring to you this weekend. Bia, that's only two days away. Can you sit tight 'til then for me, cuz?"

"Yo, this phone about to cut off, but alright, I'ma fall back."

"Bia, don't come back to Phi-Fuck!"

After his cousin's cell phone went dead, Splash stuffed his own cell phone into the side-pocket of his denim, Rag & Bone cargo shorts.He pulled his keys out of his other pocket as he swung his right leg over the top of his royal blue,2010 Aprilia motorcycle. When he twisted his key in the ignition, the bike quickly came to life with a roar that intensified when he used his right hand and played with the throttle.

Before his garage door could close, Splash released the clutch on his motorcycle with his left hand and steered his pretty bike out into his driveway, leaving Tia's pink and white motorcycle all alone in their garage. His car was blocking Tia's Cadillac station wagon in their driveway, so if Tia didn't ride her motorcycle, she was going to be stuck at home, unless Splash called their insurance company and told them to send a tow truck for his car, but that was the last thing on Splash's mind as he rode shirtless on his motorcycle to Philly to see an old friend of his.

"Shit!" Splash cursed, realizing that he had left home without his gun. As the thought of doubling back home crossed his mind, his eyes spotted a Muslim woman in all black, standing beside her car on the shoulder of the expressway up ahead. "Damn. Fuck it, though. It ain't like somebody else gon' see if she cool. Mu'fuckers just drivin' past her like she ain't even fuckin' standin' there 'n shit. Nigga, you can use a good deed anyway."

Splash pulled his motorcycle over onto the shoulder lane behind the gun-metal gray,2011 Lincoln MKX. As he climbed off of his motorcycle, he looked at the white, Audi A8, that was slowly braking to a stop in front of the stalled Lincoln MKX.

When the driver of the Audi A8 stepped out of his vehicle, the Muslim woman got back into hers. Her displeasure was visible in the way that she moved her body, which was covered in a loose, black material, that hung all the way down to the ground. Her head was covered with a black scarf, and she had a black veil hiding her face from the bridge of her nose on down. After lowering her window, she stuck her two hands out of her car and told the driver of the Audi A8 something in sign language.

"Ay, yo, that's ya peoples?"

The driver of the Audi A8 nodded his head at Splash, then he crouched down beside the flat tire on the Lincoln and shook his head. His long dreadlocks danced around his face as the hot wind from the passing cars on the expressway blew over to the shoulder lane.

Splash hopped back on his motorcycle and started it back up. He was in the presence of Yasmeen Bey, and her son, Kenyatta, and was completely unaware of it. His coincidental encounter with the two of them was only the beginning to the many future episodes that were about to reshape his destiny in some unimaginable ways. The worst of Splash's days were yet to come. As he merged back into traffic, for a reason unknown to him, something compelled him to look over his right shoulder at the white, Audi A8.

He had an odd feeling in his gut that was telling him that he had left something behind.

Shockingly, Splash did leave something behind. Fifteen minutes earlier, while he was at the gas station filling up the gas tank on his motorcycle, Kenyatta Bey had been abducting Tia from their front lawn. She was laying unconscious under a sheet in the trunk of Kenyatta's Audi A8. Two days earlier, during a prison visit, in exchange for a lawyer and twenty thousand dollars, Tia's brother Angelo had given up her address and description to Kenyatta Bey.

Snookums was the only one that had been there to witness Tia's kidnapping. He was still whimpering beside her cell phone on Splash's and Tia's front lawn, where the early morning abduction had occurred.

Chapter Twenty

At the stroke of midnight, every light inside of Gossip Alley went out. This darkness in the crowded nightclub lasted for a full-minute, and no one panicked, or appeared to have any problems with it. All of the regulars in the club knew that the best part of the night had just arrived, so with growing anticipation, all of them began to cheer, whistle, and holler, as the sixty seconds came to an end, and every light inside of the nightclub came back on.

"Yo, what the fuck was that shit about?"

"Naw, they do that shit every-Nigga, go look down at the fuckin' dance floor."

Taking his bottle of Ciroc with him, Prep walked over to the glass wall that provided an overlooking view of the nightclub's dance floor from the VIP section, where him and Robbie were by themselves. What Prep saw when he got to the glass wall impressed him right away, and even left him speechless for a moment.

To the sound of Usher's song, "Love in this Club," thirty exotic dancers were taking control of the club's huge dance floor. It was a sight to see. There were fifteen female strippers, and fifteen male strippers. Ten of the exotic dancers took to the stage, where they all started to gyrate and go into their performances,while the rest of the strippers began to work the excited crowd, who were all waving fistfuls of money at them. During the synchronized-sixty second blackout, all of the women in the nightclub had moved to one side of the dance floor, and all of the men in the club had done the same exact thing.

"Yo, the bitches snappin' more than the niggaz is."

"They always do."

"Man, fuck this VIP shit."

"Yo, watch this bitch shoot milk out her-"

"Yooooo,"Prep exclaimed, not believing what his eyes were seeing. His eyes grew wider as one of the female strippers on the stage finished pouring milk into a funnel that was sticking out of the ass of another female stripper, who was down on her hands and knees. "Ay, yooooooooooooooooo!!"

After the pink funnel was removed from her asshole, the black stripper arched her back, and to the building drumroll that the D.J had mixed in with the music that he was playing, she began to squirt the milk back out of her ass up into the air. To the cheers of all of the men, a young, white guy opened his mouth real wide, and positioned himself on the dance floor, where the milk started to fall.

"Prep, do you mind if I talk to Robbie for a minute?"

Instead of answering Jen, Prep raised his bottle of Ciroc up to his lips and gulped down the Vodka, until his insides told him to stop swallowing.

"Prep,it ain't like that, I just wanna-"

"Jen, get the fuck out my face," Prep demanded, stepping between her and Robbie. Them being together in front of his face made him think about the pain they had caused his cousin Camay. "Robbie,you a fuckin' nut, dog. Straight up. Yo, I shoulda knew you was on some nut ass shit. First, you ain't wanna come to this fuckin' club, but I guess this bitch made you forget all that shit you was sayin' about how you ain't want me and Tia husband to go through nothin' up in this mu'fucker, huh?"

"Prep, it's not like-"

"Bitch, I ain't fuckin' talkin' to ya smut ass, so mind ya-"

"Oh, so you gon' call her a smut, but chu just told me that Cam had a fuckin' threesome wit' Tia and Splash, and she pregnant by that nigga, and you ain't speakin' on that, though, Prep!"

Having one of his own admissions thrown back in his face made Prep feel like shit. The thought of cracking Robbie over the head with his bottle of Ciroc crossed Prep's mind, but instead of acting off of that impulse, he walked out of the VIP section and left Robbie and Jen alone.

"Bitch ass nigga," Prep thought, gulping a mouthful of Ciroc as he followed the metal, spiral stairs that led down to the dance floor. Two more gulps of the Ciroc made him angrier. "Somethin'-"

"Yo, my peoples up there?"

"Ay, little man, these guys with you?"

Prep looked up at the tall, burly bouncer, who was blocking the bottom of the spiral stairs that led up to the VIP section, then looked back at the faces of Robbie's cousin, Maniac, and his friend, Idris. A premonition of the two of them killing him for his money flashed in his head, but his drunken arrogance replaced that flash warning with the naive belief that Robbie didn't have the heart to cross him like that.

"Yea, they can go up."

Prep hadn't been inside of a nightclub in almost two years. As he began to walk around the dance floor, he smiled to himself, and nodded his head in appreciation of the moment that he was experiencing. His ego rose when a pretty stripper up on the stage started to follow him with her eyes. The music was so loud that he couldn't hear himself think. His eyes became glued to a female stripper that was giving some guy a lap dance in the shadows beside the end of the bar.

"I know that ain't Prep!"

At exactly 12:15 p.m. all of the lights inside of Gossip Alley went out again, and the D.J switched the music back to some normal songs.

"Prep?!"

Prep dropped his bottle of Ciroc and started shoving his way through the crowd.

"Yo, man watch where the fuck you goin' at!"

"Nigga, slow down!"

"Ouch!"

"You just made me drop my damn drink, boy!"

"Somebody grab that pussy for me!"

"Prep?!"

Ignoring every complaint, Prep kept moving. He didn't want to face the female that was calling out his name. She was Gary's cousin, and his son's mother's best friend.

"Prep, I know you fuckin' hear-"

All of the lights in the club came back to life, and Prep, with his heart slamming against his chest, stopped running and turned around to face his hunter.

"Dag, you act like I'm the cops, or somethin'."

"Damn, what's up, Honey?"

"Do I really need to answer that question, 'cause I'm sure you know I ain't for the bullshit, Prep."

"Let's go talk in one of the bathrooms."

"Right here is just fine with me."

Prep and Gary's cousin were in the middle of the staircase that separated the first and second floor of the club. They were standing closer to the first floor, and were opposite each other with their backs against the walls.

"I see you makin' good use of that money you and my cousin took."

"I still got his half."

"You fucks me up, Prep."

"On what tip?"

"What I gotta spell it out for you?"

"You gon' have to, 'cause-"

"So, after all these years, you standin' there tryna tell me that you never figured out that I liked-"

All of the male and female strippers started coming down the steps. Prep pressed his back against the wall, because the male strippers were in the lead, and he didn't even want their breaths to touch him. He didn't relax, until the female strippers at the end of the line began to pass him on their way down.

"Girl, you had me up there lookin' all around for you, and you right-"

"Prep, this my roommate, Bella."

The last stripper coming down the steps was the one that had been following Prep from the stage with her eyes.

"Hi."

"What's up?"

"Honey, this club is the shit, girl."

"I told you."

"I made a stack in twenty-"

"Yo, here this nigga go right here, Robbie."

Robbie's cousin came down the steps with two, unopened bottles of Nuvo in each hand. His friend, Idris, had an unopened bottle of Ace of Spades in his left hand, and as they both passed Prep, they gave him nasty stares. Robbie descended the stairs last with two bottles of Ciroc in his hands. He stopped on the same step that Prep was standing on, and looked at Gary's cousin with a smile on his face.

"What's up, Robbie?"

"Yo, why you ain't dance tonight?"

"I let my girlfriend take my place."

Meanwhile, in Cape   May, New Jersey, six faces

were smiling under the glowing, full moon. While the waves from the Atlantic ocean were running up on the beach, and retreating back to its origin, its peaceful sound was joined by the harmonious voice of Sabia's friend, Moo, as he recited Arabic to his wife, as they both walked hand-in-hand behind Trixie and Sabia, who were also walking hand- in-hand. Up ahead, Splash's friend, Bleach, was walking beside his girlfriend, with his arm draped over her shoulder.

"Moo, can I ask you somethin'?" Trixie asked, using the most respectful tone of voice she could muster up, after Sabia's friend became silent. She was curious about something that she had always wanted to know. "I couldn't, um, help but notice that every time I hear Arabic somewhere, it always sound like it rhyme to me. Is that just me, or-"

"Naw, you right."

"I am?"

"Kind of."

"If it's not too much to ask, can you explain it to me?"

"Alright, you ever heard-"

"And I promise, I won't bother you about nothin' else for the rest of the time we here."

"Naw, it's cool."

Trixie squeezed Sabia's hand and flashed him a bright smile. Informative things always aroused her interest.

"You ever read the Bible before?"

"Not all of it, and the parts I did read was so long ago, I-"

"Alright, well, uh, do you remember any of the stories of the prophets, and how they all started out?"

"I remember the story about Noah."

"Alright, well, what about Moses and Jesus . . . alayhi salaam?"

"Moses, Jesus, and who?"

"Oh, naw, I said, "Alayhi salaam. That's what we say, after we mention one of the names of the prophets."

"I ain't never know Muslims believed in Jesus."

"Me, neither."

"Straight up, Moo. I ain't know that shit either, dog."

"I did."

"Bleach, you ain't know that shit, dog."

"Bia, my celly over the 'F' was just goin' in on me, tellin' me all that stuff."

"Why you ain't become Muslim, then?"

" 'Cause, I ain't wanna do that shit in jail, dog. Damn."

"Yo, you can take ya shahadah now. Can't he, Moo?"

"If he want to."

"Yo, I'm-Ay, Bia, you drawin', dog."

"Sabia, can you stop messin' with Bleach, and let Moo finish?"

Sabia smiled and picked up a clam from the wet sand, and threw it out at the ocean.

"Alright, so, look, God blessed all of his prophets and messengers with whatever was prevalent during their time, or whatever."

"I don't get it."

"You ever hear of Pharaoh?"

"He's the guy that was a tyrant ,and who Moses saved the Children of Israel from, right?"

"Exactly. Alright, so, now, during his time, magic was a real big thing, so God blessed Moses . . . alayhi salaam, with a staff to compete against all of the magicians that Pharaoh had on his team."

"Ain't that the stick he used to split the sea, or somethin' like that?"

"Yup."

Trixie looked past Sabia at the vastness of the Atlantic Ocean. The thought of a great body of water being split in half by a magical stick touched her soul in a way that she had never felt before.

"With Jesus, God blessed him and his mother with-"

"You didn't say, "Alayhi salaam," Moo."

"Huh?"

"You forgot to say-"

"Oh."

When Sabia's friend, Moo, and his wife beamed proud smiles at her, Trixie cheesed back at them.

"What does that mean anyway?"

"May Allah's peace be upon him."

The three couples were almost back at Trixie's brother's lavish beach house. They were on their way back from enjoying the rides on the boardwalk. Behind them, the brightness of all of the tall rides were illuminating the night sky.

"So, what was God reason for makin' the Qur'an rhyme, Moo?"

After his question, Sabia picked up another seashell and threw it at the crashing waves.

" 'Cause poetry was real heavy back then, so God revealed the-"

"Ay, Trixie come-Ashley, put her on speaker-phone real quick, so Bia and Trixie can hear what she just said."

Everyone stopped walking, and gave Bleach's girlfriend's cell phone their undivided attention, except for Moo's wife. She stood back from the small circle and lowered her eyes down to the sand.

"Ashley, who was that?"

"Man, it's ya fuckin' brother."

"Oh, my God! Bleach, when the fuck you-Ashley, why you ain't-"

"Honey, where that nigga at?"

"If y'all hurry up, y'all can catch-"

"Yo, we ain't even in-Just tell me what that nigga drivin'."

It wasn't until that moment that Trixie realized who Bleach and his sister were talking about.

"Bleach, I don't know yet, but tell Ashley this his cell phone number."

"Alright, what is-"

"Do Mommy know you home?"

"Honey, man, what's the fuckin' number?"

"What?"

"What's that nigga number?"

"Dummy, I meant that this his cell phone I'm usin' right now, but I'ma have to erase Ashley number from his outgoing calls, so he won't know-"

"Where the fuck you at, anyway?"

"At Gossip Alley in the bathroom."

Trixie and Sabia looked at each other with wide eyes.

"Honey, I need you to find out what that nigga dri-"

"Ask her is that a pre-paid cell phone she talkin' on."

Bleach nodded his head at Trixie, but the look on his face said that he thought her question was meaningless. When Bleach asked his sister to find out what Prep was driving again, Trixie snatched his girlfriend's cell phone out of his hand and stared at its screen. After she memorized the seven digits, she handed the cell phone back, grabbed Sabia's hand, and took off running for her brother's beach house.

At exactly 1:26 a.m., Trixie was staring at her iPad with three faces over her shoulders.

"So, if you gotta mu'fucker phone number, all you gotta do is go to that website, and you can get they address?"

"It's like doing a reverse search, but because most people use phony info when they buy pre-paid phones, it won't work."

"But that shit work for house numbers, and mu'fuckers that got bills on they cell phones, though?"

"Bleach, it'll work like a charm every time."

"Ill, that's mean."

"That's where his cousin live."

Trixie, Sabia, and Bleach, all looked at Bleach's girlfriend. They were still ignoring the sounds of love making that were echoing from the bedroom upstairs, where Moo and his wife were.

"So, when we out there, Trixie?"

"A week from today."

Chapter Twenty-One

"Hello?"

"Splash?"

"You still haven't heard from Tia?"

It was 8:03 a.m., and no one had heard from Tia, or had any idea where she might possibly be. Splash had found Tia's cell phone lying next to Snookums on their front lawn when he arrived home the night before.

"Nope."

"Splash, I think you should call the cops and make a missin' person's report."

"I-Cam, hold on . . . this Rhonda on my other line."

"Okay."

Splash accepted his second call and sat up in his bed. Both of his eyes were bloodshot-red from him not getting any sleep.

"What's up, Rhonda?"

"I'm at the door."

"Alright, here I come."

Snookums hopped up at attention when Splash got out of bed. He followed Splash out of his bedroom, down the hall, and when Splash started going down the spiral stairs without him, he began to make whimpering noises.

"See what I'm sayin'?"

"What?"

"Yo, somethin' ain't right, man," Splash cried, switching his cell phone to his other hand, so he could scoop Snookums up with his right hand. When Snookums licked his forearm, he felt his heart tremble in his chest. "Cam, even when Tee not here, Snookums still be trippin' when I come home. This nigga been actin' way different on me. He followed me everywhere I went last night in this mu' fucker. Yo, man, somethin'-"

"You think he saw somethin'?"

At the bottom of the spiral stairs, Splash returned Snookums to his feet.

"He had to, Cam."

As Splash walked through his Roman-styled foyer, he wiped his tears. When he opened his front door and looked into the face of his wife's cousin, the fear and concern reflecting from her eyes almost crippled him.

"Who that?"

"Cam."

"Let me talk to her."

Splash handed Tia's cousin his cell phone and walked past her outside. Snookums was right behind him. Together, the two of them walked across the lawn. They both stopped at the multi-tiered, white stone, fountain, that stood in the middle of the grass. Here, Splash sat down on his lawn and pulled Tia's cell phone out of his pocket.

"What the fuck happened, Tee?" Splash wondered, as Snookums made a whimpering sound and climbed on his lap. Blinking back tears, he looked around his lawn for any clue that he might have overlooked the night before. "You ain't no where in the house. Ya car here. You ain't goin' nowhere without ya fuckin' phone. I done called any and every fuckin' body, and don't nobody-"

"Camay want chu, Splash."

With a sigh, Splash took his cell phone back from Tia's cousin and put it to his ear.

"What's up, Cam?"

"I'm on my way there, okay."

"Alright."

"If you hear anything before I get there, make sure you call me."

"Alright."

"Splash?"

"Yeah?"

"Keep thinkin' positive."

"I am."

Several minutes later, Splash was staring at one of Tia's sandals that her cousin had discovered in the grass a few feet away from where he was sitting. As the sandal was handed to him, he felt an encompassing gloom fill up his soul.

"Who we killin' first?"

Splash looked up at Tia's cousin's face, but he couldn't see it. He had so many tears running from his eyes that he was blind.

"Just-Just tell me-Just tell me who we kill-"

Tia's cousin Rhonda fell to her knees and sobbed like her insides were being ripped out of her.

"They-Splash, who we killin' first?!"

Splash couldn't answer Tia's cousin, because he didn't have a voice. His mouth was open from a scream that had started from a deep place within, but after it passed his heart and reached his lips, it came out soundless. Tia was the owner of his heart.

She was him.

He was her.

They were Mr. and Mrs. Gunplay.

There wasn't a person alive that Splash wouldn't murder for Tia. His love for her didn't have boundaries. If you crossed her, you crossed him, and vice versa. Their love for each other ran deep, and because Splash knew that

Tia had been hurting from the way he had been treating her lately, this only caused him more anguish. As he laid on his lawn and listened to Tia's cousin sob beside him, he started thinking about the question that she had asked him. It was no way that he could narrow down who might be responsible for Tia's disappearance, so he came to one conclusion.

Everybody.

Must.

Die.

"Come on."

Tia's cousin and Snookums followed Splash across the lawn, and back into the house.

Later on that afternoon, a question was asked that inspired Splash to make a phone call to his cousin Sabia.

"Ay, yo, let me holla at Bia."

"Who this?"

"His cousin."

"Which one?"

"Nigga, do it fuckin' matter?!" Splash growled into his cell phone, as Tia's cousin and Camay stood beside him in his driveway, and watched with him as the tow-truck drove away with his mangled Camaro. "Tell him his fuckin' cousin Splash on the-"

"Splash, watch out!!"

The spray of a machine gun was followed by the screeches of tires biting into the street.

Splash, Camay, and Tia's cousin Rhonda, all took off running. Camay ran across Splash's and Tia's lawn to her car, and Splash and Tia's cousin ran in the opposite direction, after the white, Audi A8, with guns in their hands.

The Audi A8 was a blur of white machinery.

"Get in!!"

With balls of fire in their eyes, Splash and Tia's cousin hurriedly jumped in Camay's car when she pulled to a stop beside them at the corner of Upsal Street. Neither one of them wasted any time in lowering their windows.

On the I-76 expressway, a Highway patrol cop started chasing the Audi A8, and followed it when it raced off of the Philadelphia Zoo exit. Camay's champagne-colored, 2011 Infiniti G37 was right behind them.

At Girard Avenue, to the amazement of everyone in Camay's car, the driver of the Audi A8 slammed on his brakes and bailed out of his car, causing the Highway patrol car to rear-end it with a loud crash. Then, with his long dreadlocks swinging wildly around his angry face, the driver of the Audi A8 side-stepped over to his car and pulled out an assault rifle that had a shell-catcher attached to the side of it.

Bravely, the Highway patrol cop exited his vehicle shouting demands for the driver of the Audi A8 to drop his weapon, but that only earned him a team of bullets that sent his brown, uniformed body falling down to the ground.

"Rhonda?! Splash?! No!!"

Camay panicked when Splash and Tia's cousin jumped out of her car and started trading bullets with the driver of the Audi A8. It completely shocked her when Tia's cousin jumped inside of the Audi A8, and continued shooting out of the window at the guy with dreadlocks, while at the same time, trying to run him over with his own car, as he ran out into the two lanes of westbound traffic on Girard Avenue.

"Bocka! Bocka! Bocka! Bocka! Bocka!"

After letting off five more shots, Splash lowered his Glock 50 and ran back to Camay's car, and got inside of it quickly.

"Hurry up, before this car that's comin' see ya license plate, Cam!"

"That cop dead!"

"Cam, fuck that cop!!" Splash hollered, looking over his shoulder through Camay's rear window. The sound of a loud car crash made his neck whiplash forward. "Yo, drive! What the fuck-Man, don't chu hear-"

"Okay!!"

The loud car crash had been Tia's cousin crashing the white, Audi A8 into a blue, Mercedes SUV, that the owner of the Audi A8 had ran behind. The accident made it impossible for other cars to pass by, but this only forced people to abandon their vehicles at the places where they had stopped, and sent them scrambling for their lives. People in the Philadelphia Zoo's parking lot were doing the same thing as well. The same couldn't be said for the white man that owned the soft pretzel stand at the entrance of the Zoo's parking lot. He had succumbed to a gunshot wound that had entered the back of his neck, and had tore through his right eye socket.

With Splash shouting instructions at her, Camay drove her Lexus around the Highway patrol car, up onto the pavement, and over the small, grassy hill, which came to a descent beside a large tree that she barely missed when she steered her car between it, and a parking meter, to make it back out onto the street. This brought Camay's car within ten feet of the crashed up Audi A8.

"Fuck!!" Splash cursed, after he got out of Camay's car. Disregarding the sounds of police sirens that seemed to be coming from everywhere, he ran over to the driver's side of the white, Audi A8, and snatched the door open. "I'm right here, Rock 'n Roll. I'm right here. I got chu. This fuckin' air bag! Aargghhh!"

"Splash, hurry up!!"

"Did I-Did I get him, Spl-Sssss, ouch."

"Naw, that pussy got the fuck away."

"Drop me and-Ouch. Just leave me here and go get him, then."

Splash carried Tia's cousin over to Camay's car, and after he managed to get the back door partially open, he used his elbow to get it open all the way, then slid Tia's cousin across the backseat, and got in next to her.

"I left my gun in that car."

"Splash, which way do I go?!"

"The way the fuckin' cops ain't goin'!"

Chapter Twenty-Two

"So, y'all seriously not gon' talk to me?!"

Splash's shout caused some of the birds that were perched in the trees in the cemetery to fly away. After a brief flight in the gray sky, many of the small, black birds returned to their places. The rest of them landed on the tops of different tombstones. One of these selected tombstones was two feet behind Splash.

"Dad, I-"

"Do you notice anything that look different about me and your gran 'father?"

"No."

Splash's father and grandfather were sitting on the grass with their backs against the opposite sides of the same tombstone. Splash's grandfather was crying tears of blood, but because he had his head down, the red teardrops falling from his eyes weren't visible for Splash to see. Splash's father had his head tilted against the tombstone. His knees were pulled up to his chest.

"Why Gran'mom not here?"

"She'll be here after her funeral."

"Dad, why y'all look like that?"

Splash's father raised his right hand and turned it from side to side. It looked like a hologram. He did the same thing with his left hand, then returned them both to his lap.

"Why y'all look like y'all disappearin'?"

"'Cause we are."

"W-Why?"

Splash's grandfather raised his head and looked at him.

Splash fell to his knees.

Splash's father stood up.

"Dad, what's happenin'?"

"My agreement with God has run its course, Splash."

"But chu said as long as I keep ya jeep, we-"

"I lied."

"But chu said we would always-You said we would always have this."

"I know, but I should've told you the truth."

"What's the truth?"

Splash's father dropped down to his knees beside Splash and hugged him.

"Dad, what's the truth?"

"I made a deal, and I didn't keep my end of the bargain."

"Who you made a deal with?"

"God."

"What was the deal?"

Splash's father stood back up and looked around the land of the dead. Splash followed his gaze.

"I know you can't see, or hear them, but under most of these tombstones, and in them mausoleums, it's people gettin' tortured in their graves, Splash."

"That's what happened to Gran 'pop eyes?"

"Ask him."

"Gran 'pop, what happened?"

Splash's grandfather lowered his head.

"Gran 'pop?"

"He can't hear you."

"Why not?"

"All of us have real deep, and special connections, Splash."

Somberly, Splash nodded his head and looked over his father's shoulder at his grandfather.

"Your grandfather heard your grandmother screamin' when she was gettin' raped, Splash."

"He heard her here?"

Splash's father nodded his head.

"Them tears?"

Splash's father nodded again.

"Why-"

"Her screams was so loud they made him deaf."

Splash pushed past his father and crawled over to his grandfather. His love and respect for the man was the premiere force behind his character and value system. Since the age of three, after the death of both of his parents, his grandfather had done all he was able to do to mold him into a decent man.

"Gran 'pop?" Splash spoke, lifting his grandfather's chin with his hand. The vision of the bloody tears crawling down his grandfather's face made his heart twist itself into a knot, but beyond the pools of redness, Splash could see the disappointment that his grandfather was feeling. "I'm sorry, Gran 'pop. You know I wouldn't let nothin' happen to Gran 'mom. You know I wouldn't. I was tryna to get there, but-"

"This is the last time you gon' get to see us, Splash."

"Why?"

"Because I made a commitment to God that I wouldn't let you turn out like me, and you-"

Splash rose to his feet ,and after wiping his face clean of his tears, he gave his father an incredulous look. What he was hearing didn't make any sense to him.

"You turned out worse than me."

"What that got to do with-I made my own choices to be who I am, though."

"As your father, it was my responsi-"

"So, you tryna tell me that you thought you could steer me in whatever direction you wanted to?"

"It's what fathers do, Splash."

As much as Splash hated to hear it, he knew that his father was ultimately right, because had Tia given birth to his son, his priority would have been to guide his own son down a positive, and productive path. Nonetheless, this still didn't comfort the pain that he was feeling. Knowing that he was seeing his father and grandfather for the last time put a thousand regrets on his mind.

"I should've let you go to that college when you had the chance to."

"Dad, why you ain't never-"

Splash's father and grandfather started disappearing right in front of Splash's eyes.

"It's my turn to get tortured, Splash."

"Dad?!!"

All of the little, black birds in the cemetery took flight.

"Wait!" Splash begged, wrapping his arms around his father's vanishing frame. Missing the chance to hug his father, he ran over to his grandfather, but he got there too late. "Aaaaaahhhhhhhhhhhh!!! What about my mom?!! Dad, what about-What about my mom?!!! Wait!! I- I'ma change!! Tell God I'ma change!!! Dad, tell him I'ma change!! I'm gon' change! Dad, come back!! Gran 'pop?!! Come back, Gran 'pop!! Come back!!!"

Because God's wisdom was so infinite, Splash would never grasp and fully understand the unique design of his life, or realize how influential he was to all of the lives that surrounded his own. He still had a lot of growing up to do. His willingness to change his life had been an empty pledge brought on by his emotions, but his destiny was about to lead him down a road that was going to force him to reshape how he looked at the entire world.

Chapter Twenty-Three

"And you gon' bring her here out of all fuckin' places?!"

"Man, Mommy told me to!"

"Yatta, some-Yo, somebody on they way over here to look at the fuckin' apartment right now!"

"Just say the basement ain't finished, yet!"

"Why the fuck y'all ain't tell me y'all was gon' do that shit anyway?!"

"Ask Mommy that shit!"

"Man, I'm askin' you!"

"I'm out!"

"Did you even check to see if she still fuckin' alive?!"

"Go down there and see, since you so concerned about that dumb ass bitch!!"

"Where the fuck you goin'?!"

"Don't worry about it!"

"You and Mommy gotta get her the fuck outta here, Yatta!"

"Well, tell Mommy that, then!"

"You brung her here!"

"Mommy told me to!"

"Alright, watch!"

Like the conversation held between Malcolm and Kenyatta Bey, the sound of a door slamming forcefully had echoed through the heating vent that was above Tia's head.

All night long, and for most of the morning, Tia had been listening to all sorts of noises. Most of what she was hearing was coming from outside. Besides the sounds of buses, that were stopping and pulling off every twenty-eight seconds, on a corner somewhere nearby, Tia could also hear cars as they drove up and down the street, and every so often, the faint conversations of people walking by made its way to her ears as well. Throughout the night, things had been eerily silent. The hours had passed by like years for Tia, and because she had regained consciousness with something covering her head, each time she had heard a car door being shut, her heart jumped up into her throat, and she had assumed that her executioner was coming to end her life.

Tia's ankles were handcuffed to the legs of the wooden chair she was sitting on. Her hands were cuffed behind her back, and under the black pillowcase that was over her head, she had the arm of a thermal shirt stuffed in her mouth.

Knowing that her existence to the world was on borrowed time, Tia was using the happy moments from some of her memories as an anchor to keep her sanity from drifting away.

The sound of a door being opened, and the flipping of a light switch was followed by descending footsteps, which instantly sent Tia's nerves scrambling. As her entire body tensed up and went rigid, and her heart did backflips in her chest, she began to piss on herself. When the material covering her head was snatched off, she started vomiting.

"What the fuck?"

The thermal sleeve in Tia's mouth was causing her to choke on her vomit. Her eyes felt like they were about to pop out the front of her face as her upper and lower body began to convulse. Even when the gag was removed from her mouth, she continued to purge for several minutes longer.

"You cool?"

"I'm-I'm preg-I'm pregnant."

"Ya name Tia?"

Swallowing, Tia nodded her head and began to cry. Her closest run-ins with death had come from the hands of both of her estranged brothers.

"You know who I am?"

Tia nodded her head again.

"Who am I, then?"

"My brother."

"So, you knew about me all this time?"

"No."

"When you found out?"

"A few weeks ago."

"From who?"

"The same-The same person that told-"

"Salvatore?"

After nodding her head, Tia looked up into her brother's eyes for the first time. What she saw in them, besides that they were gray like her own eyes, was the questions that he wanted her to give him the answers to. He wanted her to tell him about the man that was their father. She could remember a time when she had been desirous of the same knowledge. She could remember crying her eyes out every night when she was younger, because each night before she went to sleep, she had wished that she had her father there to read her a bedtime story.

"You look like him."

"Like who?"

"Our dad."

Tia followed her brother's eyes down to the small puddle of piss that had her right foot encircled.

"I'm pregnant, Malcolm."

"Who told you my name?"

"Uncle Salvatore did."

"You don't look pregnant to me."

"I-I know, but-But I am."

"That shit ain't gon' win you no fuckin' sympathy with-"

Malcolm Bey reached into his pocket for his cell phone when it started ringing. He kept his eyes on Tia, and Tia kept her eyes on him.

"Hello? What? Who the fuck-What? How you get this phone?"

In her brother's silence, Tia started observing her surroundings. She was in the rear, right corner of a finished basement. The floors were hardwood, and three of the walls were painted white. The wall not painted white was under the staircase, where the heating tank, and washer and dryer were. All of these appliances were brand new. The wall behind them was exposed bricks. In the ceiling, there were two rows of spotlights, that were spaced three feet apart from each other, and went from the back of the basement up to its front.

Through with looking around her prison, Tia brought her eyes back to her brother. The smell of her own vomit and urine was burning her nose, and making her nauseous.

"Who the fuck is Rock 'n Roll Rhonda?!!"

Tia flinched when her brother charged at her and pulled a gun off of his waist.

"Huh?!"

"She-She my cousin."

"Where the fuck she from?!!"

"As much as I wanna live to give birth to this baby inside of me, you gon' have to kill me right here, and right fuckin' now, if you think I'ma tell you anything else about-"

"Bitch, shut the fuck up!"

Tia glared at her brother's back when he walked away from her and placed his cell phone back to his ear. It was visible in his body language that something was wrong, and as her eyes followed him over to the red, Kenmore washing machine, and dryer, where he stepped and switched his cell phone to his left ear, she wondered why he had asked her about her cousin Rhonda.

"Yatta?! I fuckin' told you!! Man, them mu'fuckers got Mommy!!"

A smile teased Tia's lips.

" 'Cause some bitch name Rock 'n Roll Rhonda just called me from Mommy fuckin' cell phone!!"

Forty-six minutes after that, Tia felt the promise of survival growing inside of her heart as she listened to her cousin speak. Her voice was coming through the speaker of her brother's cell phone.

"I ain't even get her husband involved, yet. All this my work."

Kenyatta snatched the cell phone from his brother.

"God created way more killers than just y'all two-"

"Bitch, how the fuck we suppose to know our mom still-"

"Call me out my name again, and I'ma send this deaf bitch head to the fuckin' radio station, and all ten of her fingers to that Daycare center, where I got her nonhearin' ass at!!"

"Yo, alright!"

"Which one is this?!"

"The one you spoke to earlier. Yo, we just wanna know our mom-"

"Send a video of my cousin to y'all mom phone, and I'll send one of y'all mom to yours, and trust me, if my cousin gotta scratch on her, expect y'all mom to be bleedin' from the same fuckin' places."

"Alright."

Tia traded hard stares with Kenyatta Bey, as he reached for the vomit-stained, thermal sleeve in her mouth, and yanked it out.

"You should've just left me alone."

The balance of power had shifted, and Tia was happy that it had. The whole ordeal had taught her new things about herself that had bleached some of the bright colors in her personality. It had unpeeled some of the thick layers that she had around her heart, softened the layers that still remained, and had scared all of the evilness out of her bones.

"Move, Yatta."

Before stepping aside, and behind his brother, Kenyatta Bey let a mouthful of spit fly from his mouth.

"Bitch, this shit far from over."

"Obviously, you seem to have me in the wrong category," Tia responded, feeling a new fire igniting in her chest with saliva oozing down her face, and tears rolling from her eyes, she looked at the back of her brother's cell phone, as he began to record the video her cousin Rhonda had requested. "This mother fucker just spit in my face, Rhonda, and he did it after you told them that it better not be nothin'-"

Malcolm Bey lowered his cell phone down to his side. He could see his mother's fate in Tia's eyes.

"Whether this shit over, or not, don't for one second think I won't let y'all mom feel some of this same type of sufferin' I'm goin' through."

"Yatta, go upstairs."

"I ain't goin' nowhere."

All attention went to Malcolm Bey's cell phone when it began to ring.

"Shit."

"What?"

Tia's eyes zigzagged from Malcolm, to Kenyatta, then back to Malcolm, as the ringing of his cell phone filled the cool air in the basement.

"Damn, this the chick that supposed to come look at the fuckin' apart-Hello?"

Malcolm and Kenyatta stepped to the front of the basement, because Tia started vomiting again. When someone outside knocked on the front door, both of them raised their eyes up to the ceiling.

"You here? Oh, um, damn. Uh, alright. Alright, here I- Alright, here I come right now. Wa laikum As Salaam."

The entire two-story building belonged to Malcolm Bey. It was a property that was the third house from the corner of 7th and Tree, in South Philadelphia. The first floor apartment was vacant, and the second floor unit was used by Malcolm when he didn't feel like driving the long distance to his house in Mt. Laurel, New Jersey.

"Yo, I'ma be right back."

Malcolm darted up the basement stairs, taking them in threes. In his absence, his little brother walked up behind Tia, pulled his dick out, and pissed on her back. Once he was done, he used the torn thermal sleeve he had put in Tia's mouth to gag her the night before as a rag, and wiped it through his piss-puddle on the floor, then shoved it into Tia's mouth.

Not even two seconds after that, like a cavalry, and looking like ninjas, six Muslim women came rushing down the basement steps holding two guns a piece.

"As Salaamu Alaikum, ohki. Stop oppressin' the sister, and back away from her, Insha Allah."

Tia recognized her cousin Zainab's voice right away.

With a Muslim woman in front of him, and behind him, Malcolm Bey came walking back down his basement stairs.

"Y'all know we gon' find out who the fuck y'all is, right?"

"Yatta, shut the fuck up, and worry about gettin' Mommy back!"

"Ohki, my name Zainab Abdur Rahman, and I attend every salafi masjid in this city, so you ain't gotta waste no time tryna find out who I am, 'cause I just told you."

"Yatta, give them the keys, so they can uncuff her."

"I ain't givin' 'em shit, until I know Mommy alright."

Tia's eyes watered as her cousin approached her. She had never felt more valued in her whole life. In her cousin's eyes, she was able to see how much she was worth.

"You okay?"

Crying, Tia nodded her head when her cousin removed the filthy sleeve from her mouth. Able to breathe through her mouth again, and beyond sick to her stomach from having Kenyatta Bey's piss in her system, she started vomiting down the front of her lavender, Via Spiga tunic again. Sitting in the same restricted position for so many hours had every joint in her body stiff. Her muscles were under her skin screaming for mercy.

"Shahadah, go out to the car and get that bag of clothes."

"Ain't nobody goin' no fuckin' where."

"Ay, Yatta, what the fuck I told you?!!"

Fourteen guns were aimed at Kenyatta Bey.

One gun was aimed at the back of Tia's head.

Malcolm Bey's cell phone started to ring in his pocket.

"You shoot her, we shoot you."

"Yatta, put down ya-"

"Ohki, that should be my cousin callin' you."

Malcolm Bey pulled out his cell phone and answered it. His own gun was sticking him in the ribs.

"Hello?"

Unable to see Kenyatta Bey, because he was standing directly behind her, Tia cast glances at everyone else in the basement that she could see. She looked at her cousin Zainab first. Their knees were touching. This physical contact was allowing her to feel the currents of tension that were racing through her cousin's body. As she shot quick stares up to the front of the basement, where the seven Muslim women were standing with their guns aimed, where she assumed Kenyatta Bey was standing behind her, she wondered how she had been found by them and her cousin. That thought vanished when her brother raised his cell phone in the air.

"Zay?"

"I hear you."

"She there?"

"Yeah, she-"

"She about to be dead, if you don't send that video of my-"

"Yatta, man, shut the-"

"Man, fuck these bitches!!"

"Use some hikmah! They got Mommy!!"

"Zay, what's goin' on over-"

"Rhonda, just send them the fuckin' video of they-"

"Tia?!"

"Yeah?"

"They hurt chu?"

"Rhonda?"

"'Cause I'm starin' this bitch in her eyes as we speak, and-"

"Rhonda, I gotta gun pointed at the back of my head."

Silence.

"I'm about to send them the video right now, Tia."

"Hurry up, Rhonda."

"Did they hurt chu?"

"No!" Tia lied, certain that if she told her cousin the truth, all hell would break loose. The look in her cousin Zainab's eyes confirmed to her that she had done the right thing by not telling their cousin the truth. "They didn't do nothin' to me, Rhonda. I'm okay, and just want all this to hurry up and be over. Okay? Just do what chu told them you was gon' do earlier, so they'll know that their mom is okay, then we'll decide what to do next."

"What's the one name that got all the mouth?"

"His name-"

"My name Kenyatta."

"Somebody showed me that spot up Mt. Airy, where you be gettin' them plated, Audi A8s from, boo boo."

"I 'on't give a fuck."

"You will when you see the news later on. I set that shit on fire, and I rocked that old head bitch you was fuckin' two doors away from there, too."

"That bitch ain't mean nothin' to me."

"What about the one that live on 2nd Street down Northern Liberty, who you bought that engagement ring for two weeks ago?"

Kenyatta Bey looked at his brother in shock and lowered his gun.

"I'm pregnant by her brother, but over that one you kidnapped, him, her, and they fuckin' mom can get it."

Twenty minutes later, Tia was standing under the warm water of the shower in Malcolm Bey's 1st floor, apartment bathroom.

"How did they find out where your house was?"

"Your guess is better than mine."

"Well, the stuff I brung you right here on the toilet seat."

"Okay."

No matter how much Tia washed her hair, or scrubbed her skin, she couldn't seem to get the rancid smell of her vomit, and Kenyatta Bey's piss, off of her. Once her cousin was out of the bathroom, and she was left alone, she raised her face to the falling water from the showerhead, and stopped washing up. Mixed with the relief of having her destiny changed, and emotionally damaged by what could have been, she placed her hand over her stomach and released tears of gratitude for what would be now.

"Tia, you okay?"

After turning off the shower, Tia stuck her head out from behind the shower curtain and looked at her cousin, who was standing in the bathroom's doorway.

"Rhonda here with they mom, yet?"

"They should be here in like a half an hour."

"Everything okay out there?"

"We about to pray."

"With them?"

"Well, the one that kidnapped you not, but the one that's your brother-"

"Leave me a gun in here, Zainab."

"I did already."

"Where at?"

"Under your towel."

"Oh."

"You want my cell phone, so you can let Splash know you okay?"

"Leave it on the sink for me."

"Okay."

"Zainab, what if the other one try somethin',while y'all prayin'?"

"Trust me, it might cross his mind, but he ain't gon' bother us out there."

In that moment, Tia became a pessimist. She didn't put anything past Kenyatta Bey. So when she stepped out of the shower, after her cousin had placed her cell phone on the sink, and left her alone in the bathroom again, the first sensible thing she did was go for the gun that was hiding between the folds of the white towel laying on the base of the toilet. She only sat the gun down once, and that was to free her hands, so she could dress herself, and even then, her eyes never left the handle of the chrome, pearl-handled, Republic Arms 9mm.

Tia picked up her cousin's cell phone when it began to ring. The caller was her cousin Rhonda.

"Y'all here?"

"Tia?"

"Yeah."

"Oh, un uh. We comin', though."

"Where y'all at?"

"Comin' down 8th Street. We just crossed Washington Avenue."

"I love you, Rhonda."

"And that's exactly why I did everything I had to do to find you."

Tia sat down on the toilet seat and stared down at her bare feet. Water from her wet hair was dripping down her shoulders and back, wetting the ruby-red, Nicole Miller dress, that her cousin had brought for her to put on. As she stared down at the plum-colored nail polish on her toenails, she thought of asking her cousin about Splash, but decided against doing so, because despite everything that she had just gone through, it didn't make her forget all of the hurtful stuff Splash had told her the night he came home drunk.

"What chu in there doin'?"

"Starin' at my bare feet."

"We can stop down South Street on our way back."

"Where y'all at now?"

"Dickinson Street."

Tia sighed and wiped at a teardrop that slid out of her right eye.

"You hungry?"

"Food the last thing on my mind."

"We at Mckean now."

"Alright, call when y'all out front."

"Wink ya right eye at me, if you want me to rock all of 'em when we get there."

With a heightened sense of anticipation, Tia walked out of the bathroom carrying her cousin's cell phone in one hand, and her cousin's gun in the other. The twist of events she had just experienced seemed unreal to her. As she walked down the short hallway, which opened out into a nice-sized, empty living room, the idea that her life was being swapped for another person made her shake her head from side to side. Her wet hair was still dripping water. Her wrists and ankles still had the double-lined imprints of the handcuffs she had been freed of forty minutes earlier, and as she laid her gray eyes on the man that had put them on her, a voice in her mind screamed for her to shoot him in his smiling face.

Tia blew Kenyatta Bey a kiss, and just like she had thought, this got him to stop smiling. Leaning her shoulder against the living room wall on her left, she turned her attention to the congregational prayer that was taking place, and she understood why her cousin Zainab had told her that Kenyatta Bey wouldn't try anything, while she was praying.

Malcolm Bey was leading the prayer.

Zainab, Tia's cousin, and three of her Muslim companions were in a straight line three feet behind Malcolm Bey, following his motions, each time he uttered "Allahu Akbar." Behind them, the remaining four sisters were holding their guns and looking silently at Kenyatta Bey. Five minutes earlier, they had been the ones who were praying.

"As Salaamu Alaikum wa Rahmatullah . . . As Salaamu Alaikum Wa Rahmatullah."

Tia answered her cousin's cell phone in the middle of the second ring.

"Y'all here?"

"Yup."

Hearing Tia's question, Kenyatta Bey stormed over to the door, opened it, stepped out into the vestibule, and snatched open the front door.

"Tia, come on."

Tia felt her heartbeat speed up, as she walked with her cousin and all of the Muslim women out of the apartment. She looked over her shoulder to see if her brother had gotten up yet, but he still had his face prostrated on the floor. His long dreadlocks made it impossible for her to see his face. It seemed like things were happening so fast. Her and Yasmeen Bey crossed paths on the steps of the apartment, and it wasn't until her left foot came down on a small piece of a glass on the sidewalk, that she stopped being ushered so quickly by her saviors.

"Ssssss," Tia hissed, removing the tiny piece of green glass from the heel of her feet, as soon as she sat down in the backseat of her cousin Rhonda's car. They were parked directly in front of her brother's apartment, so when she looked up, their eyes met when he came to his front door. "Wait, Rhonda. Stop. Rhonda?! I wanna say somethin' to-Rhonda?!"

"Rhonda, slow down!"

Tia's cousin ignored Tia, and her cousin Zainab, who was right beside her in the passenger seat, and continued racing her car down the narrow street.

"That wasn't they mom!"

"What?!!"

Tia's cousin, Rhonda, made a hard left off of Tree Street and sped up 7th Street. Behind her, Tia's cousin, Zainab's, Muslim companions were driving just as fast, in a navy blue, 2011 Ford Explorer.

"Who was that you gave them, Rhonda?!"

"I paid some dopefien' lady a hundred dollars to wear all that Muslim stuff, and I duct-taped her dumb ass mouth, and-"

"Rhonda, where they fuckin' mom at?!"

"In the trunk!"

"I gave them my word, Rhonda!"

"Well, I didn't, Zainab!!"

Closing her eyes, Tia took a deep breath and laid across the backseat of her cousin's speeding car.

"Tia, you still wanna stop down South Street?"

"I sure do."

Chapter Twenty-Four

Splash's aura was darker than the black, Fratelli Rosetti suit that he had on. The tinted lenses on his Carrera Aviator sunglasses were hiding the emotional storm that existed in his eyes. His heart was in his chest fighting everything near it. In painful silence, he looked on as his grandmother's coffin was being lowered down into the earth. Beside him, his aunt stood on unsteady legs. She was using his left shoulder as a crutch. His aunt squeezed his hand when his grandmother's coffin reached the very bottom of the dirty grave, and at that moment, being in the same jail cell, where Angelo Masino was being held by the authorities, was the only place on earth Splash wanted to be.

A little under two hundred people had attended Splash's grandmother's funeral. Some were friends of hers from her North Philadelphia neighborhood, but it was really all of the members from her church, who made up the large gathering in the cemetery. For it to be such a sad day, the weather was extremely nice. The sky was cloudless, and the sun was fulfilling its obligation as it always did in early August. It was a muggy 93 degrees, and the temperature, according to the forecasters at all of the local news stations, was going to reach a high of 99 degrees by late afternoon.

After Splash's grandmother was laid to rest, and the pastor said some final words, everyone began to somberly disperse, and return to their cars.

"You know you don't have to come back to the church to eat with everybody, if you don't want to, right?"

"I know, Aunt Steph."

Sighing, Splash responded to his aunt's hug by kissing her on the cheek, and hugging her back tightly. The finality of his grandmother's funeral came with the sobering reality that she would never be coming back. Seventy-five percent of his heart was now a big void.

"Walk with me to the limousine, Splash."

Splash gave his aunt his right hand when she reached out for it as they both began to walk. The grass was making it difficult for his aunt to walk steadily in her high heels.

"Ay, Aunt Steph, I need to tell you somethin'."

"If it got anything to do with why Tia didn't come to your grandmother's funeral, I still think it's real disrespectful that she didn't-"

"Tia got kidnapped, Aunt Steph."

"She-What? Kidnapped?"

Splash took a deep breath and released his aunt's hand. They were almost at the limousine that had driven his aunt from the church out to the cemetery.

"Some lady and her sons from South Philly mad, because-"

"What lady?"

"This Muslim lady that got all these Daycare-"

When Splash pulled the rear, passenger door of the limousine open for his aunt, she readjusted the strap of her pocketbook on her shoulder, then pushed the limousine door closed and crossed her arms over her chest.

"Nephew, what the hell is goin' on?"

"Me and Tia used to kill people for a livin', Aunt Steph."

For the next couple of minutes, Splash told his aunt bits and pieces of what he was comfortable with her knowing.

"They gotta reward out for-"

"We ain't have nothin' to do with that highway patrol cop-"

"Did anybody see you?"

"No, Aunt Steph."

"So, how much money are they askin' for?"

"Who?"

"The lady and her sons."

"They don't want money, Aunt Steph."

"Well, what-"

"They want us dead."

"Dead?"

Looking away, Splash clenched his jaws and nodded his head.

"Do you think they already-"

"I 'on't know."

"Splash, you have to call the-"

"I ain't callin' no cops, Aunt Steph."

"You standin' there, and you don't know if your wife alive or dead, and you-"

"Aunt Steph, if Tia not alive, I swear on every grave in this cemetery, I'ma send her enough company to fill up half of hell."

"In memory of your grandmother, please think this through and call the cops and let them handle-"

Splash's aunt grabbed his arm when he turned to walk away.

"Nephew, please?"

"I ain't the one that started all this shit, Aunt Steph."

"And do you honestly think that's gon' matter to one of them judges in one of them goddamn courtrooms?"

"It's gon' be bullets flyin' when they catch me, Aunt Steph," Splash responded, removing his sunglasses. He wanted his aunt to see the raw pain in his eyes. "Right now, I don't give a fuck about no cops, standin' in front of no judge, or nothin' else. Aunt Steph, look at me. Look in my eyes. My own life breakin' my heart. My own life, Aunt Steph. I'm startin' to feel like God pickin' on me. Aunt Steph, I'm gon' end up in this cemetery, before I make it to any of them courtrooms they got. I don't live no life, where I can call the cops for help. Aunt Steph, if I did, what would I tell them? Can I tell them everything I just told you?"

"You remind me of your father so much right now."

"Aunt Steph, I gotta go."

"Splash, where you-Wait!"

"I gotta go find Tia!"

Minutes later, Splash was sitting behind the steering wheel of Tia's Cadillac sports wagon. Her car was the only one left in the entire cemetery. Splash had his face on the steering wheel, and he was crying loud and hard. From the cemetery, he was going straight down South Philly to visit every Daycare center that Yasmeen Bey owned, starting with the one that she used as her headquarters on 21st and Passyunk Avenue. He wasn't going to stop his search, until he was face to face with her, or one of her sons. Since Tia's cousin Rhonda hadn't returned any of his calls in the last two days, he had decided that he was going to go to war all by himself.

Splash had a Glock 50 on his waist, two Glock 45s under the driver's seat, and two more under the passenger's seat. In the console, he had three, live-hand grenades, and in the backseat, he had two SKS assault rifles, a bulletproof vest, and a Celeste silenced-machine gun, all hiding beneath a white and blue-striped comforter.

Tia and her cousin Rhonda pulled up slowly beside her Cadillac sports wagon and looked inside of it. Both of them gasped and looked at each other when they saw how hard Splash was crying.

"He ain't in there just cryin' about his gran 'mom."

"I wonder why he still here."

"Tia, you wrong for not lettin' him know that you was okay all this time."

Tia looked at her cousin and let out a sigh.

"Now, he gon' be mad at me when he find out I was ignorin'-"

"Rhonda, just shut up and gimme a hug."

"It's Rock 'n Roll Rhonda."

"Well, you definitely earned that name now."

After sharing a tearful hug with her cousin, Tia took a deep breath and stepped out of her cousin's black, 2010 Buick Lucerne, and shut the passenger door behind her. Four steps brought her within inches of her own driver's side door. As she listened to her cousin's car drive away, she stared into her own car at her crying husband. He still hadn't noticed that she was standing outside of her car. Naturally, she was happy to see him, but she wasn't able to forget that before her abduction, their marriage had come to a crossroad, so as she grabbed the lever on her driver's side door and pulled it open, she swallowed the lump in her throat and fought back the tears that were trying to flood her eyes.

Mid-sob, Splash looked up at Tia and just stared at her. He thought that his eyes were playing with his mind. Because weirder, and unimaginable things had happened to him in his life, he felt compelled to reach out and touch her to see if she was actually standing right there in front of him. That one-handed touch turned into a two-handed grab, and that two-handed grab quickly became a bonafide bear hug. This hug lasted for nine minutes. Inside of that small window of time, Splash apologized to Tia and said sorry over twenty times.

For Tia, all of Splash's heartfelt apologies were like the gentlest of kisses to her bruised heart.

"Tee, I love you so fuckin' much, man."

He was her.

"I love you, too."

She was him.

"How-Where-Tee, how you get here?"

They were Mr. and Mrs. Gunplay.

"Take me to where y'all buried ya gran 'mom, Bay."

"Man, what the fuck."

Tia broke down crying when Splash wrapped his arms around her again and squeezed her tightly. Her heart knew its owner. The harder Splash squeezed her, the more loved she felt. So badly, she wanted to tell him that she was pregnant, but she made the conscious decision that she was going to wait until they got home. Again, as Splash hugged her and ran his fingers through her hair, he began to tell her how sorry he was over and over again. Each utterance of that apologetic word was like the application of a Band-Aid to every cut he had given her heart the night he came home drunk.

"How you get here, Tee."

"Rock 'n Roll Rhonda."

"But-How-Where she-"

"Bay, take me to your gran 'mom first, then I'll tell you everything that happened on our way home."

Chapter Twenty-Five

The next morning . . .

"Do I meet your expectations as a wife?"

It was 9:53 a.m., and it was cloudy and showering raindrops outside. Splash and Tia were laying in their bed in the spoon position. The two of them had been awake for six minutes, but neither of them had spoken to each other until Tia had asked her insightful question.

"Of course you do."

"Well, why you wanted to get a divorce, then?"

"You know how I feel about chu, Tee."

"I used to think I did."

Before the moment could fully unravel, Splash felt himself becoming disappointed in it, and wanted it to go away. He had hoped that the morning would come with Tia acting a little bit more responsive to his affection, and that she wouldn't appear so distant to him like she had seemed throughout most of the night. Even as he held her body close to his, he could sense that her thoughts were somewhere else.

"Tee, I-"

"Besides Cam, who else you fucked, since we been married?"

"What?"

"You heard me."

"What chu mean who else I fucked?"

"Who else you fucked?"

"Tee, turn around."

"Why?"

"'Cause I-Yo, can you just turn around?"

Letting out an exasperated sigh, Tia turned around and faced Splash. The points of their noses kissed.

"Do you even get why I'm askin' you these type of questions?"

Splash looked intently into Tia's eyes, but he didn't answer her. Instead, he raised his hand up to her face and affectionately caressed her left cheek.

"You don't, do you, Bay?"

"Tell me, so I will."

Tia blinked.

Splash blinked too.

"I gave you my virginity, "Tia spoke, staring into Splash's eyes. She inhaled his morning breath, and exhaled her own. "Everything I did for the first time happened with you. Everything. Bay, I was eighteen when I became ya wife, and in all these years, the thought of fuckin' some other nigga never once crossed my mind. I always valued how deep our trust level was, but chu introduced the ideas of doubt from stuff you said that night chu came home all drunk, and from how you was so quick to believe that I fucked-"

"What I say?"

"Well, for one, you said you tired of fuckin' me."

"I did?"

"And you said when you fuck me, it feel like you be stickin' ya dick in a bucket of water."

Splash raised his eyebrows.

"Tellin' me stuff like that was like an indicator."

"So, since I said that, now you think I been fuckin' somebody else?"

"Maybe you found a bitch, who pussy don't feel like a bucket of water."

"I was drunk, Tee."

"That's when people tell the truth."

"Tee, I ain't mean that shit."

"That's what chu supposed to say."

Splash rolled over on his back and looked up at his mirrored-ceiling.

"I'm all for savin' our marriage, but we not gon' move forward and pretend like-"

"I ain't never cheat on you, Tee."

"Swear to God."

"I swear to God."

Like Splash, Tia rolled over on her back and placed her eyes on their mirrored-ceiling. She didn't want to believe Splash, but her heart forced her to.

"You believe me?"

"Yeah."

"Simple as that?"

"I'm not chu."

"What chu mean, you not me?"

"I'm not chu," Tia repeated, staring up at Splash's reflection. The thought of the small life forming inside of her made her put her hand on her stomach. "Your word still gold to me. Nobody just can't tell me anything, like you let Cam cousin do, and it reshape all the trust we built over all these years. Until I see you doin' some bullshit with my own fuckin' eyes, you tellin' the truth and they the fuck lyin'. Now, that's the page you should've been on that night-"

"I know, Tee."

"So, can we agree that you deserve some type of punishment for all the pain and suffering you took me through, then?"

"Like what?"

"Well, you can start off by puttin' ya face in my bucket of water, and while you doin' that, I'ma think of some other ways that chu can compensate me."

"That ain't no punishment."

"And if I ever find out that chu fuckin' another bitch, I'ma shoot her in her fuckin' face, and leave her in ya car so you can get charged for it."

The next day . . .

Monday morning was as wet as the day before it. The sky was gray, littered with clouds, and the sun appeared to be taking a second day off of work.

"Why it's so quiet in there?"

"I'm not home."

"Where you at this early in the morning?"

"Zainab, you don't even wanna know."

"Try me."

"I'm at this abortion clinic with my friend Camay."

"For her, or for you?"

"Her."

"Oh."

"It's Splash's."

"You lyin'."

"I wish I was."

"Tia, you serious?"

"As a heart attack."

"Let me guess . . . y'all had-"

"A threesome."

"Wow."

"Spare me the lecture, Zai-"

"Girl, how messed up you sound, and how depressed you must be feelin', you don't need no lecture from me to make you feel any worse than you already . . ."

Tia's other line on her cell phone clicked.

". . . do."

"Zainab, hold on."

"Okay."

After thumbing the screen of her iPhone, Tia placed it back to her left ear and sighed.

"Fancy face?"

"What's up, Bay?"

"Us."

"You getcha new car, yet?"

"Yup."

"You like it?"

"Yo, why you sound like that?"

"Like what?"

"Like-I 'on't know, You just-"

"Bay, I got Zainab on my other line."

"Alright, but answer ya phone, if you see a funny number callin' you, 'cause ya uncle Salvatore said he gon' call you today."

"How you know?"

" 'Cause I just got off the phone with him."

"Did you feed Snookums, before you left out?"

"Nope."

"Bay, why not?"

" 'Cause that little mu'fucker back on his bullshit, and his ass tried to fuckin' bite me when I got out the fuckin' shower, that's why."

"Alright, bye."

"Damn, where the love at?"

"In my bucket of water."

"Yo, you ain't gon' let that shit die, is you?"

"Bye."

"What time you comin' home?"

"After Robbie finish movin' all his shit out."

"Alright."

"Was that cop still parked out in front of the house when you left?"

"Yup."

"Oh, well, let me go, before Zainab think I-"

"Alright, I love you."

"I love you, too."

Tia thumbed the screen of her iPhone again, and switched back over to her cousin. She had been sitting in her car out in the parking lot of the abortion clinic that Camay was inside of , and she was beginning to feel restless as she stared blankly through her rain-splattered windshield.

"Girl, I was just about to hang up."

"That was Splash."

"He mad?"

"About what?"

"The stuff with Camay."

"He don't know she preg-Well, was pregnant."

Tia looked at the screen of her cell phone when it alerted her that she was receiving another call. The number was unfamiliar to her, so assuming that the caller was her uncle Salvatore, she sat up in her driver's seat and placed her cell phone back to her ear.

"Zainab, I'ma call you back, alright?"

"Text me, 'cause I just got to my job."

"Alright."

Ending her phone call with her cousin, Tia thumbed the screen of her iPhone to accept the incoming call from her uncle.

"Hello?"

"Tia?"

A lump formed in Tia's throat at the sound of her uncle's voice. Growing up, she had always wanted to be accepted by her father's side of her family. Having her aunt Trixie in her life pacified her as a child, but the older she had gotten, the more intense her craving to meet her other family members began to get. Only her own heart and soul knew this.

"Hey."

"Do you have a minute to talk?"

"Un-Huh."

"You okay?"

"Yeah, I'm alright."

"Listen, I really wish that this conversation between us could be face to face, which, to me would be the proper way to do this, but at this point, things aren't conducive for us to have that oppurtunity."

"I know."

"I just got off the phone with your brother Malcolm a few minutes ago."

"I talked to him last night."

"He told me."

Hours after Tia's cousins had rescued her, she had made a call to her brother Malcolm from her cousin, Rhonda's, cell phone. It was an intense dialogue, and at certain moments, because Kenyatta Bey was shouting in the background, it seemed to Tia that maybe releasing Yasmeen Bey might not be the logical thing for her to do. In one ear, she had her cousin, Rhonda, telling her not to let Yasmeen Bey go, and how she should kill her and leave her dead body on the steps of one of her Daycare centers. Then, in her other ear, she had her cousin, Zainab, explaining to her how it would be a wise choice for her to just earn a good deed by sparing Yasmeen Bey's life, and setting her free.

"Are you comfortable with this truce, Tia?"

"In some ways I am, and in some ways I'm not."

"From my perspective, the agreement will be honored and from the talk that I just had with Malcolm, your safety is one of his top priorities."

"It's not Malcolm that I'm-"

"Is it true that your pregnant?"

"Who-Malcolm told you?"

"Yep, and I bet your husband is excited as hell, isn't he?"

"I still haven't told him."

"Why not?"

Tia glanced up at her rearview mirror in time to see Camay putting up her umbrella, as she stepped out of the abortion clinic.

"Uncle Salvatore, can I call you back when I get home?"

"Uh, sure you can."

"Okay, bye."

"Okay."

"Uncle Salvatore?"

"Yeah?"

"Can I meet ya daughters?"

"Certainly, but I have them both down here with me, until I see how this thing blows over with your brother Angelo."

"Well, can you text me they e-mail addresses, so I-"

"I'ma take care of that right now."

"Okay."

After ending her phone call with her uncle, Tia sat her cell phone in her console and got out of her car to open her passenger door for Camay.

"You okay?"

Instead of answering Tia with words, Camay just shook her head and closed her umbrella, as she got into Tia's car. The expression on her face was ghostly, and she was moving her limbs like every movement hurt her down to the marrow inside of her bones.

"This shit is all your fuckin' fault," Tia thought, as she shut her passenger door and looked up at the raining sky. The guilty emotions in her heart inspired tears, and the warm raindrops that were peppering her upturned face inspired her to stand beneath them a few seconds longer when she made it back around to her driver's side door.

"Camay wouldn't've never even thought of us doin' that shit that night, if I wouldn't've brought that shit up. I wonder if she blamin' me about this, and just not tellin' me? Cam hate everything about abortions. Now, she had to get one, because of me. I'm not gon' even tell her that I'm pregnant. I'ma wait."

After a brief mental, and emotional struggle, Tia got a grip on her composure, and got back into her car.

"My doctor was related to that cop that got killed when we was chasin' that guy."

"How you know?"

"I heard him talkin' about it to one of the nurses, before-"

Unable to complete her sentence, Camay dropped her face into her hands and began to cry. Her sobs were silent at first, but as the seconds vanished, they became more audible.

"Cam, I'm so sorry you had to-"

"Tia, take-Just take-Take me home, Tia."

"Okay."

"Just take me home."

It only took Tia eighteen minutes to get to Camay's house. Camay's doctor's office was located across from Oxford Valley Mall, which was only about a half a mile from Camay's house. During the drive, Tia had received another phone call from Splash.

"What chu think about goin' back out to the cabin?"

"I'd rather go visit my uncle, so I can meet my cousins, if we gon' take a trip anywhere."

"You know he gotta yacht, right?"

"Umm-hmm, I remember Aunt Trixie mentionin' somethin' about it a long time ago."

"Yea, he was tellin' me about it when I talked to him."

"You home, yet?"

"I'm pullin' into the driveway as we speak."

"He still there?"

"Yup."

One of Splash's and Tia's neighbors had reported the sound of gunshots on the morning that Kenyatta Bey had shot at Splash, Camay, and Tia's cousin, Rhonda. That anonymous neighbor hadn't seen anything, and wasn't able to provide the cops with any other information, except that they had overheard what they had believed to be someone shooting a gun, so, naturally, because of the chaos that had boiled over on Splash's birthday weeks earlier, a cop was placed on duty in front of their house to monitor their activities.

"Bay, don't forget to feed Snookums for me when you get in the house."

"Alright."

"Is you gon' do it, or not?"

"Not."

"Please?"

"Alright."

"Bay, I'm serious."

On the other end of Tia's cell phone, Splash was dealing with his own demons. Like his mother, Zanax pills had become his remedy to help him escape from the pain and grief that he was dealing with. After he killed the engine on his new, black, 2011 Jaguar XK, he switched his cell phone to his other ear and looked up at the cop car parked across the street from his house in his rearview mirror.

"So, what chu gon' do for the rest of the day?"

"I'm about to call Tuna, 'cause he got this club promoter who wanna holla at-"

Splash glanced at the screen of his cell phone, then put it back to his ear.

"Ay, Tee, this Bia callin' me."

"Call me back, then."

"Alright."

"Don't forget to feed Snookums."

"Alright."

Eleven minutes later, Splash was sitting in the passenger seat of his father's Nissan Pathfinder. The three Zanax pills that he had in his system were making him nod off and on, in the middle of his conversation with his cousin, Sabia. Had he been sober, certain things his cousin mentioned would have caused his antennas to rise.

"We gon' do that shit as soon as it get dark."

"Yo, I told you I had you, cuz."

"What chu drunk?"

"Naw."

"Why it sound-Yo, you sound like you did that night you banged out."

Licking his lips, Splash sat his cell phone in his lap and closed his eyes. Within seconds, his chin was resting on his chest, and he was snoring.

Where.

Am.

I.

There was a beautiful waterfall spilling down from a large mountain that appeared to be hollow on the inside. A flowing lake was at the base of the waterfall that separated two huge beds of fragrant plants. The water in this lake was clear as glass, and had the scent of honey. On the floor of the lake, there were diamonds of all colors, matching the bodies of all the pretty birds that were flying around in the cloudless, sunny sky.

"Splash, open your eyes."

Splash blinked several times, before he finally opened his eyes and fixed them on the face that was only inches away from his own.

"Mom?"

"Hey, baby."

"Mom?"

"Yes, Rasool."

For a moment, Splash just stared at his mother's face in a trance at the fact that she was right there before him. She had on a long dress that was exceedingly white, and she was as beautiful as any woman that he had ever seen with his own two eyes. He could see all the motherly love she had for him in her chestnut brown eyes, but he could also see the worried look that was being wet by the tears that were beginning to form in her eyes as well.

"Rasool, your wife is in trouble."

"Huh?"

"Hurry up, and come with me."

Still slightly disoriented, Splash pushed himself up from the bright bed of flowers that he had been laying on, and rose to his feet. The mountainous waterfall commanded his attention first, but it was the sight of the awe-inspiring lake that caused him to slow up his steps as he followed his mother across a bridge made of onyx over the bejeweled, sweet-scented water. Hearing his mother speak to someone up ahead, Splash raised his eyes from the enchanting water. Who he saw at the other end of the bridge made his eyes protrude from his face.

"Hey, son-in-law."

Just like Splash's mother, Tia's mother was wearing a white dress that looked like it had been cut from the fabric of a pure, white cloud. Her eyes were gentle, and the features on her face were ageless. Around her neck, there was a string of gold that held a heart-shaped locket.

"Miss Tessa, how-"

"Splash, you have to get to Tia, before it's too late."

With tears rolling down the front of her face, Splash's mother grabbed Splash's hand and squeezed it tightly with both of her hands. At that moment, Splash knew that Tia's mother, and his very own mother knew something that he didn't. He could feel his heart as it began to climb up his throat. He was scared to find out what the future held, but because it had something to do with the love of his life, he felt compelled to learn about her destiny.

"What's about to happen, Miss Tessa?"

"Seven people about to die tonight, and unless you make it to Tia in time, she's going to be one of-"

"But-Naw, Tia-"

"Splash, Tia's pregnant again, and if you don't-"

"Baby, I know this not the way you wanted to see me, and I know that we have so much to talk about, but what Miss Tessa is telling you is far more important right now, so please-"

"You the only one that can save my daughter, and my unborn grandchild, Splash."

"But, Miss Tessa-"

"Give this to Tia for me."

After removing the string of gold from around her neck, Tia's mother put it around Splash's neck, fastened it, then kissed him on the cheek.

"You've made me the proudest mother-in-law that ever existed, Splash."

Splash hugged Tis's mother, then turned around and embraced his own mother.

"Mom, I love you so much."

"I love you, too, son. I love you, too."

After a series of bright explosions of light, Splash woke up from his paranormal dream. The Zanax pills in his system resumed control of his thoughts and his body, as he climbed out of his father's jeep. In his mind, he believed that he was moving at a fast pace, but he was actually moving quite sluggish. His eyelids were drooping lazily over his eyes, and after his garage door finished rising, he stepped out onto his driveway, not realizing that the cop was no longer parked in front of his lawn, or that he had left his cell phone in his father's jeep. Not paying attention to his surroundings, he didn't notice the silver, Audi A8, sitting across the street in his neighbor's driveway.

Tia's safety was the only thing on Splash's mind as raindrops chased him down the length of his driveway to his car.

He was her.

She was him.

They were Mr. and Mrs. Gunplay.

Chapter Twenty-Six

"What the hood sayin' about that shit?"

"That Gary did that shit with some niggaz from Logan, and that them niggaz down Mexico some fuckin' where havin' it they way."

"So, mu'fuckers around the way don't even know I'm home, huh?"

"Prep, mu'fuckers think you fuckin' upstate somewhere, dog."

"Ashley know I'm home, though," Prep spoke, after blowing out a cloud of weed smoke. Raising the Dutch back to his lips, he took three quick drags, and handed it over to his friend Gamble. "Gary cousin, Honey, do, too. All she want is-"

Prep stopped talking to exhale the weed smoke from his chest.

"Still, though, Ashley ain't said shit about chu to nobody in the hood, and me and you both know how Honey get down when it come to a dollar."

"Yo, I ain't know she was strippin'."

"Dog, you late."

"Gary must've told that bitch I was doin' that shit with-"

"Ay, yo, so, who you want me to go see first, 'cause I gotta take my mom her car back, before she start bitchin'?"

"Drop Gary mom pocketbook off first, and just go past my mom spot and Ashley house after that."

"Alright."

"Don't tell Gary mom that shit came from me, Gamble."

"Dog, just that chu called my crib outta all the niggaz down the end you could've hollered-"

"You the only nigga I could trust to do this without spinnin' me."

"Alright, let me go handle this business for you, then."

After Prep and his friend Gamble shook hands, Prep stepped out of the car and pulled the brim on his fitted hat down to his eyebrows. As he stood there in his cousin, Camay's driveway, and got wet from the falling rain, he thought of the three gifts that were about to be delivered to his friend, Gary's mother, his own mother, and to his son's mother. He was sending each of them one hundred thousand dollars inside of the pocketbooks that Tia had returned to him. There were two letters containing sincere apologies to his mother and son's mother in the expensive pocketbooks that were being sent to them, and he left his new cell phone number, and the next destination he was about to be traveling to at the bottom of both of there letters.

Prep had plans on waiting until it got dark, before he made a final exit from his cousin, Camay's, house.

"Hello?"

"Prep, what's good?"

Instantly annoyed at the sound of Robbie's voice on the other end of his cell phone, Prep sighed and pushed his cousin Camay's front door open, then closed it behind him, and locked the bottom and top locks.

"Ain't chu supposed to be comin' through with a movin' truck, or some shit like that today?"

"Yea, I'm on my way there right now."

"Oh."

"What time Cam get off work?"

"She ain't go to work."

"Naw?"

"Her and Tia in her room."

"Alright, I'ma see you when I get there."

"Alright."

Thirty-eight miles away, in the middle, northbound lane, on the I-95 expressway, Sabia, and his friends, Bleach, and Moo, were inside of Bleach's Nissan Armada, lost in their own thoughts. There was nothing that needed to be said. Money and murder was on all of their minds. The interior of the big, SUV, was cloudy with weed smoke.

"Ay, Bleach turn that shit down for a second."

After Bleach lowered the volume on the loud music that had been dumping out of his speakers, Sabia accepted his incoming call and pressed the cell phone that Trixie had bought for him to his left ear.

"What's up, Trixie?"

"Y'all okay?"

"Yea, we straight."

"Just checkin'."

Trixie was five cars behind Bleach's SUV.

"Ay, don't Camay live out here somewhere, Trixie?"

"I never been to her house before, but I think so."

"This shit gon' be sweet, watch."

"Let's just hope he's still there."

"If he not, we just gon' torture whoever in there, until they tell us where his bitch ass at, that's all."

Back at Camay's house, inside of Camay's bedroom, Tia was at a window that provided an attractive view of Camay's large backyard. Tia's mind was elsewhere. She wanted to go home and climb in her bed, but she didn't want Camay to be alone. So, while Camay laid in her bed and slept, Tia walked around Camay's bedroom remembering all of the small details of a painful moment that would forever be imbedded in her memory. She wished that she possessed the ability to turn back the hands of time to undo certain things that had occurred in her life. However, she knew that her strength and growth as a person came from all of the good and bad trials that she had endured. She knew that miscarrying her first child was going to make her extra protective about the second child she was now sheltering in her womb.

"Robbie ain't get here, yet, Tia?"

"I don't think so."

"You can go home, if you want."

Tia declined by looking at Camay and shaking her head.

"I almost did it again, Tia."

"You almost did what?"

Camay's face reflected the pain that she felt as she moved in her bed to turn over on her back. Once she was on her back, she dug her right hand down into the pocket of her pink and white, Spoylt Bette bathrobe, and withdrew it holding a small, chrome gun.

"Gimme that gun, Cam."

Only one teardrop left Camay's left eye as she put the nozzle of Robbie's gun beneath her chin and pulled the trigger.

"No, Ca-"

"Click . . ."

The hammer on the Walther PPk .380 slammed against the pin, which would have sent a bullet flying through the roof of Camay's mouth, and up into her brain, but her lack of knowledge of guns prevented this fatality, because she had never flipped down the safety accessory on the weapon, before pulling its trigger.

"Girl, gimme that shit!!"

Camay didn't put up a fight when Tia dove on her and wrenched the gun out of her hands.

"Tia?!!!!!!!"

The loud call came from outside.

"Tia?!!!!!!!"

With Camay's gun in hand, Tia scrambled off of Camay's bed and rushed over to a window in Camay's bedroom that overlooked the front of her house. Splash was nowhere in sight. How he was shouting her name had her worried, so she ran out of Camay's bedroom, taking along Camay's gun with her. Unbeknownst to her, Camay had the twin to the gun she was carrying in her left, bathrobe pocket.

Tia and Robbie crossed paths in Camay's foyer. Neither paid any attention to the other.

Fate.

Is.

Inescapable.

"Tia?!!!!!"

Catching the stares of the three men parked in a white, Acura SUV, that was sitting idle in Camay's driveway, Tia kept up her fast pace and only stopped when she made it down to the end of Camay's rain-wet driveway. There, she looked right and left.

"Tia?!!!!!"

Inside of Camay's house, in her guest bedroom, Prep and Robbie were sharing a death stare over the Glock that Robbie had aimed at Prep's face.

"Damn, this where we at with it, Robbie?"

"Nigga, shut the fuck up, and get out the bed."

"Me, though, Robbie?"

"Yea, nigga, you."

Outside, under the gray and raining sky, a priceless piece of jewelry hanging from Splash's neck had Tia mesmerized.

"Ya mom told me to-Ssssss . . . shit."

Splash had twisted his ankle and fallen between his car, and the rear of Tia's Cadillac sports wagon, while stepping up on the sidewalk.

"Let me help you up, Bay."

"My shit-Tee, we gotta-Yo, somethin' bad about to-"

"Tia?! Splash?!"

Splash and Tia looked at Trixie with confused looks on both of their faces. The gold, Buick Lacrosse that she was in had just driven past them, then it had reversed back to where they were.

Fate.

Is.

Inescapable.

All at once, fate revealed its hand. Both doors on the Audi A8 swung open. It had been sitting in the empty driveway of one of Camay's neighbor's houses across the street. Thirty feet down the street, Bleach's Nissan Armada was speeding recklessly across Camay's front lawn towards the white, Acura SUV, that was parked in her driveway. Inside of Camay's guest bedroom, Robbie still had his gun pointed at Prep, but fate had twisted itself into a pretzel, and pulled Camay into the gothic picture.

"Shoot him Camay."

"She ain't got the heart to."

"Camay shoot him."

"Robbie why you pointin' that gun at Prep?"

"He tryna take my money."

Seconds earlier, Camay had gotten out of bed, because she had overheard Prep and Robbie shouting at each other. The gun she saw in Robbie's hand had influenced her to pull out her own.

"What money?"

"The money in that bag right-"

"Bitch, you had a fuckin' threesome with Tia and Splash, and got preg-"

The sound of gunshots outside, mimicked the ones that began to roar in Camay's guest bedroom. Robbie's gun jammed after his first shot.

Camay's didn't.

Outside, fate was treating Splash and Tia terribly. The two of them were in between their own cars, and they had the angel of death waiting beside both of them, to see which one of them was going to die first. Splash had Tia wrapped tightly in his arms beneath him, making it impossible for Tia to get Camay's gun out of the front pocket on her spring, Armani hoody. Hot bullets were flying at them from the guns that Kenyatta Bey and his female companion were shooting.

Down the block, Trixie was driving beside Sabia, as he chased after Robbie's cousin, Maniac, across the lawns of Camay's neighbors. All of the shooting had brought many people out of their houses into the rain.

"Sabia, fuck him, and come on!!"

In Camay's driveway, Sabia's friend, Moo, lay dead. His killer was the man that Sabia was shooting at down the street.

When Camay's garage door shot up, and her Lexus came speeding out, Bleach hopped out from behind the rear of his SUV and lit up the windshield with his SKS assault rifle. The driver of the Lexus got sprayed across the chest, but didn't stop. After slamming head-on into the white, Acura, Camay's Lexus sped across her lawn. Because the driver wasn't the person that he had a personal vendetta with, Bleach ran into Camay's garage in search of the man that he so desperately wanted to lay his eyes on.

When Camay's Lexus skidded out into the street, it rammed into the passenger side of the Audi A8 that was racing by. Jen's body was thrown from the Audi A8 onto the hood of Camay's Lexus. Bleeding from his mouth, Kenyatta Bey staggered out of his car and took several steps, before falling down to the ground.

Up the street, Tia was screaming for help at the top of her lungs.

"Somebody help!!"

Melissa Circle was the home of some of the richest people in Yardley, Pennsylvania. Camay and Robbie had been the only two black people to live amongst them. Their community was outlined with tall trees that stood on the landscapes of all of their spacious lawns. Some of these huge trees blotted out the sun and provided spots of shade all around the street that curved into a circular stretch of road all around the upscale community.

From their lawns, and out of their houses, people came out in droves to help Tia with Splash. An elderly, white man even played his part by taking the gun that Tia had laying beside her, and disappeared with it.

Off to the shoulder, on the I-95 expressway, Trixie and Sabia sat and looked through the windshield at all of the cop cars in the opposite lanes that were racing back to the scene they had just left. When a gust of wind blew through the shattered rear window of their rental car, Sabia looked at the car that had sped by them.

"Yo, that's fuckin' Camay right there!!"

Trixie put her rental car into drive and mashed down on the gas pedal. Within seconds, her and Sabia were beside Camay's Lexus.

"Oh, shit!"

"She shot Sabia!"

As Trixie matched speeds with Camay's mangled, and shot up Lexus, Sabia lowered his window and stuck out his hand in an effort to get Camay's attention.

"Trixie, hit the horn!!"

When Trixie pressed down on the horn, Camay looked left and noticed her and Sabia racing beside her. Immediately, she slowed down, and pulled her car over onto the shoulder of the expressway. Several cars hit their horns in protest of their reckless driving.

"Oh, my God," Trixie thought, as she shifted her rental car into park and cut it off in the shoulder lane. She broke down into tears when Sabia jumped out of the car and slammed the passenger door behind him. "God, please let them be okay. Jen, you fuckin'-"

"Bocka! Bocka! Bocka! Bocka! Bocka! Bocka!"

Trixie flinched and backed herself against the panel of the driver's side door when Sabia got back into the car and swung a big bag into the backseat.

"Sabia, what did you do?!"

"She had the fuckin' money!!"

"But that-That was Camay, Sabia!!"

"Man, she was about to die any-"

"Are you a fuckin' doctor?!"

Not wanting to see his own actions, Sabia jammed his gun in Trixie's side and closed his eyes.

"Bocka! Bocka! Bocka! Bocka! Bocka!"

Back at Camay's house, a lot was going on. A SWAT team was on the scene, and two police helicopters were up in the sky. Several EMT units were also on the scene, including a handful of detectives, that were scouring the premises and asking questions to any of Camay's neighbors that were willing to talk.

In Camay's guest bedroom, Prep was laying on his side next to Robbie's lifeless body. His own blood, and Robbie's blood, were mixing together and creating a pool of blood, where his bag of money once was.

"Look at me."

Prep looked up into the eyes of the man that his son's mother was now in love with. It was one of the most humiliating moments of his life. He could feel his spirit easing its way out of his bleeding body, as he held eye contact with his friend, Gary's cousin.

"What chu got to say for ya self now, nigga?"

"I-I sent-"

"What?"

Bleach crouched down beside Prep.

"I sent some-M-Money to Gary mom, and to Ashley th-This mornin'."

This statement only earned Prep a face full of spit.

"You know who that's from, right?"

Prep closed his eyes and just breathed. The gunshot wound to the left side of his chest felt like the devil was tickling his lung with one of his hot fingers. He wanted to be back on house arrest at his mother's house, or even back in jail. He wanted to be anywhere, but the place where he was.

"You look like you want death to speed up, so I'ma do ya nut ass a favor, and I'ma get chu outta here, alright?"

Prep opened his eyes and looked at Bleach as he stepped back and pointed his SKS at him.

Out of nowhere, Camay's guest bedroom door flew off its hinges, and three members of the SWAT team stormed in squeezing their triggers. Bleach took thirteen bullets to his chest and legs, but he still managed to spray a few shots of his own, before he melted down between Robbie and Prep's bodies. He died with his eyes open just like Prep.

Their lifeless orbs were looking at each other, over a pool of their own shimmering blood.

Chapter Twenty-Seven

August 11th, 2010-2:24 p.m., New Haven Hospital (Bucks County, Pa.)

Pain.

"Let me see my fuckin' husband!!"

Silence.

Teardrops.

"I wanna see my fuckin' husband!!" Tia screamed, struggling to raise her heavily bandaged forehead from the hospital's hallway floor. Her entire body trembled from the agonizing pain that she felt, but she let her concerns for her husband take precedence over her own physical suffering. "I'm not gon'-I'm not gon' stop 'til I-I wanna see my fuckin' husband!! I wanna see him right now! Somebody take me to my fuckin' husband!!"

Silence.

More pain.

More teardrops.

Unable to crawl any further, Tia slowly returned her face back down to the glossy, hospital floor. Its cold surface tinged her right cheek. After closing her eyes, she pulled her lips into her mouth, forcing her breaths to escape her nostrils in short, quick exhales. Waves of pain were rippling through her veins as she laid there motionless. Her long hair hid the pained-expression that was on her face, as well as her countless teardrops, that were creating small puddles on the hospital floor all around her face.

"Splaaaaaaasssshhhhh?!!!"

Tia's sudden outburst startled the hospital staff that were slowly surrounding her sprawled out body. All at once, they all began to exchange tentative stares.

"Where the fuck is my husband?!!"

Tia's intuition was ringing like a fire alarm. She could feel Splash's pain under her own skin. Every single fiber in her body was telling her that something was wrong with him, and her not knowing where he was at in the hospital had her terrified.

"Baaaaay?!"

He was her.

"Where y'all got my fuckin' husband at?!!"

She was him.

"Splaaaaaaasssshhhhh?!!!"

They were Mr. and Mrs. Gunplay.

Exchanging guilty glances, some of the hospital staff blinked away their tears, while the rest of them stared down at Tia sympathetically. All of them knew that her husband was undergoing major surgery in an opposite wing of the hospital ,and that his chances of coming out of it alive was next to impossible.

Just an hour and seventeen minutes earlier, the EMT unit had rushed Tia and Splash into the hospital's emergency room. Both of their bodies were riddled with bullets. Tia had been shot once in her right forearm, and twice in the left side of her upper back. Above her right eyebrow, a nasty graze-wound disappeared into her hairline, displaying just how close death had come to snatching away her young life. Sadly, in Splash's case, things were much more serious, and a lot more complicated. Splash had gotten shot eleven times. Since his arrival to the hospital, he had died twice on the operation table, and the dime-sized bullet lodged inside of his left cheek had nothing to do with his complications ,and neither did the removal of his left lung. His young life was being threatened by three bullets that were lingering dangerously close to his heart, and eerily, it seemed as if his heartbeats were summoning their fatal connection.

Everyone on the hospital's staff had sent up their prayers to the afternoon skies, but, as of yet, the heavens still hadn't sent down any miracles to rescue Splash from the shadows of death.

After wiping away a falling teardrop with the back of her hand, the white, middle-aged doctor, who had personally removed the bullets from Tia's arm and back, took a deep breath, and slowly knelt down beside her. Up until this point, she had never dealt with a hospital patient like Tia before.

"Mrs. Barnes?"

More doctors and nurses were beginning to gather at both ends of the hospital's long corridor. They stood in small groups, engaging in hushed-whispering as they all somberly looked on. Most of them were married women, so by being wives themselves, they all couldn't help but feel responsible for not submitting to Tia's heartfelt pleas to see her husband. Their hearts went out to her, but none of them had been able to muster up the courage to give her the sad news about her husband's unfortunate situation.

"Mrs. Barnes?"

When Tia didn't respond to her again, the doctor looked over her shoulder at her colleagues. This got her nothing but heavy sighs and shrugging-shoulders. This was the third time that Tia had regained consciousness, climbed out of her hospital bed, and had managed to crawl out into the hospital's busy hallway. All three times before, she had passed out soon afterwards.

"God, please don't take Splash from me," Tia silently prayed, as teardrop after teardrop squeezed through her closed eyelids, and trickled sideways down her face to the hospital floor. She was daring to speak to a higher power that had been disappointing her for most of her life. "He all I got. God, you know he is. Please, don't do this to me. You already took my dad and mom. Don't take Splash. Not now. God, please, not now. I'm sorry for everything we ever did. I'm sorry. Don't chu love Splash? You let him be able to see his dad and them. You even let him see my-"

"Mrs. Barnes?"

Tia opened her eyes.

"Mrs. Barnes, you can't keep doing this."

Tia's audible sobs made her chest vibrate against the hospital's hallway floor. Pieces of her heart were breaking away and falling to a place deep in her soul.

"Mrs. Barnes, we're going to put you in a wheelchair like we did before, and take you back to your-"

"Take me to my husband."

"I'm sorry, but I can't do that, Mrs. Barnes."

"Why not?"

"Because your husband is still in surgery."

"All this time?"

"Yes, Mrs. Barnes."

"Why?"

"I'll explain everything to you, once we get you back-"

"Explain everything now."

"Mrs. Barnes, can we please discuss this in your room?"

"No."

Silence.

It took Tia a few seconds to realize that the teardrops falling on the hospital floor near her face didn't belong to her own eyes. Slowly, she tilted her head and looked up at the doctor's face.

"Mrs. Barnes, your husband has three bullet fragments very close to his heart," the doctor confessed, sighing as she fixed Tia's hospital gown with a nervous hand. With her other hand, she tried her best to stop the many tears that were chasing each other from her eyes. "The bullets are moving, and our surgeons are having a difficult time trying to-Mrs. Barnes, we don't think-It's-It's not looking good, Mrs. Barnes. I'm-Mrs. Barnes, I'm sorry, but-"

"No!!"

"Mrs. Barnes, please?"

"Shut up!!"

"Mrs.-"

"Noooooooooo!!!"

Invisible wings carried Tia's scream up and down the hospital's crowded corridor. Some hearts shook at the sound of it. Those same invisible wings left the hospital and ascended up to the heavens. A prayer was attached to them. The owner of the prayer was asking the Lord of the worlds for a favor. Tia's cousin, Zainab, had once told her that fate can sometimes be altered, because when a prayer is sent up, it must then wrestle with fate between earth and the heavens, to see which one will ultimately manifest.

Tia knew that if she lost Splash, it would destroy her beyond repair.

"Splaaaaaaaasssssshhhhhh?!!!!"

He was her.

"Bay, where you at?!!"

She was him.

"I'm pregnant, Bay!!!"

They were Mr. and Mrs. Gunplay.

Later that afternoon, to the surprise and awe of everyone on the hospital staff at New Haven Hospital, Splash pulled through. For Tia, it was an answered prayer. For Detective Konn, who was in Splash's hospital room with Tia, it was a grand opportunity for him to display the measure of his wrath.

"I already told the detectives everything I know earlier."

"And you and I both know that that's far from the truth."

"I wanna be alone with my husband."

Tia's voice was only a few volumes above a whisper. She was sitting in a wheelchair, facing Splash's hospital bed, and she was shell-shocked and completely devastated down to the core of her soul. Before Detective Konn's arrival, several Bucks County detectives had questioned her about what had happened. Playing the victim, she told them that someone tried to carjack Splash for his car, after the two of them had pulled up to go visit her friend, Camay. When they began to question her about all of the rest of the carnage, and started showing her pictures of Jen, Camay, Prep, Kenyatta Bey, Bleach and Moo, Robbie, and her aunt Trixie, she fainted.

"Did your husband ever mention anything about me to you?"

Tia ignored Detective Konn and kept her stare on Splash. He had a see-through, plastic tent surrounding his hospital bed. There were machines all around him, making different electronic sounds, and he had tubes coming out of more places on his body than she could count.

"My name is Detective Konn."

"Bye, Detective Konn."

"Your aunt and best friend were murdered by the same person, you know."

Tia closed her eyes and saw Sabia's face behind her eyelids.

"And several neighbors identified your friend, Jennifer Mai, as one of the people that shot up you and Rasool there, but you probably know all that already, right?"

"Get out."

Silence.

"Your brother Angelo wasn't lying . . . you are a cunt."

Tia didn't have the strength in her to argue, and she only looked in Detective Konn's direction, because she heard the clicking sound of handcuffs.

"Lucky for him, you're in here, 'cause I had my mind set on unplugging all of those fuckin' machines that's helping his ass breathe when I came through that door."

Horrified, Tia watched as Detective Konn stuck his hands under the plastic tent around Splash's bed and cuffed Splash's right wrist to the metal arm on his hospital bed.

"Why the fuck are you puttin' handcuffs on him?!"

"I'm placing him under arrest."

"For what?!"

"For the murder of your cousin Mikey, and your brother, Angelo, has already given me a statement, and is willing to testify that he seen him do it."

"But-But-"

"You and your husband have a nice day, Mrs. Barnes."

After Detective Konn walked out of Splash's hospital room, Tia fixed her stare back on Splash and broke down into tears. Her answered prayer had come with a curse attached to it. Like an unrelenting avalanche, Tia felt all of her emotions tumble down her chest to her stomach, where her unborn fetus was. In tears, she wheeled herself closer to Splash's hospital bed, and reached under the plastic and laid her hand over his handcuffed-wrist.

"Bay, Jen tried to kill us with that guy Kenyatta," Tia whispered, as she stroked the back of Splash's hand with her fingers. Touching him sent chills through her body. "Everybody dead, Bay. Sabia killed Aunt Trixie and Camay. Why-Why would he do-"

Tia's chin dropped to her chest as she sobbed uncontrollably. Around her neck, she had the necklace that was given to her by one of Splash's surgeons. It was the same string of gold that her late mother had always worn in memory of her father. A picture of him was inside of the locket. Her mother had died wearing it, and now there she was with it around her very own neck, all because of her husband's special gift from God.

He was her.

She was him.

They were Mr. and Mrs. Gunplay.

www.ingramcontent.com/pod-product-compliance
Lightning Source LLC
Chambersburg PA
CBHW070310260626
47160CB00003B/791